GALDONI BOOK 2
Into The Fire
By Cheree L. Alsop

ISBN: 9781494956202
Cover Image by Celairen and peroni68
Cover Design by Andrew Hair
www.chereealsop.com

ALSO BY CHEREE ALSOP

The Galdoni Series
Galdoni
Galdoni 2: Into the Storm
Galdoni 3

The Silver Series
Silver
Black
Crimson
Violet
Azure
Hunter
Silver Moon

The Small Town Superheroes Series
Small Town Superhero
The Small Town Superheroes
The Last Small Town Superhero

Heart of the Wolf
Keeper of the Wolves
Stolen
The Million Dollar Gift
Thief Prince
Shadows
Mist

PRAISE FOR CHEREE ALSOP

The Galdoni Series

"This is absolutely one of the best books I have ever read in my life! I loved the characters and their personalities, the storyline and the way it was written. The bravery, courage and sacrifice that Kale showed was amazing and had me scolding myself to get a grip and stop crying! This book had adventure, romance and comedy all rolled into one terrific book I LOVED the lesson in this book, the struggles that the characters had to go through (especially the forbidden love)...I couldn't help wondering what it would be like to live among such strangely beautiful creatures that acted, at times, more caring and compassionate than the humans. Overall, I loved this book...I recommend it to ANYONE who fancies great books."

—iBook Reviewer

"I was pleasantly surprised by this book! The characters were so well written as if the words themselves became life. The sweet romance between hero and heroine made me root for the underdog more than I usually do! I definitely recommend this book!"

—Sara Phillipp

"Can't wait for the next book!! Original idea and great characters. Could not put the book down; read it in one sitting."

—StanlyDoo- Amazon Reviewer

"5 stars! Amazing read. The story was great- the plot flowed and kept throwing the unexpected at you. Wonderfully established setting in place; great character development, shown very well thru well placed dialogue- which in turn kept the story moving right along! No bog downs or boring parts in this book! Loved the originality that stemmed from ancient mysticism- bringing age old fiction into modern day reality. Recommend for teenage and older- action violence a little intense for preteen years, but overall this is a great action thriller slash mini romance novel."
—That Lisa Girl, Amazon Reviewer

"I was not expecting a free novel to beat anything that I have ever laid eyes upon. This book was touching and made me want more after each sentence."
—Sears1994, iBook Reviewer

"This book was simply heart wrenching. It was an amazing book with a great plot. I almost cried several times. All of the scenes were so real it felt like I was there witnessing everything."
—Jeanine Drake, iBook Reveiwer

"This book was absolutely amazing...It had me tearing at parts, cursing at others, and filled with adrenaline rushing along with the characters at the fights. It is a book for everyone, with themes of love, courage, hardship, good versus evil, humane and inhumane...All around, it is an amazing book!"
—Mkb312, iBook Reviewer

"Galdoni is an amazing book; it is the first to actually make me cry! It is a book that really touches your heart, a romance novel that might change the way you look at someone. It did that to me."

—Coralee2, Reviewer

"Wow. I simply have no words for this. I highly recommend it to anyone who stumbled across this masterpiece. In other words, READ IT!"

—Troublecat101, iBook Reviewer

The Silver Series

"Cheree Alsop has written *Silver* for the YA reader who enjoys both werewolves and coming-of-age tales. Although I don't fall into this demographic, I still found it an entertaining read on a long plane trip! The author has put a great deal of thought into balancing a tale that could apply to any teen (death of a parent, new school, trying to find one's place in the world) with the added spice of a youngster dealing with being exceptionally different from those around him, and knowing that puts him in danger."

—Robin Hobb, author of the Farseer Trilogy

"I honestly am amazed this isn't absolutely EVERYWHERE! Amazing book. Could NOT put it down! After reading this book, I purchased the entire series!"

—Josephine, Amazon Reviewer

"Great book, Cheree Alsop! The best of this kind I have read in a long time. I just hope there is more like this one."

—Tony Olsen

"I couldn't put the book down. I fell in love with the characters and how wonderfully they were written. Can't wait to read the 2nd!"

—Mary A. F. Hamilton

"A page-turner that kept me wide awake and wanting more. Great characters, well written, tenderly developed, and thrilling. I loved this book, and you will too."

—Valerie McGilvrey

"Super glad that I found this series! I am crushed that it is at its end. I am sure we will see some of the characters in the next series, but it just won't be the same. I am 41 years old, and am only a little embarrassed to say I was crying at 3 a.m. this morning while finishing the last book. Although this is a YA series, all ages will enjoy the Silver Series. Great job by Cheree Alsop. I am excited to see what she comes up with next."

—Jennc, Amazon Reviewer

Keeper of the Wolves

"This is without a doubt the VERY BEST paranormal romance/adventure I have ever read and I've been reading these types of books for over 45 years. Excellent plot, wonderful protagonists—even the evil villains were great. I read this in one sitting on a Saturday morning when there were so many other things I should have been doing. I COULD NOT put it down! I also appreciated the author's research and insights into the behavior of wolf packs. I will

CERTAINLY read more by this author and put her on my 'favorites' list."

—N. Darisse

"This is a novel that will emotionally cripple you. Be sure to keep a box of tissues by your side. You will laugh, you will cry, and you will fall in love with Keeper. If you loved *Black Beauty* as a child, then you will truly love *Keeper of the Wolves* as an adult. Put this on your 'must read' list."

—Fortune Ringquist

"Cheree Alsop mastered the mind of a wolf and wrote the most amazing story I've read this year. Once I started, I couldn't stop reading. Personal needs no longer existed. I turned the last page with tears streaming down my face."

—Rachel Andersen, Amazon Reviewer

"I truly enjoyed this book very much. I've spent most of my life reading supernatural books, but this was the first time I've read one written in first person and done so well. I must admit that the last half of this book had me in tears from sorrow and pain for the main character and his dilemma as a man and an animal. . . Suffice it to say that this is one book you REALLY need in your library. I won't ever regret purchasing this book, EVER! It was just that GOOD! I would also recommend you have a big box of tissues handy because you WILL NEED THEM! Get going, get the book..."

—Kathy I, Amazon Reviewer

"I just finished this book. Oh my goodness, did I get emotional in some spots. It was so good. The courage and love portrayed is amazing. I do recommend this book. Thought provoking."

—Candy, Amazon Reviewer

Thief Prince

"I absolutely loved this book! I could not put it down. . . The Thief Prince will whisk you away into a new world that you will not want to leave! I hope that Ms. Alsop has more about this story to write, because I would love more Kit and Andric! This is one of my favorite books so far this year! Five Stars!"

—Crystal, Book Blogger at Books are Sanity

". . . Once I started I couldn't put it down. The story is amazing. The plot is new and the action never stops. The characters are believable and the emotions presented are beautiful and real. If anyone wants a good, clean, fun, romantic read, look no further. I hope there will be more books set in Debria, or better yet, Antor."

—SH Writer, Amazon Reviewer

"This book was a roller coaster of emotions: tears, laughter, anger, and happiness. I absolutely fell in love with all of the characters placed throughout this story. This author knows how to paint a picture with words."

—Kathleen Vales

"Awesome book! It was so action packed, I could not put it down, and it left me wanting more! It was very well written, leaving me feeling like I had a connection with the characters."

—M. A., Amazon Reviewer

"I am a Cheree Alsop junkie and I have to admit, hands down, this is my FAVORITE of anything she has published. In a world separated by race, fear and power are forced to collide in order to save them all. Who better to free them of the prejudice than the loyal heart of a Duskie? Adventure, incredible amounts of imagination, and description go into this world! It is a 'buy now and don't leave the couch until the last chapter has reached an end' kind of read!"

—Malcay, Amazon Reviewer

"I absolutely loved this book! I could not put it down! Anything with a prince and a princess is usually a winner for me, but this book is even better! It has multiple princes and princesses on scene over the course of the book! I was completely drawn into Kit's world as she was faced with danger and new circumstances...Kit was a strong character, not a weak and simpering girl who couldn't do anything for herself. The Thief Prince (Andric) was a great character as well! I kept seeing glimpses of who he really was and I loved that the author gave us clues as to what he was like under the surface. The Thief Prince will whisk you away into a new world that you will not want to leave!"

—Bookworm, Book Reviewer

The Small Town Superhero Series

"A very human superhero- Cheree Alsop has written a great book for youth and adults alike. Kelson, the superhero, is battling his own demons plus bullies in this action packed narrative. Small Town Superhero had me from the first sentence through the end. I felt every sorrow, every pain and the delight of rushing through the dark on a motorcycle. Descriptions in Small Town Superhero are so well written the reader is immersed in the town and lives of its inhabitants."

—Rachel Andersen, Book Reviewer

"Anyone who grew up in a small town or around motorcycles will love this! It has great characters and flows well with martial arts fighting and conflicts involved."

—Karen, Amazon Reviewer

"Cheree Alsop has written a great book for youth and adults alike. . . *Small Town Superhero* had me from the first sentence through the end. I felt every sorrow, every pain, and the delight of rushing through the dark on a motorcycle. Descriptions in *Small Town Superhero* are so well written the reader is immersed in the town and lives of its inhabitants."

—Rachel Andersen, Amazon Reviewer

"Fantastic story...and I love motorcycles and heroes who don't like the limelight. Excellent character development. You'll like this series!"

—Michael, Amazon Reviewer

"Another great read; couldn't put it down. Would definitely recommend this book to friends and family. She has put out another great read. Looking forward to reading more!"

—Benton Garrison, Amazon Reviewer

"I enjoyed this book a lot. Good teen reading. Most books I read are adult contemporary; I needed a change and this was a good change. I do recommend reading this book! I will be looking out for more books from this author. Thank you!"

—Cass, Amazon Reviewer

Stolen

"This book will take your heart, make it a little bit bigger, and then fill it with love. I would recommend this book to anyone from 10-100. To put this book in words is like trying to describe love. I had just gotten it and I finished it the next day because I couldn't put it down. If you like action, thrilling fights, and/or romance, then this is the perfect book for you."

—Steven L. Jagerhorn

"Couldn't put this one down! Love Cheree's ability to create totally relatable characters and a story told so fluidly you actually believe it's real."

—Sue McMillin, Amazon Reviewer

"I enjoyed this book it was exciting and kept you interested. The characters were believable. And the teen romance was cute."

—Book Haven, Book Reviewer

"This book written by Cheree Alsop was written very well. It is set in the future and what it would be like for government control. The drama was great and the story was very well put together. If you want something different, then this is the book to get and it is a page turner for sure. You will love the main characters as well, and the events that unfold during the story. It will leave you hanging and wanting more."

—Kathy Hallettsville, TX, Amazon Reviewer

"I really liked this book . . . I was pleasantly surprised to discover this well-written book. . .I'm looking forward to reading more from this author."

—Julie M. Peterson, Amazon Reviewer

"Great book! I enjoyed this book very much it keeps you wanting to know more! I couldn't put it down! Great read!"

—Meghan, Amazon Reviewer

"A great read with believable characters that hook you instantly. . . I was left wanting to read more when the book was finished."

—Katie- Goodreads Reviewer

Heart of the Wolf

"Absolutely breathtaking! This book is a roller coaster of emotions that will leave you exhausted!!! A beautiful fantasy filled with action and love. I recommend this book to all fantasy lovers and those who enjoy a heartbreaking love story that rivals that of Romeo and Juliet. I couldn't put this book down!"

—Amy May

"What an awesome book! A continual adventure, with surprises on every page. What a gifted author she is. You just can't put the book down. I read it in two days. Cheree has a way of developing relationships and pulling at your heart. You find yourself identifying with the characters in her book...True life situations make this book come alive for you and gives you increased understanding of your own situation in life. Magnificent story and characters. I've read all of Cheree's books and recommend them all to you...especially if you love adventures."

—Michael, Amazon Reviewer

"You'll like this one and want to start part two as soon as you can! If you are in the mood for an adventure book in a faraway kingdom where there are rival kingdoms plotting and scheming to gain more power, you'll enjoy this novel. The characters are well developed, and of course with Cheree there is always a unique supernatural twist thrown into the story as well as romantic interests to make the pages fly by."

—Karen, Amazon Reviewer

When Death Loved an Angel

"This style of book is quite a change for this author so I wasn't expecting this, but I found an interesting story of two very different souls who stepped outside of their "accepted roles" to find love and forgiveness, and what is truly of value in life and death."

—Karen, Amazon Reviewer

"When Death Loved an Angel by Cheree Alsop is a touching paranormal romance that cranks the readers' thinking mode into high gear."

—Rachel Andersen, Book Reviewer

"Loved this book. I would recommend this book to everyone. And be sure to check out the rest of her books, too!"

—Malcay, Book Reviewer

The Shadows Series

". . . This author has talent. I enjoyed her world, her very well developed characters, and an interesting, entertaining concept and story. Her introduction to her world was well done and concise. . . .Her characters were interesting enough that I became attached to several. I would certainly read a follow-up if only to check on the progress and evolution of the society she created. I recommend this for any age other than those overly sensitive to some graphic violence. The romance was heartfelt but pg. A good read."

—Mari, Amazon Reviewer

". . . I've fallen for the characters and their world. I've even gone on to share (this book) with my sister. . .So many moments made me smile as well as several which brought tears from the attachment; not sad tears, I might add. When I started Shadows, I didn't expect much because I assumed it was like most of the books I've read lately. But this book was one of the few books to make me happy I was wrong and find myself so far into the books that I lost track of time, ending up reading to the point that my body said I was too tired to continue reading! I can't wait to see what happens in the next book. . . Some of my new favorite quotes will be coming from this lovely novel. Thank you to Cheree Alsop for allowing the budding thoughts to come to life. I am a very hooked reader."

—Stephanie Roberts, Amazon Reviewer

"This was a heart-warming tale of rags to riches. It was also wonderfully described and the characters were vivid and vibrant; a story that teaches of love defying boundaries and of people finding acceptance."

—Sara Phillip, Book Reviewer

"This is the best book I have ever had the pleasure of reading. . . It literally has everything, drama, action, fighting, romance, adventure, & suspense. . . Nexa is one of the most incredible female protagonists ever written. . .It literally had me on pins & needles the ENTIRE time. . . I cannot recommend this book highly enough. Please give yourself a wonderful treat & read this book… you will NOT be disappointed!!!"

—Jess- Goodreads Reviewer

"Took my breath away; excitement, adventure and suspense. . . This author has extracted a tender subject and created a supernatural fantasy about seeing beyond the surface of an individual. . . Also the romantic scenes would make a girl swoon. . . The fights between allies and foes and blood lust would attract the male readers. . .The conclusion was so powerful and scary this reader was sitting on the edge of her seat."

—Susan Mahoney, Book Blogger

"Adventure, incredible amounts of imagination and description go into this world! It is a buy now, don't leave the couch until the last chapter has reached an end kind of read!"

—Malcay- Amazon Reviewer

"The high action tale with the underlying love story that unfolds makes you want to keep reading and not put it down. I can't wait until the next book in the Shadows Series comes out."

—Karen- Amazon Reviewer

"Really enjoyed this book. A modern fairy tale complete with Kings and Queens, Princesses and Princes, castles and the damsel is not quite in distress. LOVE IT."

—Braine, Talk Supe- Book Blogger

". . . It's refreshing to see a female character portrayed without the girly cliches most writers fall into. She is someone I would like to meet in real life, and it is nice to read the first person POV of a character who is so well-round that she is brave, but still has the softer feminine side that defines her character. A definite must read."

—S. Teppen- Goodreads Reviewer

"I really enjoyed this book and had a hard time putting it down. . . This premise is interesting and the world building was intriguing. The author infused the tale with the feeling of suspicion and fear . . . The author does a great job with characterization and you grow to really feel for the characters throughout especially as they change and begin to see Nexa's point of view. . . I did enjoy the book and the originality. I would recommend this for young adult fantasy lovers. It's more of a mild dark fantasy, but it would definitely fall more in the traditional fantasy genre . "

—Jill- Goodreads Reviewer

To my husband who is also my best friend,
Our kids' greatest role model, and
A miracle worker in the lives of so many.

To our family and friends who have supported
Us in all of our adventures;
We love you!

CHEREE ALSOP

Chapter One

Fire rolled around me in waves. It flickered on the drapes, creating a battle of shadow and light as the flames devoured the cloth. The fire would win the battle, but shadow would win the war. The darkness always won.

I turned away from the heat that pulsed at my exposed face and hands. I was no stranger to what fire would do if it captured a live victim; those thoughts kept me focused whenever I glanced into a room already engulfed in dancing orange and yellow. It may look beautiful and mesmerizing, but fire was a cobra whose venom had no antidote once it truly caught hold.

A scream halted my progress down the hall. No one was supposed to be home. Jake had said the place was clear. The scream had been feminine and young.

I jogged up the hall in the opposite direction from the study. The stairs were already being consumed. My sneakers heated as I ran up them. There would be no going back down.

Another scream directed me to the second bedroom on the right. The door stuck. I wasn't sure if it was the heat or stubborn hinges, but I had to hit it twice with my shoulder before it gave up and burst open. My heart pounded as I stepped into the room and searched quickly for its occupant.

Smoke poured in around me. I dropped to the floor and made my way toward the bed in the corner. "Who's in here?" I called out.

"Help me!"

I turned toward a closet across from the bed. When I opened the door, a pair of dark brown eyes stared up at me. She was around eleven or twelve and wore a pink and purple nightgown with the word 'Princess' on the front. Tears streaked her cheeks.

A crash sounded below. The fire had taken over. There was no way I could make it to the study. Foreboding filled my chest.

"Come on," I told the girl.

She grabbed my outstretched hand. I led the way to the window in a crouch. The pane wouldn't budge. I picked up the small folding chair next to her bed and threw it at the window. It shattered, sucking smoke out into the night air.

The girl ran to the window. "It's too high," she said. "We'll get hurt!"

I shrugged out of my coat and shoved it quickly into my satchel. "Hold onto me," I told her.

"I don't understand," she protested, her eyes filling with tears.

I spread my wings just enough for her to see them through the smoke.

"You're a Galdoni!" she exclaimed, her eyes wide.

Fire crackled behind us. The floor was starting to sink. There wasn't time for me to reassure her. I wrapped my arms around her waist and dove out the window.

The fall was short. I barely had enough time to turn and catch the air. The girl squealed in fright. The night breeze filled my wings just before we hit the ground. My heart thundered in my chest as we were lifted above the aspens on the east side of the house. I landed on the road to the sound of sirens.

"Are you alright?" I asked.

She stepped back, the reflection of her burning home in her eyes. She nodded wordlessly.

"Go to the sirens. They'll get you to your parents."

She nodded again.

I spread my wings and pushed down hard. Within seconds I was far above the city watching the smoky haze turn the lights below brown and dull. I circled once, then followed the road a few blocks south. A green light blinked three times, then went dark. A few seconds later, the same pattern repeated. I landed next to the gray car and Jake shut off the light.

"I saved a girl," I said, still filled with adrenaline at the close encounter. "She was trapped in the fire."

"Where's the bag?" Jake demanded.

I took off the satchel and handed it to him, my thoughts still on the girl. "She was scared and would have been killed."

Jake pulled out my trench coat and threw it on the ground. "Where's the money?" he shouted.

Jolted back to the present, I stared at him. My gaze shifted from his angry glare to the empty bag in his hand. "I, uh, I couldn't get to it. The flames were out of control."

His eyes narrowed; my stomach tightened at the look.

His voice took on the deadly cold tone that made my blood turn to ice. "You set the fire like I instructed?"

I nodded.

"You should have had plenty of time to reach the safe before the fire took hold."

I nodded again. I no longer dared to look at his face. I could feel the anger rolling from him in waves. The consequences of my actions would be heavy.

"You left the money to rescue a girl?"

"She would have died." My answer was a whisper, a mere brush of breath from my lips.

His fist connected with my face. The pain flared through my cheekbone. I wanted to fight back, to make him pay for the punch. I could have made him so sorry he would never lift a finger again; but if I did, I would lose everything. I wouldn't go back; I could take anything if it meant not going back.

"Get in the car," he barked.

I slid into the backseat with my wings held tight against my back so the door didn't catch them when he slammed it shut. Trees and cars rushed by in a blur. I felt numb, frozen. I heard the girl's cry for help over and over in my head. Jake's reaction told me I shouldn't have rescued her, yet I couldn't have left her there to burn. I buried my face in one hand, too numb to fear what lay ahead.

***

Five lashes later, I lay on my back on the ratty couch. I could feel the blood dripping down my chest. It hurt to move. One lash had sliced along my shoulder, so it hurt to move my right wing, though they were fine; he never touched my wings or my back. He had said often enough that my ability to fly was his road to riches. He would never do anything to damage that.

"Tell me why I did this, Saro."

I gritted my teeth, but to ignore him would only invoke his anger once more. I let out a slow breath and turned my head to face him. Jake leaned in the doorway with an unaffected expression on his face.

"I shouldn't have left the money."

He nodded. "Why is that?"

"Because of the fines you pay to keep me."

He nodded again. "That's right, my boy. I pay huge amounts of money so that they don't take you back to the Academy." He spoke slowly as if I was a child who didn't understand, but I was seventeen. His condescending tone made me even more frustrated. "Do you want to go back?"

"No, Jake."

A hint of a smile showed on his face. "Good. I don't want you to."

There it was, that glimmer of truth. My heart reached for it; I wanted it to be true so much I pushed aside all that had happened. He wanted me to stay. Even though I had messed up and didn't bring him the money to pay the fines, he would let me stay.

"I'll do better next time."

He smiled, showing perfectly straight teeth. "I know you will, my boy."

He left the room and silence flooded the space around me once more. I closed my eyes, but the pounding of my heart beat a rhythm along the whiplashes that crisscrossed my chest and stomach. I was always surprised how much it hurt. I avoided looking at the wounds. The few glimpses I had taken showed skin that looked like little more than hamburger meat after all the lashings I had received over the last year and a half. Even my back carried a few marks, remnants of the nights he went into a true rage.

I was lucky. Though I had messed up, I had gotten away with only five lashes. There was another house he wanted to hit in a week, and I had to be fit enough to do it. He said we had to or we wouldn't make the payment; I didn't want to go back to the Academy. Keeping a Galdoni was expensive.

Sleep tugged at the corners of my mind. The girl's scream echoed as my thoughts were obscured by tendrils of smoke and flame. Light and shadow warred as it always did. This time, the shadows won quickly and I was pulled away to blissful unconsciousness.

***

"You remember where the safe is?"

I nodded and checked my pack for the twentieth time to ensure the tools I needed were there. The Molotovs Jake had made smelled strongly of gasoline and the alcohol he had used to soak the wicks. The three bottles were separated with towels to keep them from breaking, though I had lost more than one pack to accidents that were later branded on my skin in whiplashes.

I slid a hand into my pocket to reassure myself that I had the lighter. I slid the tan trench coat over my wings, then looped the satchel over my head and one arm.

"The green light will guide you home."

"Got it."

Jake had repeated the same statement at every robbery for the last year. No matter how chaotic the smoke, fire, fire engines, and police became, I could always fly high above whatever city we were in and locate the green light.

His reaction to the girl still sat in the back of my mind. He hadn't cared that she had been in the house. He wanted me to let her burn alive. I hoped he had been more careful to make sure this house was empty.

I followed his directions to a large home in a cul-de-sac with yellow siding and black shutters. Four white columns stood along the front porch. I peeked into the garage window. Two cars were missing of the four that occupied the place. I checked the door. It was unlocked. I had found that most people were careful with the front and back doors, but their garage doors were often left open.

I knelt near one of the two remaining vehicles and took out the first Molotov. I withdrew it carefully from the towels and set it under the car. I laid the extra-long piece of alcohol soaked wick on the ground and lit the end. I hurried into the house.

The alarm began to beep when I opened the door that led from the garage to the kitchen. I entered the code Jake had given me. The alarm stopped beeping and the light on top turned green. I never questioned where Jake got the codes; I was just grateful for them. They definitely made my life easier.

I lit another Molotov in the kitchen next to the well-stocked pantry and put the last one in the living room before following Jake's directions to the master bedroom. It wasn't hard to find the safe embedded in the wall behind the end table. I knelt and pulled out my tools.

The months of practicing with a stethoscope would pay off with the older safe. I listened carefully as I turned the dial to the left. A faint click sounded. I let out a slow breath and turned it to the right. The explosion from the first Molotov made my heart jump. I pushed down the adrenaline and concentrated. I couldn't rush or I would miss the click and have to start over again. I didn't want to risk more lashes.

I felt the second click through my sensitive fingertips, and turned the dial back to the left. The second Molotov exploded. I held my breath, willing the click to sound. I could already hear the fire tearing through the house. The cocktail Jake put in the bottles made them spread quicker than the combination we used when I first started. I only had a few minutes before the place would be entirely up in flames.

I forced my fingers to slow on the dial. I closed my eyes and put all my attention toward the lock. Each tiny click as it turned made my heart race. I rotated the dial at a maddeningly slow pace. I had just about given up to start over when the slightly louder click sounded. My heart leaped. I yanked open the door. Stacks of cash, gold coins, and a few documents filled the safe. I pulled open my bag and dumped everything inside.

A crash shook the floor. The fire was raging. I stepped out of the bedroom to see flames racing up the hallway. I ducked back inside and threw off my trench coat. Shoving it in my bag, I hurried to the window. The sound of a siren wailed faintly through the crackling flames. I pushed open the French doors and stepped onto the small balcony. The rush of fresh air through the house brought raging flames into the room.

I glanced back and realized I had forgotten to shut the safe. One of Jake's rules was to close the safe to give us more time before they realized it was the focus of the robbery. I ducked inside, running low to avoid the fire now snaking along the ceiling, and slammed the safe door closed. I darted back to the open French doors and dove over the railing just in time to avoid the reaching tendrils.

The rush of air filling my wings never ceased to thrill me. I raced low over the lawn, then pushed down hard to send myself high above the neighboring houses. I circled the house once and noted that the lights of the emergency vehicles were drawing closer. I wheeled slowly south. The green light blinked lazily along a back road not too far away.

"Did you get it?" Jake's gruff voice carried a hint of threat, warning that I had better not have failed him again.

Luckily, I had succeeded. I handed him the bag.

He grunted at the weight. "Good job, my boy." He set the bag on the front seat and began to look through it.

I smiled and slid across the back seat. Satisfied with what he found in the bag, he shoved it to the passenger seat and started the car.

"Keep this up and we'll be able to keep you out of the Academy for good," Jake crowed as he took us slowly down the road. He always drove five miles per hour under the speed limit; his way, he said, of balancing out the robberies we had to do in order to keep our lives afloat. I wasn't quite sure how not speeding related to theft, but he seemed perfectly happy with the explanation. I closed my eyes and tipped my head back.

Chapter Two

The streets below didn't look anything like they had from the barred windows of the Academy. A chill filled me even though I knew it was a dream. The dream came from memories all too fresh. Dead-end alleys were filled with trash, and a scent rose into the air that made my stomach curl. I pushed my wings harder, fighting to get as far away as possible from the cold stone building behind me.

A part of me trembled at the thought of leaving. I shouldn't be afraid to go; I shouldn't have any fear left in my body after the rigorous training regimen. Fear was weakness, and weakness was scorned behind the gray walls.

I pushed my wings harder, flying faster than I ever had before. My soul soared. I had never flown with such freedom. We had been allowed to fly inside the Academy in the Arena for the few minutes a week we were given to strengthen our wings. Such flights were done with swords, chains, and armor to weigh us down and prepare our muscles for the battles for which we had been raised.

Freedom had never crossed my mind. It was a forbidden word, because to talk of freedom meant to acknowledge captivity. We weren't captive; we were raised within the confines of the Academy to better teach us the honor and nobility of battle. Every second was given toward perfecting our art. Each fight was a form of worship, and honing our strength and skill showed true dedication.

Yet we were free. What did that mean? When they had thrown the Academy doors open and forced us from the walls, they had shattered everything I knew about the world. I didn't know where to go or what to do. The streets and buildings that passed below me were foreign places I had never wondered about. What did the people who looked up do, watching our forms fly past in the twilight? Why did they go inside the buildings or walk the streets? How was I to fit among them?

Terror filled me at the unknown. My wings faltered. The further I flew from the Academy, the faster I left the known and dove headlong into the unknown. I circled once. Galdoni I had known since my first steps continued past. No one spoke or acknowledged each other, the same as it had been within the Academy. Perhaps it wasn't the building that dictated our actions. Maybe Galdoni were naturally antisocial.

I fought back a smile as I landed on the rooftop of a building. It was my insubordinate thoughts that had often gotten me into trouble at the Academy. The beatings I had received until I learned to keep them in my head instead of voicing them aloud were lessons in self-preservation.

Psychoanalysis was a subject of study because Galdoni had to find whatever weakness they could exploit in their enemy. Psychoanalysis of myself showed that I used humor as a form of defense. I may not have been the quickest or strongest among the fighters, but my ability to laugh at my mistakes and berate myself until I stood back up helped me win with perseverance. I wasn't sure how my enemies could use that against me, but the teachers and duel instructors had been quick to beat me for it.

Maybe they didn't like my jokes. I grinned and walked to the edge of the roof. Down below, ladders and small metal balconies lined the path to the alley. A pair of voices drifted up to me.

"I don't want you to go." The voice was feminine, something I hadn't heard often during my life. There were two teachers and one administrator at the Academy that had been female. The lighter tones and gentleness of the voice held my attention.

"You don't want me here." I guessed the male to be my age by the youthfulness of his voice, somewhere around seventeen.

"I don't want you to fight with your brother or hide beer and cigarettes in your bedroom, that's what I don't want." By the tightness of her voice, she sounded close to tears.

"You don't accept me for who I am, Mom," the boy shouted.

A step on the metal balcony, then, "I love you for who you are; I just worry about where you're going."

"You don't like my friends, you don't like my girlfriend, and you always think I'm up to no good!"

"I just think they're bad influences on you."

"Maybe I can be a good influence on them."

"It doesn't work like that, and you know it."

The metal of the balcony rang as someone kicked it. "There is no one else, Mom." The boy's voice was quieter as if he admitted something that was hard for him to say.

"What do you mean?" the woman asked.

The sound of metal being kicked again followed. "They're the only friends I have. If I turn away from them, I'll be alone." I recognized the loneliness in the boy's heart.

I shied away from the thought. I didn't need anyone or anything. I was free of the Academy and the Galdoni and humans who beat me. I didn't need anything else, but the fact that humans warred with the same loneliness broke something inside of me. Had I hoped it would be different? I scoffed at the thought. Galdoni didn't hope. Hope was insubstantial, as meaningless as loneliness. Dwelling on either got me nowhere.

***

Jake dropped me off near the next house a few nights later. We usually didn't hit so many for fear that we would be tracked down, but Jake had gotten a good lead that he said would pay off very well if we played our cards right.

Trepidation filled me with each step. I usually wasn't nervous to hit a house. The healing lash marks across my chest burned as the strap of my satchel rubbed them, reminding me not to mess up. Jake had been fidgety in the car; he was usually calm and rational. He said that the money cache in this house held twice as much as the last, and said that I had to be sure to grab the envelope that was with the money. His excitement made me anxious to do good and prove my worth to him.

I studied the house that rose before me. White false shutters outlined windows curtained against the night. My steps echoed faintly against the beige siding. No lights showed in the interior. Jake had reassured me that the family had left on a vacation; nobody was expected home for at least two more days. That should have made me feel better, but instead my chest tightened as I drew near to the garage door.

It was locked. I let out a slow breath and drew my lock picking tools from my trench coat pocket. A Molotov shifted in the pack at my side, its glass chinking quietly against one of its comrades. I hadn't wrapped them well enough. I gritted my teeth and concentrated. A few seconds later, the door swung inward. Beeping followed.

I hurried across the garage into the house, counting the seconds of my forced entry as I followed the sound. Luckily, the inside door leading to the house was open, so I stepped inside and looked around for the alarm board. The beeping came from the front closet. I pulled the door open to reveal a glowing red circle and a number panel.

I quickly punched in the numbers Jake had given me. The alarm continued to beep, signaling that I hadn't entered the right code. I hit the numbers again, saying them out loud as Jake had done.

"Six, seven, five, five. . . ."

I hit the enter button again. It continued to beep. The timer was down to three seconds. Two. I hissed a curse and tore the panel from the wall. I fumbled through my backpack for the wire cutters I hardly ever needed. The cold metal was reassuring when I pulled them back out.

"One."

I held my breath and clipped all the wires. The screen went blank and the siren I was waiting for didn't sound. I stared at the empty screen for a second. A sigh of relief left me. I glared at the destroyed panel as I shoved the wire cutters back in my pack. At least the cops wouldn't be on their way.

I followed Jake's instructions to the basement. There was a well-stocked library to the left of the hall, followed by a wide room with a projector, reclining chairs, and several gold statues of men in wrestling holds. The one closest to the door caught my attention. One man was held in a headlock with his right arm held behind his back. His face was twisted in pain.

I chuckled. He could easily slip his left foot behind his opponent's right, shift his weight to his right leg, then sweep his left foot around and duck at the same time. If he had a good hold on his opponent's left wrist, he could have the man on the ground and at the verge of a dislocated shoulder in a matter of seconds.

I continued to the small study beyond. The room was bare; only a small wooden desk, a bronze lamp, and a picture of a ship on the ocean at sunset made up the only adornments. I knelt below the desk to the safe embedded in the wall. It was a newer style and would require a bit more finesse to open.

I pulled open my satchel and removed the drill. I withdrew the three Molotovs and adjusted the length of the wicks. Drilling a safe always took longer; being rushed by fire wasn't a pleasant experience. After ensuring that I had all the tools I needed, I took the Molotovs up to the main level.

I set the first one in the garage like before. Vehicles ignited quickly and were hard to put out when trapped inside the confines of the garage. It was my safety measure to ensure that I got away because with a fire burning so furiously, the fire department wouldn't have time to look for the culprit while they ensured the protection of the houses within reach of the flames.

I ran up the stairs to the second floor. Pictures lined the walls, photographs of children increasing in age each year, pictures on a beach, and kids with painted faces. A big family picture took up the majority of the space above the stairway, a mother and father with four children, three boys and a girl all dressed in white shirts and blue pants. The pictures around it showed the same family by a car, having a picnic beneath a tree with autumn leaves, and holding balloons amid a crowd of people.

One small frame caught my attention from the end of the row. I stepped closer to get a better look. The girl's eyes were beautiful with large brown irises. Wavy dark blond hair framed her face, accentuating high cheekbones. The barest hint of a smile touched her lips, but it didn't show in her eyes.

They held my attention. There was sadness in them, loneliness. My heart echoed the emotions with a painful thud.

I blew out a breath and turned away. I had a job to do. I lit the second Molotov in the upper living room near the curtained window. I ran back down the stairs, set the last Molotov in the kitchen next to floor-to-ceiling cabinets worked in beautiful spirals that I pretended not to notice, and jogged to the basement once more.

I drilled at an angle, aiming for the wheel pack as I had done many times on Jake's practice safes. When the hole was complete, I slipped the borescope through the hole. My heart hammered in my chest. No matter how many times I had broken into houses, I was always anxious to leave. It would only take one slipup for the cops to catch me and send me back to the Academy. The thought was enough to hone my attention to what I was doing.

I turned the dial carefully, watching through the borescope as I did so. Each notch lined up as it was supposed to, and the fence finally fell into place. I let out the breath I hadn't realized I was holding and pulled the door open. I stared at the bars of gold it revealed.

A few safes had held such bars, usually one or two that were at least matched by the cash I also found. Jake's excitement was definitely justified as I pulled out twenty gold bars along with several stacks of cash and an envelope of paper.

The sound of the first Molotov exploding in the garage made me work faster. A few seconds later, the next one followed in the kitchen. I double checked the safe to ensure it was completely empty, then spread the satchel on the ground with the main pocket wide open.

Chapter Three

The third Molotov exploded. A scream sounded above me. I jerked back and looked up the stairs. The sound had definitely been feminine. Memories of the girl I had saved rushed back. My chest still burned from the whipping. I had to bring the gold back to Jake.

I took a shuddering breath and began stacking the bars inside the satchel. I wasn't sure how much it could hold. Each bar weighed roughly three pounds. I was definitely pushing the limits of the pack. Another scream sounded.

I packed faster, shoving the bars as close together as possible. I threw the cash on top, then slipped the envelope into a side pocket. Something crashed in the room above me. I was running out of time.

I grabbed the satchel; the strap tore. Cursing under my breath, I picked the bag up in both arms and ran up the stairs. Fire raced along the kitchen cabinets. Smoke billowed and burned my eyes. Jake's Molotov cocktails were definitely getting more powerful. I made a mental note to set the fuses longer next time.

I slid the lock up on the sliding backdoor and stepped outside. Fresh night air rushed into the inferno that had become the kitchen. I took a deep breath to chase the smoke from my lungs.

Another scream sounded.

I needed to fly away. I should find Jake, get the gold and money to him, and leave the house behind to burn into a pile of ash.

I threw my trench coat in the bag. I knew what I should do. I knew what Jake expected.

I would pay later. I dropped the bag and opened my wings. With one powerful push, I rose to a balcony on the second floor. I pounded on the door with my fist. There was no movement inside. I regretted leaving my jacket. I gritted my teeth and drove my elbow through the glass door. Flames and smoke rushed out.

"Help!" the girl yelled.

"Where are you?" I demanded.

I ducked beneath the smoke. It was thick and black, the kind that could steal your breath from your lungs and leave you dead on the floor. I dropped to my knees and crawled, afraid that my wings would be singed by the fire racing across the ceiling.

"Over here!"

I made it through the door. The floor was hot, telling of the fire eating up from below. I couldn't burn my hands; if I did, my ability to break into safes would be nullified. A beam fell from the vaulted ceiling to the floor. The crash of wood shook the house; embers rose to join the flames that were devouring the house much faster than I had imagined possible. I had never stayed inside to experience it.

A hand touched my arm. Instinct took over. I grabbed the hand and drove my shoulder forward, bowling the attacker to his back. I had a hand on his throat and was about to bring my fist down when my vision focused. I stared through the smoke at a pair of brown eyes. She didn't beg for her life or cry. All she did was watch me, waiting to see what I would do.

I let go and backed up. "What are you doing in here?" I demanded through the crackle of fire around us.

"I live here," she said.

She pushed up to a sitting position. A pair of gray wings rose behind her. My heart froze.

"You're a-a—"

"You are, too," she replied, her voice just above a whisper. She smiled, then began to cough.

"Stay low," I told her. "Duck under the smoke." She did as I directed, but she couldn't stop coughing. I grabbed her arm and backpedaled down the hall toward the room with the balcony. She followed, coughing so hard her eyes filled with tears.

"Keep coming," I said, though there was no other choice. The inferno behind us was so hot my skin felt like it was on fire. The floor sunk beneath our weight. I pulled her toward the black hole that marked our exit.

When we reached the balcony, I sucked in huge gulps of fresh air. The girl coughed and held onto the railing. I opened my wings. She stared at me.

"We've got to get out of here."

"I can't fly," she said as if the idea was ridiculous.

"You've got wings," I pointed out.

She lowered her gaze. I stepped back far enough to look behind her. The fire bit at my back, urging me to jump. My mouth fell open. Her feathers ended in jagged edges just below her back while mine brushed the middle of my calves.

"Someone cut your feathers," I breathed, barely daring to believe it.

She lifted her chin and gave me a defiant look. "Then let me burn."

I watched her, meeting her glare for glare. The balcony sank below us with a jerk. She let out a little shriek. I grabbed her around the waist and drove my wings down hard. We rose above the flaming house. The balcony collapsed, sending up a rush of sparks. I soared away from it and landed on a small rise near the south side of the house. Sirens raced toward us in the distance.

I turned to go.

She caught my arm. "Don't leave me here."

I met her brown gaze again. My heart gave a strange little thump at the fear in her eyes. "They'll help you. Don't you live here?"

She nodded, then shook her head. "I-I'm not supposed to be outside." She pointed to her clipped wings. "I'm not supposed to exist." The bitterness in her voice said more than the words.

I glanced toward the house where I had left the bag of gold bars. I couldn't go back to Jake without them.

"Is there somewhere you can hide?" I asked. "I'll come get you when things die down."

She nodded. "There's an overpass just west of here. I used to hide under there sometimes."

"I'll meet you there before dawn." I opened my wings.

She caught my hand again. A slight tingle ran up my arm at the touch of her fingers on my skin. "Promise?" she asked.

Galdoni didn't make promises. We had no use for them; they inspired hope, one of the vague uncertainties humans held onto. Such intangibles had no place in battle. There was only one certainty in the Academy; we would die. That hadn't happened to me.

"I promise," I said for the first time in my life. The sirens echoed off the side of the burning house. "Run!" I told her.

She ran into the darkness as if the police would shoot her. She didn't know how valuable Galdoni were. According to Jake, a Galdoni who didn't pay the fees would be thrown into the first Arena battle without weapons, slaughtered for the coward and thief they were. It had cost so much to make us that not paying our dues was stealing from the government, and politicians looked poorly on thieves.

***

"Took your time," Jake said when I landed near the car.

I let the bag of gold bars fall to the ground for effect. "It was heavier than I expected."

His eyes widened at the sound and he dropped to his knees. He pulled the bag open. He grinned at the sight of the gold and cash, then lifted the flap and glanced at the envelope there. He laughed out loud. "Well done, Saro, my boy! You don't know what you've just accomplished!"

The thought that I had accomplished more than he knew sounded in the back of my head. I opened the car door and sat inside.

Jake hefted the pack and carried it the best he could to the trunk of the car. The vehicle tipped back slightly when he lifted the pack inside with much grunting and huffing.

"Thanks for the help," he said dryly when he collapsed on the driver's seat.

"Try flying two miles with it," I retorted before I could stop myself.

Instead of snapping at me like he usually would, he merely chuckled and turned the key in the ignition. The engine rumbled to life. He shifted the car into gear and pulled onto the lonely back road. I tipped my head to look out the window, wondering if the girl was safe.

Chapter Four

I flew back to the house just before sunrise. Jake had drunk himself into a happy stupor, and he wouldn't miss me until the next evening at the earliest. I hadn't seen him so happy since the first time I opened a safe using just my fingers to feel for the clicks of the dial. It was that night he declared he would pay the fees to keep me from the Academy. My year and a half of freedom had gone by so quickly.

It took longer than I thought it would to fly back to the house. We never hit homes in the same city where Jake lived, and I had paid special attention on the ride home so I would be able to make my way back. Even so, I got turned around a few times because everything looked different from the air. By the time I found it, smoke stained the fresh breeze, but the fire engines were gone. They had prevented the other houses from catching, but Jake's Molotov cocktails burned too quickly. There had been no way to save the home.

I felt no regret. Perhaps I should have, and I wondered at my inability to feel bad for my actions. Was it so selfish to want to avoid the Academy? If the family that owned the house had been in my place, forced to face the battlegrounds and fight for their lives, would they have burned their own home to avoid it?

To me, a house was nothing more than brick and wood, a place to hang pictures of times only the occupants remembered, rooms that held the whisper of memories, of laughter, of tears. I had seen enough families visiting in such rooms while they sipped from steaming cups and snacked on morsels evenly spaced on delicate glass plates, or read from books and cozied up on couches while watching movies to know what I didn't have. Perhaps burning the houses was my way of destroying the memories that would never be my own.

I snorted at the thought. It was boring and too filled with self-loathing to be accurate. I merely enjoyed racing against the Molotovs to see if I could escape without burning to death. I grinned. That sounded much healthier.

I flew over the charred rubble high enough that the people still milling on the ground wouldn't notice me. I followed the girl's directions west toward the traffic that raced along the six-lane highway, oblivious to the winged girl taking shelter beneath their road. I landed a ways from the overpass, too cautious from my training with Jake to rush into any situation haphazardly. As if burning houses and running from the cops wasn't haphazard.

I rolled my eyes and walked slowly toward the tunnel. I scanned every scraggly clump of sage and heat-withered tree for signs of law enforcement officers ready to drag me back to the Academy. Each shadow bristled with menace. What had I gotten myself into?

I was about to fly away when a lone figure stepped out from the darkness beneath the road. The sounds of the cars screaming down the freeway, sirens in the distance, and the barking of two dogs a block further south faded away.

I had heard there were moments that took a lifetime, instances in which every beat of the heart felt like an eternity. I was lost in one of those eternities when she met my gaze. Her expression was forlorn and sad as if she had almost given up on me. I couldn't breathe; I couldn't speak. I merely stood there watching her, wondering how the world went on with the emptiness in her eyes.

"You came back."

I expected accusation, maybe scorn. I deserved it for leaving a defenseless girl under a freeway for hours. Yet there was none of that in her tone. It was merely a statement, perhaps a bit of surprise, her eyebrows pinched together to hide her fear that she would never see a familiar face again. I pitied her that the familiar face she had searched for was mine.

"Sorry it took me so long."

She shook her head. "You didn't have to come for me."

I gave an incredulous snort. "Of course I did. You think I would leave you out here?" I glanced around us at the barren ground. A wall sheltered the cars from the ground where we stood, so even their lights didn't break the gloomy dawn. Sunlight strove to push its way through the overhanging clouds, but the unfallen rain and pollution won the battle, casting even the glorious rays in half-light.

"You could have," she said.

I didn't answer. Now that I was with her, I realized I didn't have a plan. Jake's number one rule was always to have a plan. Now I stood looking at a girl Galdoni, something that didn't exist as far as I knew, and I had no plan of what to do with her, or for her.

I stood staring at a supposedly non-existent anomaly whose expression was changing the longer I stared. Was that a hint of a smile? Her head tilted slightly to the right as she studied me. I realized with a start she was mocking me. She had her arms crossed in front of her as I did and her bottom lip was pushed into her top one with her eyebrows lowered in a searching expression. On me, I figured that the look was captivating, menacing, even. On her, it looked simply ridiculous.

"Stop that!"

A whisper of hurt crossed her face and she turned away. The jagged edges of her gray wings made me wince. The wince turned into true pain when I glanced down at her feet.

They were bare. She had run all the way from the burning house to the overpass without shoes. The roads in this part of the city were in a horrible state of disrepair, and most of the gutters were filled bottles and trash. Even with the distance between us I could see blood on her heels.

"Sit down."

She glanced at me in surprise. I crossed to her, kicking myself for my thoughtlessness.

She backed away quickly, her hands raised. She reached the side of the overpass and pressed back into the cement as though she wished to disappear inside it. She looked at the ground, unwilling to meet my eyes, a completely different person than the girl who had told me defiantly when I found her cut wings that I should let her burn.

The action caught me by surprise. I froze at the look of fear on her face. "What do you think. . . ?" My stomach twisted. I knew such things happened; the look on her face answered my unspoken question all too well. It took my breath away. "I'm not going to hurt you." I said it quietly, trying to hide the discomfort I felt that she would think such a thing. I shoved my hands in my pockets. "I was worried about your feet."

She looked down without meeting my eyes. She wiggled her toes. "They don't hurt."

"Just the same," I said. She looked up at me and I shrugged. The light made her brown eyes glow and my heart turned in my chest.

She sat down on the ground. I crossed the last few feet between us and crouched down next to her. "How did you run on these?" It was more of a whispered statement than a question, and she didn't answer. I picked up her right foot gently and examined it. Bits of glass showed in the lessening darkness. Blood caked several places. Her left foot was worse.

"Come on."

"Where are we going?"

I gave her what I hoped was an encouraging smile. I wasn't too good at those. The only time I had smiled at myself in the mirror at Jake's made me look like a shark about to snack on a few swimmers. It wasn't my teeth; they were straight for the most part. It was the fact that my smile didn't touch my eyes. They stayed wary and distrustful. The smile stayed only on my lips, a lie that would fool no one.

Yet a hint of a smile touched the girl's lips in the barest answer. Maybe I was getting better at smiling. Or maybe my smile was real. I snorted at myself for my idiotic thoughts and held out a hand. "You need to get those taken care of."

"And who's going to do it? You?" she asked incredulously, accepting my hand. She rose to her feet, but it was obvious her feet hurt now that I had pointed out the injuries.

I shrugged with another smile. "Do you see anyone else here?"

She laughed. It was short, but it made me tingle all over. I vowed to get her to laugh again, no matter what happened.

Since I had already given myself over to being an idiot, I figured I had better own it. "Your ride, my lady." I picked her up in my arms and a tiny squeak of surprise escaped her. I spread my wings and pushed down. The day was lightening fast enough that I had to hurry to avoid making us a target. I flew as high as I dared and sped toward Jake's apartment. I had no plan. Making it up on the fly was against all I knew, but it was also all I had, and ironic since I was actually flying. I grinned.

"It is amazing," the girl breathed.

I realized she had mistaken my grin for enjoyment of the flight. I nodded, eager not to explain my thoughts and confirm any suspicions she might have that I was indeed a fool. "You've never flown?" I asked, though I needn't have. The truth was in her eyes.

They were filled with joy and excitement. Her cheeks were flushed and she watched the ground as though amazed that we were so high above it. I could feel her wings move against my arm, straining to join the flight. The anger I felt that such a thing had been taken from her struggled to break free. I gritted my teeth against asking her who had done such a thing. She had gone through enough; there would be time for explanations later. I needed to land before anyone reported a Galdoni in the air.

I pushed my wings hard. We soared through the early dawn above the pollution and clouds. The air was thinner and I had to work harder to keep us above it, but it was worth everything to see the look of wonder on the girl's face.

"What's your name?" I asked before I even realized I had spoken.

She glanced back at me with a true smile. "Alana. What's yours?"

"Saro."

Her smile faltered just a little. "That's a sad name."

I nodded. My reasons were my own.

We were close to Jake's apartment building. Though I couldn't see it through the haze, I felt it in my bones. I wondered if it was the same way pigeons knew when they were home. I tipped my wings and took us in a spiral toward the ground. As we reached the cloud layer, buildings began to appear around us. I heard Alana's breath catch at how close they were, but I had flown through the area only in darkness over the past year and knew the layout by heart.

We landed softly on the sidewalk behind Jake's apartment complex. The city was still locked in the early morning stillness that blanketed the world before alarms went off and work called. It was my favorite time of day. It felt as though magic coated the city; there was no cold, no loneliness, no homelessness, no yelling, no barking, and no dejection. I could imagine that Galdoni were safe inside warm apartments instead of training at the Academy for battle. They were cozy in beds instead of on pallets, with the promise of a real breakfast instead of cold gruel.

It was ridiculous, really. I hardly ever allowed myself to imagine such silly things. When I did it made the ache in my heart stronger; the need to do something more with my life burned in my veins. Yet what was there to do?

"Are you alright?"

Alana's voice jerked me back to reality. I shook my head at the stupidity of my thoughts and gave her a small smile. "I should be asking you the same thing. How are your feet?"

"Fine," she replied, her eyes searching mine. "Where are we?"

I pushed open the back door to Jake's apartment complex. Alana took a step forward. She tried to hide the wince of stepping on her damaged feet, but I saw her pain in the line of her jaw and the slight intake of breath as she stifled a whimper.

Without giving her a choice, I picked her up again and carried her inside. She remained silent, her hands soft on my shoulders. I didn't know why I cared. I hadn't cared about anyone or anything besides staying out of the Academy for as long as I could remember. I definitely hadn't learned compassion inside the walls. The Arena saw to that. Those who had compassion died; if you cared about your enemy, they would kill you for your weakness.

I carried her past the elevator that hadn't worked since at least as long as I had been there. I grabbed the door knob to the basement with one hand, but managed to bump her foot into it as I pulled it open. "Sorry," I said when her hand tightened on my shoulder.

She gave a soft laugh, a soothing sound I had never heard before. "You don't carry girls around much, do you?"

I smiled as I walked down the steps, careful to keep from running either her feet or her head into the bricks. Carrying a girl was a harder task than it looked. "Not exactly."

"I can't really complain since you saved me from the fire. That was the bravest thing I've ever seen." The awe in her voice gripped my heart in a tight fist. "Why did you go into the house in the first place?"

I was glad she couldn't see my face in the darkness. I wasn't sure I could hide the truth from her searching gaze if she did. "I, uh, I saw the smoke and worried someone might be inside." I couldn't explain why I didn't tell her the truth. I robbed houses; that's all there was to it. But there was something in the way she looked at me, trust, friendship, things I had never seen before. I was afraid if she knew I was responsible for the fire, I would lose all of it.

"That was incredibly brave," she said quietly.

I reached the bottom step to the basement. No one ever went down there. It was dirty and carried a hint of mouse in the musty smell that permeated everything. Random pieces of furniture occupied the space, remnants of tenants who had moved or passed away and left the items behind. I set Alana carefully in an overstuffed armchair. Dust rose around us and tickled my nose. I reached up and pulled the chain to the overhead light. The single bulb swayed gently from side to side, casting shadows around the room.

"You'll be safe here," I said as I turned away.

"Where are you going?" The fear in Alana's voice made me pause. I couldn't blame her for not wanting to be alone, but I couldn't help her if I didn't leave.

I took a calming breath to steel my heart against her fear. It ate at my willpower, asking me to stay beside, to reassure her that she was safe. I gritted my teeth. I had to be strong. I glanced back at her. "To get some things for your feet." I replied gruffly.

"You're going out like that?"

The concern on her face gripped my heart tighter. No one had ever cared. I pulled the trench coat from the satchel I always carried and slipped it over my shoulders. "I'll be in disguise."

She smiled as if I had revealed the world's best trick. "Good luck, Saro."

"Thank you," I replied hesitantly before heading up the stairs. They were strange words, and tasted unfamiliar. I had never spoken them before; I had never owed them to anyone before. My arrangement with Jake was give and take. I knew he used some of the money to pad his own pocket, but the fact that he kept me out of the Arena by paying the substantial fees made it all worthwhile. I didn't owe him and he definitely didn't owe me anything. Appreciation for what each did remained unspoken because each cancelled the other out.

Yet Alana's wish after my wellbeing was unnecessary. Yes, I was risking discovery to get bandages for her feet, but I had gone out many times. If I hit the convenience stores super early or extremely late, usually the individual behind the counter was weary enough not to question anyone buying sundry items. Was it her concern I was thanking or her smile? All I knew was that I had never before confronted something so powerful. I would do anything to see it again, even if it meant risking life, limb, and Jake's temper.

Chapter Five

I heard a slight scuff from below as I took the stairs two at a time a half hour later, yet when I reached the basement, it appeared empty. Had someone found Alana? Had she given up on me and left? I willed my eyes to adjust faster to the darkness. The swaying light played with my nerves that were still tense from the fear of discovery despite my bravado on my walk to the convenience store. Every trip outside meant the threat of being discovered; Jake made certain I never forgot.

"Alana?" I called quietly. I liked the way her name felt. It rolled off my tongue as though it was a foreign language and a prayer wrapped in one. I grinned at myself. Leave it to the mysterious Galdoni girl to make me take up religion.

"Saro?"

All thoughts fled my mind at the sound of her voice. How could I have missed it so much in the short time I was gone? I hurried forward. "Are you alright?"

She stood gingerly from behind a brown, green, and yellow wool couch. The relief on her face was unmistakable. Never before had the sight of myself filled someone with such obvious joy. I didn't dare get used to the sight, but it buoyed something up inside of me. It made me feel as though I mattered more than air or water. I felt like I was flying even though my worn shoes were most definitely on the cement ground.

"I'm so glad to see you," she said.

I held out a hand and she accepted it. She tried to climb over the back of the couch, but I could see a million things that could happen if she tripped. There were lamps and end tables waiting to be crashed into, a pile of tattered blankets that might upset her balance, and the unforgiving floor just waiting to break an arm or wing. I jumped onto the couch and lifted her over, amazed at how light she felt.

She laughed when I set her carefully on the cushion.

"What?" I asked, feeling a wall rise in case she laughed at me.

"I'm not made of glass," she said. "I can climb over a couch."

I grinned at myself. It wasn't a smile; it wasn't a predatory shark-like revealing of the teeth before I attacked. It was a true grin, and it felt good and strange for my mouth to turn up that way. "I thought you were going to hurt yourself."

She laughed out loud, showing her own pretty white teeth. "Are other Galdoni klutzes then?"

"No other Galdoni are like you."

I regretted it the moment I said it. She dropped her gaze and studied the floor; the wall I had felt moments ago chased the emotion from her face. I hadn't had enough social interactions to know how to bring her back from wherever she was hiding. I let out a slow breath and lowered to my knees. I could feel her eyes on me as I took out the bandages and ointment I had bought with the few dollars I always kept hidden in my pack in case of an emergency. Even Jake didn't know about that.

When everything was ready, I felt suddenly nervous. "I'm not exactly a doctor," I said.

"You could have fooled me," Alana replied.

My lips twisted again into the smile. How was it that a simple sentence from her could make me feel so happy? I glanced up at her. "Doctors have nurses."

"And you're sorely lacking in beautiful women ready to assist you."

I snorted at the thought. "It's not exactly sanitary down here."

She looked around. "It's cozy, and I'm sure the mice won't mind having a roommate if I clean up after myself."

I set one of her feet gently on my knee. I had almost forgotten how bad they were. The fact that she pretended they didn't hurt bothered me. Galdoni were supposed to be tough, to never complain, to tend to their wounds and hide their pain so it was never used against them. Yet I wanted her to be different; I expected her to be. I let out a small breath and said, "This is going to hurt."

"I know," she replied in a tight voice.

I looked up to see her eyes closed and hands tightly gripping one of the ratty blankets. I sprayed a bottle of saline solution on the bottom of her foot. She kept perfectly still. I picked up the pair of tweezers I had purchased. My hands shook. I had never doctored someone else, and my own wounds I had tended to healed as scars that still pained me sometimes. I didn't want to be the cause of more pain to her.

"I don't think I should do this."

She opened her eyes. Her brown gaze held me with a look of trust and belief I felt I didn't deserve. Her smile was small, but it touched her eyes. "Who else is there?"

I gave in. "Fine, but I don't expect you to like me much after this."

"Who says I like you now?"

The words and the way she said them brought another smile to my face. Instead of looking up to show myself grinning like a dork yet again, I ducked my head and concentrated on her foot. A gasp answered my gentle prodding. I gripped a piece of glass firmly with the tweezers and drew it out as gently as I could.

Alana kept silent, but when I looked up again I saw tears rolling down her face. I clenched my jaw and focused on her foot. I couldn't explain it, but every intake of breath or muted

54

gasp hurt me more than any wound I had ever received at the Academy. My hands were shaking by the time I was done, and the blood that coated my fingers felt more precious than the blood pounding through my heart.

I sprayed more saline solution on the bottom of both of her feet, then spread ointment across the tattered skin as gently as possible. I pressed bandages against the worst of the wounds before wrapping her feet in gauze.

I had never cared for anyone or anything. The ache I felt at the sight of the blood on the floor was as unfamiliar as the rage that burned in my chest at the thought of her cut wings. I was used to kill or be killed. At the Academy there weren't friends, there wasn't family, there were only Galdoni waiting to kill you should you make a wrong move or forget to watch your back. I didn't care about any of them.

A slight whisper in the back of my mind reminded me that I was wrong. I grimaced at the rush of memories brought by the thought.

"What are you thinking?"

Alana's quiet voice jolted through the silence. I looked up, surprised to find her watching me. The pain was bright in her eyes, her expression pleading as though she asked for a distraction.

I cleared my throat, hesitant to trust her with something as secret as my thoughts. I was Saro. I didn't trust anyone. Yet she pleaded without saying a word.

"The Academy," I replied honestly.

She nodded as though she had guessed as much. "It must have been horrible," she said.

I looked down and realized I still held her feet, one in each hand as if by touching them I could help her heal faster. I eased them gently to the ground, reluctant for reasons I couldn't explain to release my hold on her. I rocked back on my heels and felt a slight chill at being distant from her, if only by less than a foot. "Worse than you'll ever know," I replied without meeting her gaze. "At least I hope so." The thought of Alana at the Academy sent another chill racing up my spine.

"What do you mean?"

I picked up the supplies I had used on her feet and tucked them back into the plastic bag from the convenience store. "If you're captured, they'll take you there. I don't know how a girl would fare at the Academy, but they don't hesitate to send anyone to the Arena." My voice grew bitter. "Anyone at all."

Silence filled the air between us. She broke it after a few minutes. "Saro, the Academy doesn't exist anymore." She said the words hesitantly as though worried about how I would take them.

I felt a pang of remorse at her naiveté. Pretending something didn't exist didn't make it any less real. The scars across my body ached in agreement. "It exists; trust me."

I saw her shake her head out of the corner of my eye. "It used to, but it was disbanded a year ago. The Galdoni are free."

The absurdity of her statement made me laugh out loud. "Yeah, then why were you hiding from the cops?"

She shrugged her shoulders, making her gray wings move. "I thought it was obvious."

A strange feeling pitted my stomach. "Because you're a girl?"

She nodded. "Female Galdoni don't exist. The world wasn't ready for girls to fight. Even humans wouldn't have put up with that."

I studied her. "If you don't exist, why am I looking at you right now?"

She lowered her gaze. "The scientists never stopped experimenting. Their original goal was to create ultimate soldiers, but the Galdoni were too unpredictable, too *animal* in their impulses."

Her emphasis wasn't lost on me, but my mind was already spinning. "That doesn't explain why you were at that house."

She opened her mouth to say something, then closed it again. Her brown eyes searched the room, avoiding my gaze. She finally said, "They wanted to make something a little more human, but they didn't want to start from scratch."

Her gaze finally locked on mine, willing me to understand. I was still stuck on her comment about the Academy being shut down. It didn't make sense. Jake said he paid fees to keep me with him. He protected me. He couldn't have lied.

My thoughts darkened, laughing in cruel tones at the back of my mind. Had I been the one who was naïve?

I ran from the thought, pounding it down into a little black box that I locked in the far reaches of my mind to never be opened again. I focused on her words, focused on the reason for girl Galdoni. Why would having girl Galdoni make them more human? What reason could they possibly have?

The knot in my stomach hardened into a brick. I felt my eyes widened as I stared at Alana. She nodded. "Understand now?"

"Babies?" I knew enough from our biology classes about the difference between test tube babies like the Galdoni and the way human babies were born. My voice came out in a strangled whisper. "They would impregnate girl Galdoni so the babies would be more human?"

She nodded, her eyes hidden behind lowered lashes. "Less driven by animal instincts and the need for their own survival; more willing to cooperate."

My jaw clenched so hard I thought my teeth would break. I felt like I was going to explode. I wanted to hit someone; my fists tightened. I rested one on the ground, leaning on it from my crouched position.

A hand touched my arm. "It's okay, Saro."

"How can you say that?" I demanded, looking up at Alana. "How much more can they get away with? It's not okay. It's wrong, and it's not animal instincts that tell me so, it's my heart." My heart pounded as though I had trained for an hour. My chest heaved and I fought to draw in air. At the Academy it had been easy to pretend I was an animal, fit only to fight. Outside, though, it wasn't a black and white world, not by a long shot. I had never been taught how to deal with gray, yet away from the Academy, gray was the only color that existed, gray that symbolized the coming of a storm.

"You're not an animal," Alana said. Her fingers brushed my unruly dark brown hair from my face. Her palm cupped my cheek gently. I turned my face into her hand. I closed my eyes and allowed myself to feel just for a moment what a touch without malice could be like. A soft warmth surrounded her hand; my heartbeat slowed. I took a calming breath, then ducked my head, breaking the contact.

"We're not human, Alana. We're not one of them." I rose. "I'd rather be an animal than be one of them." I walked to the door. I paused at the threshold and glanced back. Pain showed on her face. Whether it was from my words or her feet, I couldn't say. I leaned my forehead against the door frame for a moment; my wings drooped against my back. No words of comfort came to me. Comforting someone wasn't a strong point of mine; I didn't know what to say to make her feel better. I shook my head and started up the stairs. "I'll be back with food," I promised.

Chapter Six

The bottles that littered the floor clinked together when I opened the door. Jake stirred on his overstuffed chair in the corner. It smelled of cigarettes and the beer he spilled on it whenever he fell asleep drinking; I also smelled urine from the times Jake way overindulged, but whenever he planned to get completely blackout drunk, that was his favorite place.

"Another beer," he demanded in his sleep.

I crossed to the fridge in the search of something other than his favorite beverage. A moldy block of cheese, several packets of ham, and bread hardened from age took up the middle shelf. There were several fast food bags stuffed along the top. I peeked into the two closest to the front and so therefore the most likely to be fresh. I about gagged at the sight of a hamburger with green meat, the tomato of which had turned into a ring of fuzz. The second bag proved more promising; it contained a few tacos that were only slightly stale.

Taking the tacos, a bottle of water, and the two blankets on the floor that made up my bed, I slipped back out the door again. I passed one man on my way back down the stairs, but despite my trepidation, he merely muttered about miscreants spray-painting brick walls and ignored me completely.

I hadn't realized how anxious I was to make sure Alana was safe until I saw her sleeping on the couch. The sight of her unharmed and resting made the tight muscles in my chest and back loosen. She slept quietly, her head tilted slightly to one side with a strand of dark blond hair crossing her cheek.

I had a sudden impulse to sweep the hair back where it belonged. My hand was halfway to her face when I realized what I was doing. I shook my head and turned away. I quickly settled the blankets on top of her before pulling over an empty dog kennel from the corner. I set the tacos and water on top of it in the hopes that the mice and rats who occupied the basement would have a harder time reaching it.

I should have her leave. Jake would kill her and probably me if he knew I was hiding a girl in the basement; or perhaps he would make her join me in the robberies. The thought made me sick as I stood there watching her sleep. She looked so peaceful. She lay on her side with her gray wings just visible over the edge of the blanket I had spread over her. The feathers looked soft in the light of the single bulb overhead. I wanted to run my fingers through them.

I walked to the door. She made me feel things a Galdoni shouldn't feel. I was an animal; she had even said so, echoing the sentiments at the Academy with words that hurt more than their whips ever had. She might not have meant the way I took them, but while my heart shied away, my teeth had ripped into flesh, and my hands had choked the life out of others. She should leave because she didn't know what I had done, what I truly was.

I sank onto the floor by the door and buried my face in my hands. The memories overwhelmed me. I saw lights overhead, cut out by a flurry of wings. They pressed me down, down, down, forcing me onto the unforgiving sands of the Arena. They meant to kill me. The bite of their weapons said it as much as their cold eyes. Blade swung his sword. They held me tight. I couldn't move. Metal glinted in the searing light. I closed my eyes.

"Saro?" Alana sounded tired but concerned.

I pushed up quickly.

"Are you alright?"

"Fine." I kept my face from the light. "There's food on the cage. I'll check on you in the morning." I stumbled up the stairs two at a time. I wasn't sure if I was running from her or the memories; at the moment, they both felt the same.

***

"The green light will guide you home," Jake said.

"Got it." I pulled my trench coat close and adjusted the satchel. The Molotovs chinked together lightly. Jake drove down the road, a single pair of taillights against the house-lined street. No lights showed in the homes around me. The inhabitants were no doubt asleep at the early morning hour. I picked the lock on the garage and slipped inside.

I left the Molotovs in the kitchen and hurried upstairs. It was my new habit, a quick check to ensure that the house was empty before I set it up in flames. I realized that should have been my strategy from the beginning, but at least I was learning. I jogged past school pictures that lined the walls like mug shots, cute kids who no doubt never smiled like that in real life. I hadn't had much experience around kids besides those at the Academy who had tried to kill me growing up; I suppose that might have skewed my perspective a bit.

The house was empty. Good. No more winged girls calling out for help or terrified cries from within the flames. I did find a cat, a black and white thing that hissed when I tossed it outside. It landed on its feet. Jake would have lashed me for taking the time to save it. At least my conscience was free, although I couldn't say when exactly I had begun to have a conscience, and I also highly doubted it was a good thing for a Galdoni to have. Accountability didn't exactly rank high in the life of killers.

I walked past the living room back to the kitchen, and something caught my eye. I turned slowly. A laptop sat on the corner of the coffee table. I glanced back at the bag of Molotovs, then at the laptop again. I knew I shouldn't. There wasn't time and Jake was swift to punish slothfulness. I took another step toward the kitchen, but Alana's words tickled at the back of my mind. I had to know.

Breathing a curse, I hurried to the laptop and opened it. The screen glowed blue with a window in one corner. It asked for a password. I shook my head as I shut it and set it back on the coffee table. I didn't set it straight; the weight of the battery pulled it over the edge. I caught it before it hit the ground. I was about to put it back when I noticed something had been written on the backside. The word 'password' had been scrawled with a black pen. Curious, I opened the laptop again and sat on the couch. With hesitant fingers, I typed 'password' into the box. I hit enter and the screen changed.

"Great," I muttered. "Using the word password for the password. This man's a genius." I grinned wryly. "And he wrote it on the back of his laptop in case he forgot."

Still chuckling to myself, I pulled up the internet and typed a few words into the search bar. My laughter died in an instant. Jake didn't own a laptop or a television. He said such things were for the lazy, though I wondered what was different from his booze-filled evenings on the couch. He did have a cell phone with the internet on it and occasionally he made me search for fast food places or the nearest bar. Depending on what city we were in, it varied widely. I had gotten used to him grabbing the phone quickly from me the second the search was completed.

My fingers shook. Had he really kept technology from his apartment because he was afraid I would find the truth? Entering the words 'Galdoni Freedom' showed a picture of KL426, a Galdoni I had known from combat at the Academy. The caption read "Kale's Fight Brings Freedom for Galdoni." He stood in front of the Arena. Its black gates hung crookedly and had been chained to prevent intruders. They hadn't been that way when I left.

I scrolled down. A button beckoned me to push play. I took a hesitant breath, then pushed it. Music started. I saw a tiny Galdoni baby with black wings sleeping in gloved hands. In the next scene, a toddler was learning to walk, then there were young Galdoni in a classroom. A teacher was in the middle of bringing down a whip to discipline the child, something so common it didn't bother me.

My heart stopped when the video shifted to the next scene. A young Galdoni boy stood with a katana in the middle of a fighting circle. The tip of the blade rested on the ground, something the enforcers at the Academy would have beaten us for. Dark blood coated the blade, trailing from the middle of the weapon to the floor. The boy's head hung low, his wings drooped against his back. The feathers of his wings had been colored black; I didn't know why. It didn't matter.

I closed my eyes. A tear slid down my cheek. I remembered the loss I felt as I stared down at VZ579. He clutched his stomach, holding in its contents that we both knew would spill out the instant he let go. Lifeblood flowed around him, coloring the sand dark brown. I remembered the feeling of it when it reached my feet. He was dying, and I had killed him. I had killed my best friend when I was only six years old.

I stood with a roar and threw the laptop across the room. It crashed into the entertainment stand, causing movies and electronics to fall to the floor. Still the music continued to emanate from the small black rectangle. I covered my ears, but I couldn't keep out the sound. I sobbed, pain wracking my shoulders. I again felt the enforcer's hand grip my shoulder and heard his gruff voice say, "Well done, SR029."

I slammed my fist into the coffee table. The glass shattered. I hit the table again and again, cracking the wood and destroying the glass panel on the other side. I fell to my knees beside the mess. An emotionless voice in the back of my mind reminded me that Jake would be mad I had left evidence that the fire wasn't normal. I shook my head. I was a fool. The evidence of the Molotovs alone would show that it wasn't a normal fire. Yet Jake never left any sign of arson on the houses; it was all mine.

I drew my legs up under my chin and rested my forehead against my knees. I closed my burning eyes. Words spoke from the laptop. "The life of a single Galdoni. Not a monster, not an animal, but a hero waiting for his chance to live. We've been taught to see them as inhuman, but we can't deny the humanity Kale has shown. Help us stop the violence that goes on behind these walls. Refuse to watch the fights; don't gamble on lives that should be spent in the pursuit of happiness, our right and theirs. Don't let Kale die because you didn't take a stand."

I rose shakily to my feet. I couldn't look at the laptop. The words had stopped, but they circled in my mind like vultures. *Not a monster. Not an animal.* I was an animal. The words were a lie. I robbed without remorse. I had fallen into Jake's trap without question. I had become his scapegoat, following him blindly because he promised to keep me from Academy. I had been so desperate not to go back that I believed anything he said. I was a fool.

I pulled the Molotovs from the satchel and lit them without bothering to check how long the fuses were. I threw all three into the living room where the laptop waited to condemn the stupidity of my actions. The roar of flames was the only comfort I felt. I stood and watched the fire consume the drapes and couch cushions. It beat against my face with the same desperate rage I felt, ready to destroy anything in its path. I finally retreated when the heat became too much. I stumbled outside into the backyard.

What would I do? Everything had been a lie. Inside the Academy, we were raised with the belief that combat was sacred, and an honorable death was the only way to reach heaven. When I left the Academy, I found that all the truths I had believed were wrong, designed to feed a greedy nation who gambled life savings on the show where they broadcasted our fights to the death. How many Galdoni had died with the belief that they would reach heaven instead of some cable box to the enjoyment of bloodthirsty viewers?

When Jake found me, he had promised to give me a purpose in life. I remembered the gleam in his eyes when he took me in. Memories danced within the firelight.

"You okay, son?"

I stood up straight despite the pain in my shoulder. "Fine."

Jake's eyebrows drew together. "You don't look fine." He indicated my shoulder with a lift of his chin. "I heard a gunshot. That's why I came."

"They outnumbered me. I had to fight back."

I had finally given up flying when my empty stomach hurt enough to drive me to search for food. I found discarded loaves of bread in a big metal bin behind a bakery. That was where they found me.

"This is our turf," a big, burly man with black marks down his arms growled.

There were seven of them. I was fast, but they were armed. A quick check showed a variety of knives and clubs. I wasn't at my full strength because I was starving and had flown for hours, circling back over the surrounding cities because for some reason fear pressed against me the further I got from the Academy. As much as I wanted to leave it behind, it still had me in its iron claws. "I don't want trouble," I replied.

"Too bad," the first man said with a chuckle, "Because we do."

My wingspan was too wide for the alley. I tried anyway. When I spread my wings, a sharp crack rang out. Fire tore through my shoulder with such force that I stumbled back against the garbage bin. The gang closed in.

I crouched and drove a fist into the first man's groin, then chopped the knee of a second hard enough to feel his joint give way. I spun back and elbowed another in the face, followed by a haymaker to the jaw of his companion. A man jumped on my back, tearing at my wings. I let his weight pull me backwards and shoved my elbow behind me as I fell. The force drove the air from his lungs as I slammed my full mass into his stomach. I rolled to the right in time to avoid a club, then caught it on my way up and punched my attacker in the stomach.

A man flipped open a knife and tried to slice my face. I ducked under his slice and caught his arm in both of my own. I brought my left hand down and drove my right arm up on the other side of his elbow, snapping it with a quick push. He stumbled back, screaming in pain.

A club caught me behind the knees. I fell on my back, but kicked out before any of them could jump me. My foot connected with a knee and another scream followed. Someone drove a fist at my face. I blocked it with my forearms and used his momentum to pull him down on the pavement next to me. I slammed my elbow into his nose. A club hit my head. Stars danced in my vision.

"What's going on back there?" a voice demanded. "I've called the cops!"

"Let's get out of here," one of the gang members shouted. They pulled each other to their feet. Some limped and several were bleeding from crushed noses or mouths. As the man from the front neared, they ran the opposite way down the alley.

I used the garbage bin to pull myself up. I held my shoulder to staunch the blood that flowed from the bullet wound.

"You okay, son?"

Jake had taken me home and introduced me to alcohol for the first time when he had me drink it as a painkiller so he could remove the bullet. He then joined me in drinking, and when his landlord pounded on the door and demanded the rent, Jake showed me the rage his drinking invoked. The next morning, we moved to a new apartment and I vowed to never touch the stuff again. Jake disappeared for two days, and when he came back, he was ready for me to get to work.

I shook my head, clearing the memories of learning how to open safes and break into houses. It had been something to do. I didn't care back then whether it was right or wrong. After the Academy, nothing seemed right anymore.

Sirens raced toward me. The safe was a loss. Trepidation filled my chest when I opened my wings. I pushed down hard and flew high above the burning house. I watched the fire engines pull up. The team hurried to save the home, but the Molotovs burned so hot and the flames devoured everything so quickly there wasn't much they could do.

I felt a pang of remorse as I turned south and searched the ground by habit for the blinking green light. I rode the wind slowly toward Jake's car. The heaviness in my chest grew when I saw him leaning against the door with his arms crossed. I didn't know what to say. I wasn't ready to confront him. As much as I hated to admit it, I had nowhere else to go.

"What happened?" Jake demanded the instant I landed.

"One of the Molotovs exploded early," I said quickly, hoping he would buy the excuse.

The cold look in his eyes chased away that hope in a heartbeat. "You didn't make it to the safe?"

"I-I had just started on the dial when I heard the Molotov explode. I tried to hurry, but I couldn't hear over the flames." I looked at the ground. I wasn't a good liar. I supposed in a normal world that would have been a good thing. In mine, however, I was as good as lost.

"Get in the car."

A chill ran down my spine at the growl in Jake's voice. I slid onto the backseat without speaking. Explanations only made him angrier. Nothing would save me from the beating his clenched jaw promised. The steel in his eyes as he watched the road buried itself in my heart. I wished I didn't need him.

Chapter Seven

I sat on the chair and gritted my teeth. The first lash cut deep across the scars of the others. The second quickly followed. If I had to guess, I would have said Jake was putting more strength into it. Each lash cut deeper than the one before, and the whip hissed through the air, splattering small drops of red across the wall closest to us.

"I wish you would just listen to me," Jake said. Lash. "You know to check the Molotovs before you light them." Lash. "You've done it two dozen times already." Lash. "You're getting sloppy." Lash. He fell quiet.

I preferred the silence broken only by the hiss of the whip. He whipped me three more times, then whispered a curse and whipped me once again. The tip of the lash cut around my shoulder to my back. I couldn't help the yell that tore from my lips at how deep the leather cut into my shoulder. Jake's face paled. "Turn around," he demanded.

I followed his command and turned. Jake let out a breath of relief. "It didn't cut your wing." He smiled. "Can't damage those money-makers. That'd be stupid, wouldn't it?"

I nodded because his pause meant he expected a response.

He let out a loud sigh. "You know I don't like to do this, Saro. Why can't you just be more careful?"

"I'll be more careful," I replied in a monotone voice.

He studied me for a minute, then nodded. "Good. Go get yourself cleaned up."

I sat on the chair for a few more minutes as he helped himself to a beer from the fridge and collapsed on the couch. He took a long swig and closed his eyes. When it was obvious he wasn't going to move anytime soon, I grabbed my tee-shirt from the floor and went into the bathroom.

My chest bled freely. I grimaced at the sight of torn flesh layered on top of the scars from both the Arena and Jake's tutelage. I grabbed a few bandages from the box by the toilet and dabbed at the blood. My mind flashed to Alana's feet. She shouldn't be alone.

I gingerly slipped my black tee-shirt over my head. The slits I had cut in the back fell around my wings. Maybe if the Galdoni were free, someone could make clothes that actually fit right. I shook my head and grinned at the absurdity of the statement. My whole world had fallen apart yet again, and I was wondering if different clothing choices were available.

I slipped into the trench coat and checked to make sure Jake was asleep before I shut the door behind me. Carrying two more bottles of water and a half-eaten box of pizza from the night before, I hurried down the stairs to the basement.

Alana was still sleeping on the couch. She had turned to her side so that one of her gray wings spread along her body. I avoided looking at the jagged edges of her feathers as I knelt beside her. "Alana?"

She stirred slightly, but didn't open her eyes. A slight smile touched her lips that I couldn't help echoing. In the light of the bare bulb overhead, her cheek looked flushed. I wondered if she had a fever. I opened my hand slowly and set it on her cheek. Her skin felt warm, but not too hot.

Alana's brown eyes opened and met my gaze. "Hello, Saro," she said in a sleepy whisper.

I dropped my hand and sat back, feeling suddenly exposed. "I was, uh, worried you might have a fever."

She nodded. "I think I'm okay." She moved one of her feet, and then winced. "Or a little less than okay."

I needed to change her bandages, but it was going to hurt. I hated causing her pain. "Do you like pizza?"

She sat up with a smile. "I love pizza."

I opened the box and set it on the couch beside her. "It'll give you something to focus on while I check your feet."

Her face paled. "Do you have to?"

I nodded. "Somebody's got to get you better."

Her gaze softened, taking on a quality I hadn't seen before. I dropped my eyes to her feet while my heart gave a strange thump. I pulled the sack of supplies over and tried to hide the pain the action caused. I could feel blood trickling down my stomach and was grateful I wore a dark shirt so she wouldn't see it.

I gently worked the bandages off from the bottom of her feet. She munched stalwartly on pizza while I eased a few stubborn pieces from the cuts. She only gasped once when I had to remove a particularly difficult piece from a gash near her big toe. "You sure this is necessary?" she asked.

I nodded while keeping my attention on her feet. "You have to put fresh bandages on to keep your chance of infection low." I gently washed the wounds with saline solution. They were healing much better than I had hoped. She would be walking around in a few days.

"I'm glad you know what you're doing."

"I've had a lot of practice," I replied, almost succeeding in keeping the bitterness out of my voice.

"I can't imagine life at the Academy," she said quietly after a few minutes had passed. "It must have been horrible."

I spread ointment carefully over the gashes. There were so many things I wanted to say, yet part of me warned that I should keep silent. Anything I revealed could be used against me. I let out a slow breath, reminding myself that I wasn't in the Arena anymore. Somehow the world seemed darker than it had a few days before, even with Alana's presence. "It wasn't easy," I concluded in a voice barely above a whisper.

Alana winced as I pressed bandages over the deepest wounds. I looked up to see tears in her eyes, but she refused to let them fall.

"It's alright to cry," I told her, touched more than I could explain at her strength.

She shook her head. "It seems silly to cry about my feet when other Galdoni have gone through so much." Her voice broke. "I can't imagine how hard it must have been."

"We survived," I told her in a gentle, but firm tone. I met her gaze. "And you weren't there." Before my words could hurt her, I hurried on, "I haven't lived your life or experienced what you have gone through." I indicated her feet. "To me, it seems like this would hurt a lot. Things you've gone through might have been a lot worse than what I did, and even if they weren't, it's your life. I haven't walked in your shoes." I gave her a soft smile, the first I had ever given anyone. "If you need to cry, go ahead."

Her eyebrows pulled together and she looked like she wanted to laugh and cry at the same time. A single tear broke free and slid down her cheek. "How can you understand?" she asked with a tremor in her voice.

"I don't," I replied.

She smiled despite the pain of me wrapping her feet with gauze. "I think somehow you do."

I shook my head. "I've never had a family." I glared at the gauze to avoid looking at her. "I've never had all you had before it was taken from you." My throat tightened. I was responsible for what she had lost.

Fierce hatred filled her voice. "They weren't my family." At my surprised expression, her features softened. "I'm sorry, Saro. I know you don't understand. But I wasn't one of them. I lived there, but it wasn't because I was a member of the family." Her tone darkened. "Cranston created me."

My stomach tightened. "He's one of the scientists?"

She nodded. There was so much in her gaze, such frustration and pain that she was keeping inside. She finally spoke, "He kept me there because he had used his daughter's DNA combined with that of a Galdoni to create me. He said because of that he couldn't let me go."

I carefully finished tying the gauze as I processed her words; I tucked the ends beneath the rest so they wouldn't catch on anything. I chose my words carefully. "Was he kind to you?"

She shook her head, then hesitated and nodded. "He was, but the men he brought over weren't." What she left unspoken told plenty.

My hands balled into fists. I wanted to tear their heads off. They should pay for what they had done. She didn't deserve any of it.

Her gentle hand touched my shoulder. "Saro, it's okay. I'm away from there now." She lifted her fingers and looked at them. They shone dull red in the harsh light. "Saro?"

I gathered up the supplies and tried to ignore her searching gaze. I was about to stand when she put a hand on my chest to keep me there. I gasped at the pain; she withdrew her hand quickly and stared at her crimson palm. "Saro, what happened?"

"I made a mistake," I replied, trying to guard against the tears in her eyes. She shouldn't cry for me. No one should cry for me.

"What kind of mistake?" she asked. She tried to rise to her feet, but a small squeak of pain escaped her.

I hurried to her side. "You shouldn't stand," I said.

She ignored her feet entirely. Instead, she caught the lapel of my trench coat. I wanted to pull back when she tried to work it over my shoulder, but the look on her face kept me still. I turned slightly, letting the coat slide down off my wings. It fell around my legs as I knelt on the floor.

Alana touched the edge of my shirt. I leaned back, ashamed to show her. It was against the Galdoni way to reveal weakness. I had done wrong and a human, a weak, pitiful human, had whipped me. I hated myself for what I had done, and hated that I couldn't leave him. I was weaker than I thought. I lowered my head.

"Let me see, Saro," she said.

I let out a slow breath. "You won't understand."

"I haven't walked in your shoes."

I bit back a wry smile. "So it's okay to cry?"

She nodded. "Definitely."

I closed my eyes as she worked my shirt up. She paused and I heard her whisper, "Oh my goodness." Before I could change my mind, she raised my shirt completely up. "Saro." I had never heard my name said that way before. It encompassed all the agony and shame I felt, as if she could read my hatred of myself in the blood that trailed down my chest.

I opened my eyes. Tears wet her cheeks. "I thought I was the one who was supposed to cry."

She shook her head and sniffed. "I'm sorry. I've just never seen anything so painful. Here I am being a baby about my feet and yet you're hiding this?" She indicated my chest. "You should have told me."

I lowered my gaze. "I failed to rob a safe when I burned the house for Jake tonight, so he whipped me. It was my own fault."

She was quiet for a moment. "You're the one that set my house on fire?" she asked.

I nodded, but refused to look up. I didn't want to see the judgment on her face. I had put her life in danger. She could have died because of me. I was scum, even lower than scum. "I should go," I said. I grabbed my bloody shirt and tried to stand.

Alana caught my hand. She shouldn't have been able to keep me there, but between the look in her eyes and the weakness I was feeling from my lacerated chest, I couldn't fight her. I dropped back to my knees.

"Somebody's got to get you better."

My eyes burned at the kindness in her voice. I studied the floor as she pulled the bag over. A slightly swoosh sounded when she lowered herself from the couch to the floor. I watched the way her fingers sifted through the contents of the sack, making the plastic rustle. "Good thing I've had a good teacher," she said.

I heard the smile in her voice and felt my lips tug in response. I smothered the feeling.

She pulled the saline spray from the bag followed by a few scraps of gauze. "Got to clean it so you don't get an infection." She sprayed my chest. I winced at the sudden brush of cold on the open wounds. "I'm sorry," she said in a whisper.

I looked at her. Her brown eyes stared up at me, so full of understanding for my pain. In that moment, I wanted to kiss her. I had never kissed a girl in my life, understandable since she was one of the very few I had ever met. Yet the urge to press my lips against hers at that moment was almost more than I could bear. I turned my head away before I followed through with something so absurd. My heart pounded and my head swam dizzily. I put a hand to it.

"Are you alright?"

"Just lightheaded," I replied, avoiding her gaze.

She scooted around me. "Put your back to the couch. It'll give you something to lean against while I work on this."

I did as she directed, then grinned wryly at how I was following the orders of someone half my size. I could easily snap her in two.

"What's that smile for?" she asked as she cleansed the blood the best she was able to from my skin.

I looked at her. "Just thinking about how I could kill you."

She gave me a bland look. "This might be news to you, but I'm not afraid of you."

"Not at all?"

She shook her head, but the smile I was looking for touched her lips. "Not at all," she replied.

I closed my eyes with an answering smile. Somehow her response meant so much to me. I didn't want her to be afraid, ever. I vowed to do whatever I could to keep from seeing fear in her eyes that I caused.

"These are deep," she said as she spread salve across the wounds. "Do they need stitches?"

I looked down at my chest. Several did look rather gaping. I nodded. "Probably, but we don't have the supplies and I'm not feeling up to doing my own stitches."

"I could do them."

I gave her a bland look of my own. "Really?"

She thought about it, then shook her head. "I've never done stitches before."

"I have."

"I noticed." Her fingers touched the scar along my side.

It ran from almost the middle of my back and ran around to my stomach. The scar had hardened as it healed, creating a thick knot of ugly skin. At her soft touch, I felt the bit of Blade's sword again, slow and sliding as he reveled in the chance to take my life. A shudder ran through me.

"What happened?" Alana asked.

"I was supposed to die," I replied. "But I refused." I closed my eyes, remembered tearing my bedding into small strips, then forcing them through my skin with the tine from a metal fork I had sharpened on the bricks of my cell. Tying the knots had been the hardest part. By the time I was done, my hands shook too hard to grasp the cloth firmly enough. The last few remained loose, and so the scarring had taken a lot longer to strengthen. When they checked on me in my cell a few days later fully expecting to find me dead, my request for water had shocked the guards and they hastened to obey.

"You don't give up easily, do you?"

"I don't know when to quit," I replied.

"That's a good thing."

I opened my eyes at the surety of her tone. "Why is that?"

"Because who else would have taken care of my feet?" she asked.

I chuckled and she laughed out loud. The sound was so carefree and happy I felt better just by being near her. She laid bandages across my chest, then proceeded to use half the gauze in the bag by wrapping it around my middle and shoulder to keep the bandages in place.

She worked around on her knees to my back and I sat up so she could finish tying off the gauze. She paused, and I felt her fingers run through my feathers.

"I've never seen golden wings," she said. "They're so beautiful."

"It's what keeps me going," I replied. A tingle ran along my wings as she caressed my feathers. I fought to keep my thoughts focused. "Flying is what I live for."

"I want to fly." Her words were so soft as if she barely dared to speak them.

I wondered how miserable she had been, trapped in that house at the whim of her creator; unable to escape from the realities of her life. Life at the Academy had been so similar I ached for her. "You will fly," I promised.

She nodded, but the look in her eyes said she didn't dare to believe it. Perhaps lack of hope was a Galdoni trait instead of something the Academy had to demolish. She tucked the supplies back into the bag, then scooted back on her knees to get a good look at my chest. "I guess that'll have to do."

I gave her work an appraising glance. "You did a good job."

"Don't sound so surprised," she rebuked with a laugh.

I smiled. "You did have a good teacher."

She nodded, then her smile faltered. She reached out and touched an exposed place near my stomach that hadn't been cut. "So many scars, Saro."

I followed her fingers. "Sometimes I wonder if it's the scars holding me together or if it's the other way around."

"They must come with a price."

"All of them do," I responded in a whisper.

She moved next to me so that her head rested under my arm. The action surprised me. I sat with my arm raised unsure of what to do. She reached up and took my hand, then lowered my arm around her shoulders. "I feel safe here," she said.

"You are safe here," I replied. I kicked myself mentally. I had to quit making so many promises. I had never kept a promise in my life, nor made one for that matter. What made me think I was able to do so now? Her hair tickled the bottom of my chin. I stifled a sigh.

"How old are you?" she asked.

I thought about it for a moment. We had trained in age groups at the Academy, and that was over a year and a half ago. "Seventeen," I told her.

She nodded. "I'm sixteen. If I was human, I'd be driving."

I chuckled. "You have wings; when the feathers grow out, you won't need to drive."

"I like that idea," she said.

She fell silent. I wondered if she could hear the way my heart pounded in my chest at her nearness. Having her lean against me made my whole side warm. I could have sat there for a year without moving.

"Saro?"

"Yes?" I was inordinately happy about the way she said my name. It sounded familiar, like we had talked for years. "Yes, Alana?" I repeated, just to say her name.

I could hear the answering smile in her tired voice when she said, "We're going to be okay, right?"

"We're going to be just fine." Dang it. I couldn't stop with the promises.

"Good." The word lingered sleepily in the air.

I remembered about Alana's feet and the slight fever I had felt in her cheeks. She must have been exhausted, and yet she had taken the time to care for me. I slipped my arms beneath her, then stood, ignoring the way the action pulled against my chest and made the lash marks reopen and bleed.

I set her gently on the couch and tucked the blankets around her. It felt right to have the blankets that had kept me warm settled across her. I didn't want to leave her, but I couldn't risk Jake awakening to find me gone. I stopped near the door and studied her sleeping form. I could still feel the gentleness of her fingers along my chest. I put a hand to it, aware of the bandages that sat beneath my shirt.

"What am I going to do with you, Alana?" I whispered out loud.

She merely smiled in her sleep and rolled to her other side. An answering smile spread across my face and I hurried up the stairs.

Chapter Eight

"The green light will guide you home."

I stood near Jake's car. I didn't want to go to the house in the distance. I hated doing it for him when he had lied to me. I pulled the satchel tighter across my chest. The strap slid across the healing wounds Alana had bandaged a week ago. Her feet were healing as well. My only comfort from what I did was that I had saved her from her horrible life, although the one I had given her wasn't that much better.

Jake must have seen something in my expression. His eyes narrowed. "Go, Saro. We have another house to hit in two days. You've got to make up for the safe you failed to crack at the last house."

I nodded because he expected me to. I started up the street. Jake sat for longer than he usually did, probably making sure I actually went to the house. When I disappeared through the shrubs that lined the backyard, I heard the sound of pavement on tires and listened to him drive away.

I tripped the alarm at the house. It was an accident. I was usually able to enter the code in time, but either Jake's numbers were wrong or my mind wasn't in it. A few seconds later, a wailing siren emanated from the alarm panel.

I covered my ears. I had a few options. I could still attempt to crack the safe before the police arrived, but it was a newer model and would require drilling, something I definitely wouldn't have time for. I could set the house on fire and tell Jake there was a problem with the safe. I could give up and wait for the police to arrive; they could do whatever they wanted with me.

I wandered through the kitchen to the hallway with my hands over my ears. It was lined with pictures. Two curly-haired little boys stood on a big dog in one. In the next, a young girl sat on a swing with a huge smile on her face. All three kids played in a small swimming pool filled with bubbles in the yard. The next showed the mother and father holding hands.

I turned away. The Molotovs shifted in the satchel, but I couldn't do it. I couldn't destroy another home just to appease Jake's greed for money. It didn't improve his lifestyle, and he merely became more demanding, finding more houses to hit despite his reassurances that the fees at the Academy were covered. There wasn't an Academy anyway. Everything he had told me was a lie.

I stepped outside in time to hear the police cars pull up. I shrugged out of my jacket.

"Stop!"

Ice ran through my veins.

"Drop what you're holding!"

I wasn't sure dropping the bag of Molotovs would be smart. The police officer advanced from the side of the house. "Put the bag on the ground and step away."

Jake would kill me for leaving such evidence behind. I glanced back to see the officer raise his gun. My shoulder throbbed in an angry reminder that I didn't want to be shot again. I set the bag on the sidewalk.

"The coat, too," the officer demanded.

"I don't think—"

"Do it!" he shouted.

I tossed the coat down.

"Kids your age should know better than to break into houses," the officer said, advancing. "Put your hands over your head and kneel on the ground."

Alana's brown eyes flashed in my mind. I needed to be free so I could help her. I had promised her she was safe. I had to keep my promise. I took a step back.

The officer shook his head. "Don't run. It'll only be worse for you. You didn't get away with anything, so you'll get off light if you go in with me now."

He took another step forward and I mirrored it with another back.

He lifted a hand. "Son, you don't want to do this. I've got a boy your age and I know how easy it is to make stupid decisions that you regret. The best thing to do is to come with me so we can get this taken care of."

"It's not that easy," I told him. I was surprised I had spoken at all, but there was a look on his face like he really wanted to help me. I didn't know how to tell him that nobody could help me anymore.

"It is that easy," he replied. He lowered his gun. "Just come in and I promise you it won't be as bad as you're thinking."

"I can't do that."

"Why not?"

He sounded like he really cared. He was a stranger. Why should he care at all?

"I've got someone I have to take care of."

He motioned toward the house. "This isn't the way to do it."

I nodded. "I realize that now."

"Then come in. I'll make sure whoever you're caring for is alright." The compassion in his voice ate at me.

Commotion sounded from the front of the house as another police car pulled up. I glanced in that direction.

"Don't worry about them," the officer reassured me. His nametag read K. Donaldson. He gave a patient smile. "What do you say? Care to make this easy on an old man?" He ran a hand through grizzled gray hair in emphasis.

"I wish I could," I replied. I was shocked to find that I really meant it. "But like I said, it's more complicated than that."

"How—" Officer Donaldson's words were cut off when I lifted my wings. He took a step back, and his gaze searched mine. He raised his shoulders in a slight shrug. "Okay. No big deal."

The sound of footsteps came from around the house. I needed to grab the satchel. Jake would kill me if I left it. I reached for it just as two more officers appeared around the corner.

In hindsight, I realized it must have looked like I was attacking Officer Donaldson when I leaned toward him. A shot rang out. A searing pain tore along the side of my head as the bullet missed my eye by inches. I stumbled back.

"Don't shoot!" Officer Donaldson yelled. "He's not armed!"

I shoved my wings down and rose into the air, blinded by the pain in my skull.

"Wait," the officer called.

I flew higher until I could no longer make out the individual forms on the ground in the darkness. I had left my bag and my coat. Jake was going to kill me. But I had to go back; I had to get Alana out of there. Where would we go?

My head pounded too hard to think. I put a hand to my hairline. It came away wet with blood. I had almost died. I soared in a circle searching for the green blinking light. Straining my eyes made my head hurt even more. I finally found it and dove, unable to focus to fly any longer.

Instincts made me pull up just before I slammed into the car. I fell to a heap on the ground near the back tire.

"What happened?" Jake demanded.

"The alarm went off," I mumbled.

He shoved me with his foot, rolling me over. His face was red with anger. When he leaned down, I could smell alcohol on his breath. "Where's the bag?" he shouted.

"Officer Donaldson took it," I replied. The glare of the streetlight overhead knifed into my eyes like daggers. I shielded my face with my arm.

Jake kicked my arm away. "You robbed the safe and left it?"

I shook my head. The feeling of gravel beneath my skull grated uncomfortably. "I couldn't get to the safe. The numbers were wrong."

"The numbers were right," Jake growled. "You did this on purpose."

Lights exploded in my brain when his fist connected with my cheekbone. I tried to put my arms up to protect myself, but my limbs responded sluggishly.

"Not on purpose," I forced out. "I tried."

"You failed," Jake said, punching me again. "You're worthless, you know that? You've never amounted to more than a headache."

I wanted to point out that at that moment he was the one causing the headache, but I couldn't clear my mind enough to speak.

"Why come back?" he demanded. "Why not let them arrest you and take you back to the Academy where worthless scum like you belong?"

That brought a line of clarity to my thinking. "The Academy is shut down." I replied. "You lied."

Hatred twisted his face. "You finally figured it out, genius. Congratulations." He kicked me in the ribs and I felt them give. "Then why come back? Do you enjoy this, you useless animal?"

"Alana." The name came out of my muddled mind before I could stop it.

Jake froze with his fist raised over his head. "Alana?" I didn't know how he could destroy her beautiful name, but it came off sounding flat and ugly. I hated that he said it. "Who's Alana?"

I shook my head. He drove a haymaker into my jaw. Blood filled my mouth. I tried to shake him off, but I could barely think, let alone get my body to do what I asked of it. The bullet gash had probably given me a concussion, the unemotional side of my mind noted. I appreciated the medical updates as Jake battered me with punches and kicks.

"She's in the basement," I finally replied. Tears trailed down my bloody face. I couldn't hold the truth in any longer. He was going to kill me, and I didn't care. What I cared about was telling him the truth about her. I had promised to protect her. I had failed. I blacked out to the feeling of hands dragging me into the car. My head hit the window, and it was the last thing I remembered.

Chapter Nine

"I told you he'd come to."

Jake's voice pierced the black depths of unconsciousness. I was sitting up with my chin resting on my chest. I tried to move my hands, but they were tied behind me. I rocked my head to one side and squinted in the light of a single bulb.

We were in the basement. The fact made my heart begin to race. I looked in the direction of the couch. Alana sat there with her arms and legs tied. Terror showed on her face.

"Alana," I croaked.

She opened her mouth to speak, but Jake cut her off.

"Yes, Alana," he responded. "Who would have thought you'd be hiding a Galdoni in the basement? And not just any Galdoni, a *female* Galdoni?" He chortled, a gross, gut-twisting sound. "Do you know how much money I can make off of her?"

"You better not touch a hair on her head," I growled.

His eyebrows lifted. "Well, now. Look who's suddenly motivated?" He looked at Alana. "I told you he'd do it."

Trepidation filled my aching chest. It hurt whenever I breathed. The beating Jake had given me had definitely cracked a few ribs. The light overhead pierced my eyes like daggers. I could barely keep them open with the pain in my head. I forced myself to focus. "Do what?"

Jake rubbed his hands together. "You've been a bit, shall we say, reluctant to rob the safes as of late."

I met his gaze. "I won't burn houses for you anymore, Jake."

"I think you will." He looked at Alana. "I think you'll do whatever I say."

I bared my teeth, feeling more animal than ever before. "What do you want with Alana?"

He shrugged as though my rage was miniscule. "Motivation, for now. I have a feeling you'll do whatever I say to keep her safe. If not, I'm sure she'll bring a fetching price on the black market."

Alana shook her head. "Don't do it, Saro. Don't listen to him."

Jake struck her across the mouth with the back of his hand. She let out a small cry of pain and ducked her head.

"You'll do it," Jake said, meeting my gaze. "Trust me."

I shook my head. I had to keep his attention from her so he wouldn't hurt her. "You lied to me about everything. I'm done hurting people and destroying their homes. I'm done stealing for you. Rob the safes yourself."

He hit me again. I rocked back in the chair. My foot hit something that chinked lightly against the cement ground. I glanced down in time to see a shard of glass from a bottle. "You're a loser, Jake. You don't have the guts to do it alone; you have to lie to get your work done."

His fist slammed into my healing chest so hard I gasped for breath. When his next punch connected, I kicked out. The shard of glass skittered across the ground toward Alana. I saw her bend over to pick it up and knew I had to keep Jake's attention so that he wouldn't catch her.

"You're nothing but a sorry loser," I said. "You deserve to be shot by the cop who let me go."

Anger twisted his face into a rage I hadn't seen before. He advanced on me, his fists raised. "You ungrateful scum! I took you in, and this is how you repay me?"

I heard Alana call my name, but Jake's first fist connected with the side of my head where the bullet had grazed. My head rocked back and darkness surrounded me once more.

***

The scent of smoke tickled my nose, demanding to be recognized. I opened my eyes.

"Good timing." Jake's features were lit by dancing orange and yellow. "I was wondering if we'd get the chance to say goodbye."

I glanced around. We were in a house that was already on fire. The shattered remains of a Molotov bottle sat near the blazing kitchen cupboards. I tried to move, but I sat in a chair with my hands tied behind me. My feet were bound together by a cable.

"Kind-of ironic, isn't it?" Jake asked. "Going up in the same flames you used to burn down so many houses?"

"You mean *you* used," I said. The words ate through my skull. I fought not to show the pain.

Jake shook his head. "I merely made the Molotovs. This is the first time I've used them to actually set something on fire." He indicated the roaring flames. His eyes were wider than usual, and there was a look on his face I had seen many times in the Arena. The fire reflected in his eyes; Jake was no longer sane. "It's beautiful, isn't it?"

Fear twisted in my stomach. It wasn't the first time I had faced death, but it was the first I wanted to live to prove that I wasn't the destroyer he made me out to be. I wanted to be the person I saw in Alana's eyes. I might not have lived up to her belief in me before, but I was determined to now. I had a lot to make up for. "Where's Alana?" I demanded.

"You mean my new meal ticket?" he replied. "Thanks for that, by the way."

I glared at him. "Let me go, Jake."

He laughed, and there was a maniacal edge to the sound. "Have a nice death, Saro," he replied. "I wish I could stay around to see it, but things are getting a bit uncomfortable in here." He tugged at the collar of his shirt meaningfully.

"Jake, get me out of here," I pleaded. I tried to work my hands out of the bindings, but the ropes cut into my wrists. I pulled harder, ignoring the pain.

"Nice working with you," Jake replied. He lifted the bag at his feet and hefted it over his shoulder. "These are heavy. How'd you ever fly with them?" He laughed again. "At least you won't have to worry about that now."

He opened the sliding glass door that led to the backyard. The fire rushed forward, drawn higher by the fresh air. "Goodbye, my boy." His words twisted, and his gaze darkened. The smile that lingered on his face reveled at my pain. He stepped into the darkness.

I pulled harder at the ropes. Blood slicked my wrists. I hoped that it would make them slippery enough to work free of the bindings. Fire ate at my wings. I smelled the scent of charred feathers. I tried to back up to avoid the worst of the flames. The chair caught on a throw rug. I fell onto my side. A yell tore from my lips as the fire that snaked from the remains of the Molotov raced up my arms.

Fresh air met my face. "Saro!" a voice called. I looked up to see Alana standing in the doorway. Relief rushed through me so strong I could barely breathe.

She dropped to her knees and tugged at the cords that bound my feet.

"A knife," I forced out from my smoke-filled lungs. I began to cough and couldn't stop. My lungs felt like they were tearing from the inside. I gasped for breath.

Alana disappeared for a moment, then pressure tugged at my legs. I glanced down between coughs to see her sawing at the cords with a steak knife. The bindings broke. She helped me to my knees. "Hold on, Saro," she said. She crawled behind me. "Your hands," she gasped. She pulled at the ropes. I bit back a cry as they tore into my burned wrists.

When they broke free, Alana pulled me to my feet. I stumbled, unable to get my bearings with the pain in my head. "I've got you, Saro," she said.

She helped me to the door. I fell to the grass, gulping in huge breaths of air into my ragged lungs. They burned with every breath. Police sirens filled the night sky.

"We've got to get out of here," Alana said. She pulled me to my feet.

I shook my head, fighting to keep from passing out. "I can't fly," I protested.

She ducked under my arm. I felt the force of her wings as she pushed them down. We rose into the air. Alana laughed, the sound light and young. "I'm flying, Saro!" she gasped. "I'm really flying!" She soared higher.

"Saro!"

The shout drove terror into my heart. I squinted against the flaming house and saw a form shaking a fist at us from the ground. Jake's face twisted as he cursed us. He lifted something. My heart skipped a beat at the sight of a gun. The sound of a gunshot ricocheted through the air. Alana gasped. We plummeted toward the ground.

I held her tightly to my body and forced my burned wings to move. Every beat hurt so badly I could barely breathe. We lifted slowly. Another gunshot rang out. The bullet sped past, missing me by inches. I flew higher and higher until Jake's silhouette was lost far below. I pushed on blindly, unsure where I was headed.

"Kale's place," Alana whispered.

I ducked my head so I could hear her, ignoring the way the movement sent agony through my skull. "Where?"

"The internet said Crosby, a black building with gold windows." Her shirt was soaked with blood. It flowed from a bullet wound near her heart. I could hear the way she had to force herself to breathe. I shifted my grip so that her wound was pressed against my chest to help staunch the blood.

"Hold on, Alana," I said. "Don't give up on me now."

"Never," she whispered, her lips colored red.

Chapter Ten

Crosby was an hour south by car. I didn't know how much time I had made up flying. It may have taken longer. All I knew when I landed on the lawn outside the building was that I was on the verge of unconsciousness. The pain of my burned hands had faded into a blur that echoed the roar in my head. I carried Alana toward the front doors. Each step felt like it took an eternity.

The doors opened, lighting the lawn in an expanse of white that tore into my skull. People came out of the building. I squinted, and recognized Kale. He looked older than I felt, though there was only a year separating us in age. His black wings rose as he flew from the steps with several other Galdoni close behind. They reached us sooner than the humans.

I couldn't hold Alana any longer. I fell to my knees, letting her rest gently on the grass. I stumbled back to give them room. The Galdoni landed. Several made their way toward me.

"Don't touch me," I yelled. Fury filled my eyes with hot tears. I gestured with my burned hands toward Alana. "Save her, please." The last word fell strangled from my lips. I pleaded for someone else instead of myself. She was all that mattered. Darkness pounded around me. I sunk to my knees on the grass.

"We'll save her," Kale's voice promised. There was something about it I could hold onto. He spoke in full honestly; my heart recognized it even though the quality had been scarce in my life. I could believe him.

I lifted my head from my chest and forced my eyes to focus. Forms lifted Alana carefully and hurried toward the building. She stirred slightly in their grasp. She was still alive, for the moment at least.

A hand touched my shoulder. I looked up into Kale's face. "I know you," he said, his eyes tight with concern.

I nodded, which set my head pounding even harder. "I whooped you once," I said with a cough that made my lungs ache.

Kale's lips lifted in a smile. "I think I recall it the other way around."

I shrugged. "Details." My head swam and I fell forward.

Kale caught me before I could hit the ground. "Let's get you taken care of," he said in a kind voice.

"Alana first," I protested as I was lifted in strong arms.

"Alana first, I promise," he replied.

I nodded and let myself go to the welcoming embrace of darkness.

***

My mouth felt as dry as cotton when I awoke. My head itched. I lifted a hand to it only to find that my hand was covered in bandages. I stared, trying to remember why.

It came to me all at once, my confession to Jake, his beating, awakening in the basement, Alana tied on the couch. The glitter of the glass on the cement was bright in my mind. It grew into a roaring flame which ate at my hands and wings. A gunshot rang out. My heart thundered at the memory.

"Alana?" I pushed up from the bed. My knees gave out the instant I put weight on them. I fell to the ground. The sound of footsteps running up the hall came to my ears. I tried to push up, but the pressure on my hands tore another cry of pain from my lips.

"Easy, Saro." Kale's strong arms raised me up. He helped me back to the bed.

I fell onto the mattress and willed the air to stop burning my lungs. "Alana?" I forced out.

"She's stable," he reassured me.

I met his gaze, searching for any sign that he was lying. A kind smile crossed his face, something I had never seen at the Academy. "It's alright. You can trust me."

I shook my head, but it was the wrong move. I put both wrapped hands to it to make it stop spinning. The pressure hurt the burns. "How can I be sure?" I asked with my eyes closed.

Kale was quiet for a moment. I heard the sound of metal chair legs across a linoleum floor. Kale sat down, his movements slow and careful so as not to startle me. "You came to me," he said after a few minutes had passed.

"I had nowhere else to go." I chuckled at how lame it sounded, and then began to cough.

Kale left quickly and returned with a cup of water. He held a straw to my lips. I drank a few swallows and the coughing eased. He set the cup on a side table.

Kale waited until I was able to breathe somewhat normally before he sat back down. "What name do you go by?"

With the state I was in, there was no reason to hide the truth. "Saro."

He nodded. "You've had a rough time."

I smiled without humor. "Did it take you a while to figure that out?"

He laughed and sat back in the chair, crossing his arms in front of his chest. It looked strange to see him sitting there so calming with his wings out to each side as though he didn't fear a stranger walking in at any moment. He was in his element; that much was certain. "You're not the first I've had officers calling to find."

Fear twisted my heart. We weren't safe.

Kale lifted a hand. "Don't worry. Officer Donaldson was more concerned about your well-being than interested in taking you in. He said one of his men shot you." He indicated the bandage around my forehead. "I assume that's where you got that."

I nodded.

"Is that how Alana got shot?"

The memories rushed against me. The elation in her voice when she realized she was flying, coupled by the pain of her gasp after the gunshot rang out. We were falling, plummeting to the earth. My wings didn't want to respond. The feathers were charred. I couldn't hold her.

"Saro." A hand touched my shoulder. "Saro, it's alright."

I had to catch her. I struggled to force my wings free of the bandages that bound them against my back. I had to break free, to save her from falling.

"Saro, you're okay; Alana's okay!"

I blinked through the tears of pain and helplessness. Kale stood over me, one hand on my chest and the other on my shoulder, holding me down so I didn't hurt myself. My eyes focused on his face.

"It's alright, Saro. Just breathe." Kale blinked as his own eyes filled with tears. "You've been through too much."

I took in a shuddering breath. It took all my self-control to keep from coughing again. I let it out slowly, willing my pounding heart to calm. I could barely think past the pain that threatened to break my skull. Kale eased me back against the pillow. I couldn't remember ever having a pillow beneath my head in my entire life. The softness helped to drive away the panic in my chest. They didn't give you a pillow if they were going to kill you, right? I nodded. "I'm okay."

Kale lifted his hands slowly, ready to hold me down should the need arise again. "You're sure?" His gaze was uncertain, watching my every move.

I took in another breath and let it out with only a small cough. "Sorry about that." I felt more ashamed than I could bear. Galdoni weren't supposed to show weakness, yet that was all I felt under Kale's searching eyes.

"Don't do that."

His sharp tone surprised me. "What?"

"Don't categorize your faults. I've seen it too many times."

I looked away, angry that he could read me so well.

"Saro, don't hide inside yourself and destroy all that you've accomplished in getting here."

A wry, bitter smile twisted my mouth. "What have I accomplished?" I asked, glaring at the wall.

"You're here, Saro. Do you know how many Galdoni never make it here? Though I must admit I've never seen anyone arrive in the condition of you two. It must have been quite the feat to reach us."

I thought of Jake and the fire. "You have no idea," I said softly.

I heard Kale sit back in the chair. "Galdoni are a stubborn lot," he said.

He sounded more amused than angry. I clenched my hands at the thought that he was laughing at me. The action sent fiery pain racing up my arms. I looked back at him without bothering to hide my anger.

His brow furrowed and he sat forward. "It's a good thing," he said. "If we weren't stubborn, we would have died when the Academy closed. As it is, we have a survival instinct that forces us to keep fighting. That's what brought you here. You saved Alana's life."

It was her beating heart that kept my wings moving when every brush of air made me want to plummet to the earth to stop the pain. I had promised her safety. I wouldn't give up until she was taken care of. "She saved mine."

He nodded. "I figured as much." When I turned my head away, he set a hand on my shoulder. "If it wasn't for a girl, I wouldn't be here either."

I looked back and read the honesty in his eyes.

He smiled, his gaze distant. "Brie gave me a reason to keep going. She believed there was more to me than just a stupid animal raised to kill."

He lifted an eyebrow. I had to nod. "She thinks I'm better than I am."

Kale smiled. "Our job is to match that belief." A soft tune played from his pocket. He pulled out a cellphone. "Hello?" He continued to watch me as he listened to the caller. "No problem. Make them comfortable in the A block. I'll be there in a few minutes." He hung up the phone.

"You can go," I said, wondering why he bothered with me when there were obviously other things he needed to do.

"You sure you're alright?"

"I'm fine." Sleep beckoned. As much as I didn't want to stay in the bed, weariness pulled at my eyelids, beckoning for me to close them.

"I'll be back," he promised.

For some reason, the words reassured me. I nodded and let my eyes close. "Kale?"

The sound of his footsteps paused by the door. "Yes, Saro?"

"Take care of Alana."

I could hear the smile in his voice when he replied, "I will."

Chapter Eleven

The next time I awoke, darkness showed through the small window near my bed. My hands ached, but my head had cleared enough that I could think through the pounding. I sat up. The only thought that mattered was checking on Alana. I had to make sure she was alright, that they were taking care of her and that she was truly stable.

A tube ran into my arm near my elbow. It took a few minutes to get my gauzed hands to cooperate, but I was finally able to remove the needle. I swung my legs off the bed and stood slowly. My knees wavered. I leaned an elbow against the wall to keep from falling. After a few minutes, I was able to will myself to stand straight. I walked gingerly toward the door. It was shut. Thank goodness the door had a latch instead of a knob. I pressed my elbow against the latch and the door clicked. I stepped back and worked my toes into the crack. The door swung silently inward.

The linoleum floor was cold to my bare feet. I felt exposed in a hospital gown tied loosely around my bound wings. With my hands damaged and wings in who knew what condition, I would have little chance of fighting off an attack. The thought made me wary.

No one wandered the halls at the late hour. I checked every door I passed, but they were either empty or housed Galdoni I barely remembered from the Academy. It seemed like so long ago that I had fought for my life against them. Forgotten shreds of hate and regret stirred in my chest, but I shoved them aside; nothing mattered except getting to Alana.

By the time I ensured that Alana wasn't at my level of the building, I had to lean against the wall to keep walking. I nudged open the door to a stairwell. I wanted to cry at the sight of stairs rising above and below me. I sank to my knees on the landing. I was never going to find her. I tipped my head against the brick wall and closed my eyes in defeat.

The door snicked softly open. "Saro?"

I opened my eyes to see Kale watching me.

"Don't you ever sleep?" I asked.

He answered with a smile. "That's what I thought you were doing."

I shook my head. The rough brick against the back of my skull reminded me of the gravel beside Jake's car. "I need to see Alana."

Kale crouched next to me. "She's sleeping."

I shrugged, a minute lift of the shoulders. "Just the same, I need to see her."

He nodded. "Alright then." He ducked under my arm and helped me to my feet.

"How did you know I was here?" I asked tightly in an attempt to hide the pain at the movement.

He gestured to a small camera in the corner of the stairwell. "The Galdoni have enemies. It helps to be prepared."

"I'm glad we made it," I admitted somewhat grudgingly.

"You're sure about that?"

A wry smile touched my lips at his tone. "For Alana's sake."

"Good enough," he concluded as he helped me carefully down the stairs. When we reached the door, he opened it without waiting for me to ask. Even the pressure of the bandages on my burned hands made them throb almost unbearably. I could only imagine what I would be left with after they healed.

"They've kept Alana in a coma state to help her heal. The bullet removal was touch and go, but Dr. Ray is the best physician on our staff." Kale gave a small smile. "He saved my life and my wings. I wouldn't be here if it wasn't for him."

The heaviness to the way he said it spoke of a lot more that he was leaving out. I didn't know why he bothered to confide in me, but it meant something. The fact that he felt I was worthy to talk to after everything shook me.

Our pace was slow. I figured Kale would probably rather be sleeping, but he set a speed I could keep up with and didn't ask me to push myself harder than I was able. I wasn't used to such consideration. I broke the silence to clear my uneasiness.

"You didn't ask where we came from."

He glanced at me. "Officer Donaldson told us what he knew about the robberies. I figured you would fill me in on the rest when you were ready. For now, we should concentrate on yours and Alana's recoveries." His gaze was troubled despite his light tone.

"There's something you're not telling me."

We stopped in front of a window. Alana slept on the bed, an oxygen tube in her nose and other tubes running to various machines. Monitors showed numbers and I could hear soft beeps through the glass, but I didn't know what they meant. I rested my forehead against the window, grateful to find her sleeping and out of pain.

Kale watched her for a moment in silence, then said, "You weren't the only Galdoni roped into theft."

I glanced at him. His eyes were on Alana, but his gaze was distant. "There were others?"

"There *are* others," he corrected. "There's an entire theft ring of Galdoni led by the most well-known criminal filth on this continent. We're working with law enforcement to track down the leaders, but it's been a slow process." He met my gaze. "You're the first to actually break free."

"I was a fool," I said with all the self-loathing I felt.

Kale shook his head. "You were misinformed." I looked back at Alana without answering. I saw Kale nod toward her out of the corner of my eye. "But you brought us something we haven't had before."

"Alana?" I asked.

He nodded. "We know there are other female Galdoni in the underground trade, but as of yet, she's the first who has actually gotten out alive."

The fact made my stomach twist. "You've seen other females?"

Sorrow filled his face, answering my question as much as his words. "Whenever there's a bust, we find the females already killed. They're hiding something and I'm hoping Alana can give us answers."

I watched her in silence. It hurt to see her so still. She was so filled with life, so happy despite all she had gone through. Seeing her asleep on the bed attached to all manner of equipment felt wrong. My hands clenched into fists beneath the bandages. I gritted my teeth at the pain. "Jake will pay for shooting her."

Kale let out a slow breath. "Death is the way of the Galdoni."

I looked at him in surprise. "You don't approve?"

He crossed the hall and slid to a sitting position against the wall across from me as if he guessed I was on the verge of collapsing if I didn't rest. His black wings spread out on either side, a sharp contrast to the white bricks behind him. I followed his example, easing my weary body to the floor. It hurt to lean back against my bandaged wings, but I let out an inadvertent sigh of relief for the rest.

Kale gave an understanding smile. "You've been through a lot."

"No more than those female Galdoni. We need to get them out," I replied hotly.

Kale lifted a hand. "We're trying; trust me. I want them out as badly as you do, and the rest of the Galdoni besides."

"If they're caught up in this crime ring like I was, maybe they don't deserve to be here."

Kale's eyebrows rose. "You don't think you should be here?"

I shook my head. "Alana should be. She's the only reason I came."

Curiosity touched Kale's eyes. "Where would you be if not here?"

"Taking down Jake and whoever else he was working with." The pieces began to make sense. I had never asked Jake why he lived in a rundown apartment when he could have afforded several mansions with all the money I had stolen for him. At first I had put it off to the atrocious amount of the fees for keeping a Galdoni out of the Academy, but after I met Alana and learned the truth, I knew there must have been something else I didn't know. The fact that Jake was under the management of someone else made perfect sense. He must have owed somebody a great deal with all we had taken.

Kale nodded. "I appreciate the sentiment. Revenge consumed my thoughts when I first got out of the Academy. After I learned the truth about the Arena battles and the gamboling, all I could think of was getting back at them."

"What changed your mind?"

Warmth brushed the Galdoni's face. "I realized not all humans were the same. I made friends and fell in love."

I turned my face away with a snort of disbelief.

Kale chuckled. "As cheesy as it sounds, it's true. Love can focus your drive and help you understand that there is more to life than fighting."

"Fighting is all we're good for," I replied.

Kale opened his hand in concession. "Alright, a different sort of fight then. Instead of revenge, I'm focused on the survival of our race."

"Do we deserve to survive?"

Again, a ghost of a smile followed my question. "I believe so, and so does the Constitution that eventually enabled our freedom."

I tried to make sense of his words, but my mind was muffled by weariness. I leaned my head against the wall and closed my eyes, an action against every training regime at the Academy; right behind 'Never reveal weakness to an enemy' was 'Never let your guard down'. It said a lot about the condition I was in that I did so with only a slight tremor of wariness running through my limbs.

"I'm still going to stop him," I said with my eyes closed.

"I hope so," Kale replied. I heard him push up to a standing position. "Come on. Let's get you back to your bed. You need to rest."

"I'll rest here," I said without opening my eyes. It didn't feel right to leave Alana alone. I would rest more soundly within range of her call if she needed me, even if it was on a cold floor. I had slept on worse.

"She won't wake up for a few more days."

I nodded.

Kale took a few steps away; his shoes squeaked slightly when he turned back. "I'll have the staff bring a couch to Alana's room. Scars and the cold floor don't mix well."

Chapter Twelve

True to his word, a couch was brought up a few minutes later. I was embarrassed that such a fuss was made with my comfort in mind, especially at such an early hour of the morning. If the humans who brought the couch minded, they didn't show it in the least. When the couch was set, I attempted to get back to my feet, but my burned hands and the truthfulness of Kale's statement about cold floors and old wounds brought me back to my knees.

One of the humans knelt beside me. "Can I help?"

I wanted to say no, but another hour of trying to rise didn't sound appealing. I hesitated, then nodded.

He helped me up and assisted me to the couch. I stood next to it, unwilling to let down my guard in his presence.

He smiled as if he guessed my thoughts. "Not too keen on humans, huh?"

"You're perceptive," I replied dryly.

He glanced at Alana. "Kale told me about her. Can't say I blame you in the least." When I didn't move, he asked, "Would it help to tell you I felt the same way about Kale when we found him?" He grinned. "I even slept with a knife under my pillow during the first week he was at Dr. Ray's."

"Like that would have helped," I replied before I could stop myself.

He chuckled. "I know, right? The one time we got into a brawl, I was lucky to get off with a few bruises."

"You fought KL426?" I asked incredulously.

"That's Kale out here," he corrected with an amused smile. "And I wouldn't say I fought him. More like I attacked him when I thought he put my sister in danger, and he proceeded to throw me around like a rag doll without any effort."

I laughed at his dismayed tone. "You got off lucky."

"I know," he said, "But I felt like I'd been trampled by bulls the next morning."

His references suddenly fit together. "You're Brie's brother?"

He stuck out his hand. "Jayce." I lifted a hand to indicate how they were wrapped. He chuckled. "Sorry about that."

I shrugged. "No big deal. I'm Saro."

He nodded. "I know. You're all anyone's talked about since you arrived in such style the other night."

I grimaced. "Not my finest moment."

"What is?"

Caught off guard, I studied him. He watched me expectantly, his expression easy-going. It didn't seem to occur to him that it was three o'clock in the morning and time for most normal humans to be asleep. He seemed perfectly happy leaning against the arm of the couch talking to me. I realized I didn't mind the distraction from the beeping monitors around Alana. It kept me from wondering if she would ever awaken.

Against all instincts, I eased down warily on the couch cushion furthest from Jayce. He didn't say a word, but I could tell by his expression that he knew it was a strange move for me. I still felt on edge, but I was tired of keeping up my guard at all times. I was tired of everything, actually, and I didn't know what to do about it.

"So what was your finest moment?" he pressed.

Shaken out of my dark thoughts, I studied the floor for a moment. A memory surfaced, one that I had kept inside so long it felt strange to think of it again. I closed my eyes. "I don't know if you would consider it a victory."

"Sometimes surviving is a victory," Jayce said.

Surprised, I glanced at him. He shrugged. "Let's just say that working here has given me some insight into what you guys went through, and it isn't pretty."

I nodded and let the memory settle over me. "It was a practice battle in the Arena. We weren't supposed to kill. At least that's what we were told." The bitterness of reality colored my voice. "Apparently I had caused enough trouble in the training rings to get my name on the red list." I glanced at Jayce. "I had my own way of fighting the enforcers didn't care for. They said it was too scrappy. I realized after I got out that *too scrappy* meant not showy enough for the cameras."

"What's the red list?" Jayce asked, his voice flat as if he guessed exactly what it meant.

I met his gaze. "It's one of those lists you don't realize you're on until you're ready to fight with a wooden sword and realize everyone else has been given metal weapons."

Jayce grimaced. "That sucks."

I nodded. "I held my own with my *scrappy style* even with the wooden sword until Blade's cronies ganged up on me."

At the Galdoni's name, Jayce sat up straighter. I let myself fall back to that moment. "They tore the sword from my hand and had me pinned." I felt the brush of the Arena sand against my arms and legs. I tried to fly, but a Galdoni stood on each of my wings, holding me down. They beat me until I could barely move. Gashes littered my chest and sides. I bled freely from at least half a dozen wounds that would require stitching. Blade leered at me, his smile twisted and his eyes alive with the joy of seeing a helpless victim.

"This is honorable?" I asked, struggling against their hold.

"You're vermin," Blade replied. "There is no honor for vermin."

"You're a coward," I spat. "You don't dare to face me alone."

Anger sparked in Blade's eyes. I thought for a moment that he would command his cronies to step back. I would have a chance, even with my wooden sword. Then he lowered his weapon. "Scream for me, SR029."

He angled his sword along my side so that the blade rested near my spine. The metal felt cold to my bare skin. With agonizing slowness, he drew the edge along my flesh. It bit through to the muscle beneath, opening my side and spilling my blood on the sand. I screamed. There was no way to hold in the cry as he continued to work the blade around, drawing it in a half circle up toward the middle of my stomach.

"Pathetic," he sneered, pulling the weapon away.

I watched my blood gather along the blade. Drops fell with mind-numbing slowness. The dull spat they made when they connected with the sand echoed loud to my ears.

"Want me to cut his head off?" LH308 asked.

Blade smiled. "Leave him. His death from that wound will be slow and agonizing, just the way he deserves it."

They stepped off my wings. The fog that filled my thoughts numbed the pain I knew I should feel. That alone terrified me. I remembered the sensation of my lifeblood slipping through my hands as I tried to hold the gaping wound closed.

"How are you still here?" Jayce asked, his quiet voice drawing me back.

"They carried me to my cell." I gave a bitter smile. "Apparently they didn't want any deaths in the Arena that weren't broadcasted. They deposited me on the rags that made up my bed, and left me to die."

Jayce shook his head. "I don't know what I would have done." He paused, and then concluded with a smile, "Probably died."

111

I chuckled. "I was tempted to just give up, but then they would have won." The memory of the pain stole my breath. I fought back the urge to clench my hands. "I needed to bind the wound together. I didn't have thread, so I tore my blanket into the smallest strips I could manage. I had to make the holes first with a scrap of metal from a fork tine, then I used the tine to shove the blanket scraps through. I tied them the best I was able."

Jayce face was white when I glanced up. He shook his head. "I definitely would have died. I understand why surviving was your finest moment."

I shook my head. "That wasn't my finest moment." I smiled. "That came two weeks later in the training hall. It was all I could do to walk there; if Blade had known how weak I was, he would have finished me right then."

I remembered the slide of metal against metal as I pulled the sword from the container near the wall. It felt heavy in my hands, and I knew it was from my lagging strength. I would have to be quick.

Blade was in a practice ring sword-fighting against PF220, another of his cronies. I climbed in and leaned against the chains. It took all my willpower to stand up straight. "Blade," I shouted. I hit the chains with my sword.

The shock on Blade's face when he turned around and saw me alive filled me with strength. He had left me to suffer an agonizing death, not the honorable clean loss of life from a sword. I hefted the blade. His eyes narrowed with hatred. "You were supposed to die, vermin."

I lifted my lips in a snarl. "Sorry to disappoint you."

"Guess I'll have to finish what I started."

The sword I held had a dulled edge for practice; the same applied to his. I held my side tight and raised my weapon.

Blade blocked the blow with a laugh. "You're a weakling. Why don't you just die?" He swung his sword low in an attempt to hit my side. I had expected him to do just that.

I grabbed the blade with my right hand and turned into it, pulling the weapon from his grip as I spun. I lashed out with the knife I had kept hidden along my arm as I held my side. It bit deep into Blade's back. I yanked it around, carving a half circle identical to mine. A scream tore from his throat.

Blade stumbled back, his eyes wide. Blood pooled around his hands as he fought to hold the wound. I watched him with a dispassionate gaze. "Good luck with that," I said. I ducked under the chains and made my way through the Galdoni who had stopped their practice when our fight started. They let me pass without a word; their stares said everything.

"You gave him the same wound!" Jayce looked as excited as if he had been there. "He deserved it! Too bad it didn't kill him."

His tone caught my attention. "You know Blade?"

He nodded. "Know of him. He almost killed Kale the day the Arena was shut down. He disappeared afterward; we haven't heard anything about him since."

The thought of Blade amid the human population sent a shudder down my spine. "He deserves to die."

"Kale's been looking for him, but we keep reaching dead ends. It worries him to have such a dangerous Galdoni on the loose."

"As it should."

We sat in amiable silence for a few minutes. I wished Alana would move. I would have given anything to see her smile again.

"Can I see it?"

I glanced at Jayce, uncertain what he was talking about. He pointed at my side. I nodded and reached behind me in an attempt to untie the knot at the top of my hospital gown. Jayce reached toward me. I shied back, knocking his hand away with my gauzed one. My heart thundered in my chest and my muscles tensed, ready to defend me against the perceived threat.

Jayce raised both hands. "Whoa, man. I was just trying to help."

The reasoning part of my brain argued with my protective instincts. He was unarmed and obviously carried no significant amount of defensive skill by the way he held himself. He was tall and had wide shoulders, but his reassuring smile belied any attempt on my life. If he truly wanted to hurt me, he would have stood and perhaps used one of the metal arms holding Alana's tubes as a weapon.

"You don't have to worry about me," Jayce continued. "I learned my lesson with Galdoni when I tussled with Kale. That'll never happen again."

I willed my heart to slow. Embarrassment flooded through me. For the first time in my life, I had been having a normal conversation with a human, and I ruined it by overreacting. The detached part of my mind noted that I was simply acting within the normal confines of my Galdoni training. I grimaced at the thought. I no longer wanted to be caged with only fight or flight as my reactions.

I let out a breath and dropped my gaze. "Sorry. Habit."

"Sounds like that habit saved your life."

I nodded. "On more than one occasion. But that doesn't mean your life should be at risk."

His eyebrows rose. "Was my life at risk?"

I tipped my head to indicate the string that hung from the blinds on the window near the door. "I was going to wrap that cord around your neck and choke you to death. I would have just snapped your spinal cord, but my hands are a bit useless at the moment."

Jayce stared at my unemotional appraisal of his near-death experience. The hint of fear in his gaze let me know how very far beyond a normal reaction I had almost gone. "I am sorry," I repeated without looking at him. I studied my gauze-covered hands. "You can go if you want."

"You said you'd show me your scar."

I looked at him. He waited as though nothing unusual had happened. He deserved credit for courage. I finally nodded. He reached carefully behind my back and pulled the knot loose. I eased the cloth carefully over my hands, then pushed it down to show him the thick scar that ran from near my belly button to my back.

"What happened?"

I followed Jayce's gaze to my chest. The scars of Jake's repeated whippings crisscrossed along my skin. The bullet wound he had sewn haphazardly was stark white at the front of my shoulder. The scars from the Arena were smaller and had healed better, the result of my careful stitching because I was forced to be ready to fight within days. Ironically, the supplies for wound care had been better at the Academy than I could get at Jake's.

"They whipped you at the Academy?" Jayce asked. His eyes ran from one scar to the next. "Some of these look newer than others."

I slipped my hands back into the gown, suddenly self-conscious. "The guy who took me in and taught me to steal after the Academy didn't take kindly to failure."

"That's just wrong," Jayce said.

I nodded. "I realize it now, but I didn't have much of a choice at the time."

He tied the knot again, then sat back. "I don't envy your life, Saro."

I shrugged. "At least I'm still alive."

He nodded. "I have a feeling your finest moment is yet to come."

I smiled and he grinned. "I'll bring you a blanket," he said.

I settled on my side on the couch. By the time he returned, I was already asleep.

Chapter Thirteen

The steady beeping of Alana's monitors woke me late the next day. Kale was nowhere to be found. Another human brought me a tray of food. When he left, I tried to eat with the metal fork he brought with it. I kept dropping the utensil on the floor, and it hurt too much to pick it up. I eventually set it down and ate by lifting the tray to my mouth. I was glad Alana wasn't awake to see me.

When I was done, the sounds of her machines drove me from the room. I couldn't listen to the beeping and watch the green and red lines any longer without going crazy. I made my way back to my room and found a pair of loose black pants and a white shirt waiting. I grinned when I picked up the shirt and found slits and Velcro along the back. Someone had indeed made clothing for Galdoni.

It took several minutes of inventive dressing that involved the IV arm near the bed as well as the small rolling table that held the food tray, but I was finally dressed. A pair of blue socks with white rubber paw prints on the bottom sat where my clothes had been. I turned away with a wry smile. I would rather have cold feet than be caught wearing those. They alone might get me beaten to a pulp in a building filled with Galdoni.

I followed the directions on the signs handily placed near the stairs on each level, and found myself at the door to the training rooms on the tenth floor. I watched through the wide windows as Galdoni fought against each other and practice dummies. Cloth bags swung back and forth under the force of each blow. Sweat poured off of faces locked in intense concentration. Near one corner, Galdoni fought in roped rings much like those made with chain at the Academy.

It felt different, though. It took me a few minutes to place my finger on just what that difference was. The Galdoni were smiling and jostling each other. There was laughter when someone threw a particularly good punch, and those Galdoni who watched the fighters did so with grins on their faces, calling out good shots or taunting those that were bad. The Galdoni were enjoying themselves. It felt almost wrong, but also healing at the same time. I couldn't explain it.

I pushed the door open with my shoulder. The largest Galdoni I had ever seen walked over to halt my progress. I remembered him from the Academy, but barely. He was older than me by a few years, and had always kept to himself. I was smart enough to never get on his bad side because of his size. I may have been fast, but that was nothing compared to the brute force of a bear.

"I'm Goliath, caretaker of our gym."

His eyes roamed to my hands, then back to my face. It was obvious by his expression that he found me sorely lacking. I hated that look. "Where do you think you're going?"

"To train," I replied firmly.

He chuckled, a sound that resonated from deep within his chest. "How do you plan to do that?"

I had never been good at being laughed at. My survival instincts fled, leaving me with only bitter rage at my frustratingly helpless situation. "With my elbows; what'd you think?" I replied.

He chuckled again. "That I'd like to see."

"Then let me train."

Goliath's wide brow lowered when he realized I was being serious. "I can't let you in here. My orders are to keep anyone out who may hurt themselves by training." He nodded at my hands, his glance also taking in my damaged

118

wings. "I don't know how you plan to do anything without hurting yourself."

I gritted my teeth. "Look, Gandalf," I growled.

"Goliath," he corrected.

I rolled my eyes. "I can't use my hands, my wings are burned, and I may fall over at any moment, but if I have to sit in a white-walled room any longer listening to beeping monitors waiting to tell me if my only friend in the world has died, I am seriously going to hurt someone. I need a place to vent." My chest heaved. I fought back the outrageous impulse to punch him in the face. My dispassionate voice mentioned that such an action was ill-advised as Goliath could no doubt pulverize me with a single hit given my current state.

He watched me quietly for a moment. I thought he was going to turn me away. I was almost prepared to go. Instead, he nodded. "I have a room in the back you can use."

He led the way across the training room. I felt the stares of several Galdoni as we passed, but I ignored them. Goliath passed down a side hall lined with smaller individual practice rooms. Galdoni were visible through long windows as they fought stationary bags and wooden dummies. Goliath paused by the next room and opened the door. He glanced at my hands. "There's a button on the wall if you need help getting back out."

I nodded and stepped into the room. There were three white walls, and the fourth next to the door was made up of a long glass window like the rest of the rooms we had passed. Two stationary bags, a swinging bag chained to the roof, and two wooden dummies made up the training facility. A bin containing various wooden weapons sat near the door. Goliath pulled the door shut before I could thank him. I didn't think he expected it; the urge to do so surprised me as well. I turned to face the room. A small smile crossed my face.

***

I slammed an elbow into a stationary bag, then spun and used my other elbow against the second bag. I kicked low, then high, and impacted the hanging bag in the corner with another spinning kick. I dropped an elbow into the marked abdomen of one of the wooden dummies lying on the floor, rolled heedless of the pain in my bound wings, and came up with another spinning kick.

As soon as I connected with the swinging bag, I elbowed the stationary bag behind me, turned and connected with a kick to a wooden dummy's groin, then threw myself into a spinning kick that connected with both my right and left foot across the face of another dummy. I dropped to the ground and drove my elbow once more into the stomach of the wooden dummy on the ground.

I lay there gasping for air. It had been almost an hour of intense training. My shirt was soaked with sweat and my hands burned at the constant friction against the bandages even though I hadn't used them. My elbows ached. I had never used them that way before. I grinned at the thought of my technique. It may have been scrappy, but if my hands were truly disabled, I wouldn't be left defenseless.

A slight tapping on the window sounded behind me. I pushed up gingerly to one elbow. My racing heart skipped a beat at the sight of at least a dozen Galdoni crowded around the window. The thought that they had been watching me fight twisted my stomach. Someone moved and my eyes shifted to Kale. He stood near the back with his arms crossed in front of his chest. He gave a short nod, approval in his eyes.

I rose and set the room back in order the best I could. The Galdoni slowly dispersed until only Kale and Goliath remained. They spoke together too quietly for me to hear through the glass. Goliath smiled as if they were old friends. He would definitely be a handy friend to have.

When I walked to the door, Goliath pulled it open. "I thought you were kidding when you said you'd use your elbows," he said with a deep chuckle.

Kale patted my shoulder. The gesture was oddly warming, as though I had exceeded some expectation he had of me. "You never fought like that at the Academy," he said.

I shrugged, feeling self-conscious. "I never had a face for my anger."

Goliath grunted. "Remind me not to get on your bad side."

The thought of the big Galdoni being afraid of me made me laugh. "I think you're safe," I said.

He grinned. "I sure hope so."

They walked with me toward the training room exit. "You should probably go back to Alana's room," Kale suggested. "Dr. Ray mentioned checking your wings."

The trepidation I felt must have shown on my face because Kale smiled. "Don't worry. I wouldn't have my wings if it wasn't for him. He'll take good care of you."

"Come back soon," Goliath said. "The boys enjoyed the entertainment."

I smiled at his comment. Goliath held the door open. Kale and I walked up the hall. It felt strange to have someone I trusted at my side.

"It's not my wings I'm worried about," I admitted when we were out of earshot from the training room. "They feel a lot better."

Kale glanced at my hands. "I really don't know much about burns."

I didn't either. It never fell under standard wound care training at the Academy. "That's all I was good for." I looked up when Kale glanced at me, and realized I had spoken the words aloud.

"What?" he asked.

I debated whether to keep silent, but it was too late to pretend I hadn't said anything. I looked down at the gauze. "The sensitivity of my fingers let me open safes in half the time Jake said it took anyone else. What if I've lost that?"

Kale's expression was unreadable. The back of my neck itched. I wanted to rub it, but it would only hurt. I gave a humorless smile. "What is the word the humans use? When you do something bad and it comes back to make you pay?"

"Karma?" Kale asked.

I nodded. "Maybe it's karma that my hands got burned. I did bad things, and so now I'm paying for it."

"You did good things with those hands, too," Kale pointed out.

I shook my head. My tongue felt thick in my mouth. I couldn't tell him what I felt, that everything I had ever done was wrong.

He answered my thoughts without me speaking them. "What we did in the Arena was forced upon us. We were fed lies and had no reason to doubt them, no chance to second-guess what we had been raised our whole lives to know as if it was fact. I know you regret it, and I do too."

He held open the door to the third floor. I hesitated on the landing. "I saw your video."

His mouth twitched slightly. "I have no technical expertise. My friends did that."

I nodded. "They did a good job. You almost had me convinced."

"Almost?" he asked.

I wanted to walk through the door and forget about it, but I couldn't. There was no walking away from what I had seen and experienced. He had to know. "I was the little boy with the katana."

Kale watched me, but I could see his mind working, flashing back through the video to the scene of the boy dying on the floor, the victor standing above him. Regret gripped my throat so tight I felt like I was choking. I never wanted to relive that moment; seeing it had shredded my tattered heart.

"Accidents happened," Kale said quietly.

"They gave me a real blade," I shouted. The words were too painful. I had to get them out and be free of their agony. "Why would they give a six year old a real blade, and then applaud when he killed his best friend?"

I remembered the sharp thwack of the katana on the sand when it fell out of my hand. They had beat me then; not for killing another boy, not for taking a life, but for dropping my sword.

"There are so many things I regret about the Academy," Kale said. He released the door and it closed with a quiet snick beside him. His expression was stark, his eyes bare as if he saw it all over again. He stood on the Arena floor once more, the sand at his feet and the dome overhead. How many times had I experienced that same sight?

"I knew then that it was wrong." I had been forced to hide my tears of remorse, to cry them at night with my face turned away from the all-seeing gaze of the cameras in each cell. "I knew we weren't supposed to kill, but there was no way out."

I had paced my cell so many times the bottom of my feet became as tough as leather. I was a tiger unable to fulfill its destiny to run in the savanna. I wanted to explode, to change something, to make it stop, yet I was unable to do anything but train. They beat me until I trained, then beat me again when they didn't like my technique.

"I pulled the fire alarms."

I glanced at Kale, surprised. A slight smile touched his face, but it didn't quite chase away the pain in his gaze.

"Whenever I couldn't take it anymore, I pulled a fire alarm to get us out to the Arena for a chance to breathe." His smile widened. "It got to the point that whenever a fire alarm went off, they headed straight to wherever I was training."

"I remember the fire alarms," I said, thinking back. "I wish I'd thought of that."

He chuckled. "No, you don't."

"Why not?"

"I would have been thrown in solitary twice as often."

I laughed. It felt good to laugh after talking about what we had been through. I couldn't explain how much easier I could breathe hearing about the Academy from someone else's point of view, and realizing I wasn't the only one who had felt the way I did.

"We have counseling."

I gave him a bland look. "For what?"

He smiled, correctly interpreting the look. "For talking about what we went through. Every Galdoni within these walls and without is dealing with some form of PTSD."

"What's that?" I asked warily.

"Post-Traumatic Stress Disorder. It helps to talk about it. Trust me."

I gestured toward the door.

"Catch you later," Kale said, pulling it open.

I stepped inside and he let it shut again without following me. There had been something in his gaze, loss and pain as if talking to me reminded him how bad it had been. I wondered if he was going to talk to a counselor. Part of me felt like I should follow; the other part railed against the idea as if a counselor was someone with a thousand daggers. I let out a slow breath and walked up the hall.

I paused by the doorway. A man with brown hair and glasses was checking the numbers on the monitor closest to Alana. He spoke without looking at me. "I was hoping to catch you here."

"And you are?" I asked, not bothering to hide how defensive I felt to find a stranger in Alana's room.

"Dr. Ray," he replied. "I thought I'd see how Alana's doing, and hoped I might catch you as well."

I waited in silence, unsure what to say or do.

He continued speaking as if used to poor conversationalists. "Your friend is doing much better. Her wound is healing and her respiration rates have steadied. I wouldn't be surprised if she wakes up in the next day or two."

I crossed to his side, anxious to see the progress myself. Alana looked the same, though her cheeks might have had more color than before. I wanted her to open her eyes so badly I could barely think past the longing.

"What do you think?"

I glanced up, realizing I had only caught the tail end of Dr. Ray's question.

He gave a kind smile and repeated, "I said I thought we should unwrap those wings and see if they're ready for flight. They weren't burned, just singed a bit. I wrapped them to keep you from pushing yourself too hard. If you're like any of the other Galdoni I've met, you have a tendency to think you're ready to go to battle when you're still in the middle of healing."

"Occupational hazard," I replied.

A laugh burst from him at my response. He looked surprised. "I must say I'm not used to such casual references to what you've gone through."

I shrugged. "I'm not used to being pampered in a hospital. Bitter humor's my coping mechanism."

He chuckled again. "I'm just glad you weren't awake when I was taking care of your hands."

"That makes two of us."

He smiled and motioned for me to turn around. The pressure on my wings let up as he gently unwrapped them. He was silent until the bandages were completely off. When he stepped back, I noticed he held one of my feathers in his hand. It looked dull against the neon glare of the overhead light. I definitely needed a shower.

"Go ahead," he urged. "Tell me how they feel."

I spread them slowly. They ached with the movement.

"It's normal for them to hurt a bit," Dr. Ray commented without waiting for me to ask. "They've been bound in one position for longer than I intended. You're a hard Galdoni to find."

I spread them out as far as the room allowed. It felt good to have my wings open again instead of bound tight behind my back. "What about my hands?" I asked before I got the urge to fly away and never return.

Dr. Ray motioned for me to take a seat on the couch. He pulled over a tray of supplies already set out as if he had been waiting for me. At my questioning look, he smiled. "I figured if I waited long enough, you would show up." He glanced at Alana. "She's worth checking on."

"More than you know," I replied quietly.

He began unwrapping the bandages on my left hand. "This one was burned the worst. It was hard to tell how badly when you arrived. I thought we would be dealing with third degree burns, but for the most part they ended up being first and second." At my uncertain look, he explained, "They blistered quite extensively, but should heal within a couple of weeks. I don't think you'll require surgery, which you would if they had been third degree."

"That's good to hear," I replied because I felt like it was expected of me. I fought back a wince when the gauze was removed and he gently worked the bandages off.

"Some of your blisters have popped." He glanced at me. "Where were you just now?"

"Practicing," I replied vaguely.

He looked as though he knew exactly what I meant. "You should probably give your hands a rest if you want them to heal right."

"I only used my elbows and feet."

He watched me as though waiting for me to tell him I was kidding, but it was true, so I had no reason to joke. I met his searching gaze until he finally got back to work on my hands. "I need to flush these blisters, then I'll bandage your hand back up again. It'd be best if we could do the same procedure every day for the next two weeks while the burns are healing."

He unwrapped my right hand, then I watched as he gently removed the dead skin from the blisters and flushed them with an antiseptic solution. It definitely wasn't the best moment of my life; there were a few times I had to fight the impulse to throw the doctor through the window, but I figured if Alana awoke, she would disapprove. Sweat had broken out across my body by the time he was done.

He finished wrapping both hands with gauze before looking up at me. "I know that hurt. I've taken a few punches during my time here," he said amiably. "I'm still not used to my patients being so silent. I'm always worried it's the calm before the storm."

"I may have been close to violence a time or two."

Dr. Ray smiled. "I'm glad you held back."

"Alana would have been disappointed."

He chuckled. "Good to know she has a positive impact on you." He became serious. "She's going to be alright, Saro. Stick around. I have a feeling it will mean a lot for her to have a familiar face when she awakens."

"I'll be here," I promised.

He nodded. "Good. Move your hands and fingers as often as you can bear it. It'll keep them from healing stiff."

"Got it."

He picked up a chart from the side table, made a few notes in it, then gave me a nod before he left the room with the chart in his hand. I sat back on the couch. My hands ached, but it was a healing pain. With how badly they hurt, I had expected the damage to be much worse. As it was, if I could keep from destroying them while they healed, I might be just fine.

Physically, the voice in the back of my mind said.

I grimaced and rose to my feet. As much as I wanted to sit there for hours, I needed to test my wings and there was somewhere I wanted to go.

Chapter Fourteen

After considerable searching, I finally had to ask the staff if they had seen Kale. I was directed to the sixth floor by a short nurse with curly blonde hair. She looked pleased that I had spoken to her. I puzzled over it as I made my way up the stairs.

"You'd think with a building for Galdoni there'd be outside landings to fly to," I muttered as I pushed open the door with my shoulder.

I paused in surprise. Kale and two more Galdoni stood amid a roomful of children. Galdoni children. They played with blocks, drew on white boards, and several were currently trying to guess what sort of animal Kale was acting out. Even I was at a loss until he whinnied.

"A horse?" I guessed.

Everyone looked at me. Kale grinned. "You got it!" The children cheered. Kale excused himself from them as one of the other Galdoni took over with a very good impression of an angry cat.

"Dr. Ray rewrapped your hands," Kale said by way of a greeting.

I nodded. When he waited in expectant silence, I continued, "He said they would heal in a few weeks if I was careful."

"So not at all then." I stared at him for a minute before he smiled and I remembered he had been watching me practice. He led the way through the room to a tinted glass door. "I'm glad they're going to be okay."

I watched the children we passed. It was strange to see so many together. At the Academy, we had been separated by age groups, so I wasn't even aware there had been more children there when I left. It made me glad to know they weren't going to be raised within those impenetrable gray walls.

One child in particular caught my attention. He had curly blonde hair and intense blue eyes offset by dark red wings. He looked up just as we walked by. He was older than those around him, but many of the children waited nearby as if to see what he would do. He held something close to his body. When he met my gaze, he lifted the object so I could see. The boy held a bird cunningly crafted out of a bar of soap. I realized the white scraps around him were shavings. He handed the bird to a little Galdoni with brown wings. The boy laughed and ran to his friends, showing them his prize.

"Some of the children have coped a lot faster than the others," Kale explained, holding open the door.

I smothered a smile at the sight of a balcony like I had just been complaining they needed. A few Galdoni flew to other landings. Apparently they hated stairs as much as I did.

When the door closed behind us, Kale continued, "The staff have named the little boy you were watching Koden, but he hasn't spoken."

"At all?"

Kale shook his head. "Not in the year we've been running this place. Some children cope better than others. That's one of the beauties of this Center." He leaned against the railing, watching the Galdoni below. The sun was setting, casting the horizon in red and gold. They reflected in Kale's dark eyes. "Everyone can take the time they need to go out into the world." He glanced at me. "Is that why you were looking for me?"

I nodded. I felt suddenly ashamed to ask, like I was pressing my luck. "I have somewhere I need to go."

Kale smiled. "This isn't a prison, Saro. You're free to come and go as you wish. I know Dr. Ray needs to take care of your hands. Are you coming back in a few days?"

Relief flooded me. I let out my pent-up emotions with a breath. "Only a few hours. I just need to stretch my wings a bit."

He nodded as if he had expected as much. "I'm glad you'll be back. Would you mind if I had your things moved to the residential block? You could have a private room there away from the medical floor."

I shook my head. "I don't want to bother anyone."

"It's no bother," Kale reassured me. "That's what we're here for."

I studied the ground. The impulse to jump off the balcony and test my wings the hard way appealed to me. I was about to act when Kale spoke again. "Jayce pulled me aside." He met my gaze. "He didn't want to break your confidence, but he felt I should know about the scars."

"Everyone has scars," I said quietly, my gaze on the ground below.

"Usually not received after the closing of the Academy." He looked back out at the sunrays that disappeared behind the distant buildings. "If you plan to go back to Jake's, I'd like to go with you. I told the police the directions you gave me, but he was gone by the time they arrived. We've been searching for him but haven't had any leads yet."

"Good to know," I replied quietly. "I'm planning to stick around here."

Kale nodded. He turned to leave, then said over his shoulder, "There are those who haven't quite accepted the presence of the Galdoni, so take care."

"I will."

He pressed a button on the side of the door; after a moment, it buzzed and opened to release the sounds of childish laughter. It closed quietly behind me with a soft shush. I took a deep breath, then jumped off the balcony.

***

I spread my wings just before I reached the ground. The sudden tension made the minor burns and new feathers ache, but it felt so good to have them filled with wind again. I pushed hard, anxious to lose myself in the clouds that drifted across the rapidly falling night. Even though I had said otherwise to Kale, I had only one destination I needed to visit.

It took me much less time to reach the apartment than my flight to the Galdoni Center with Alana. I circled the building, trepidation rising in my chest. Now that I had arrived, I wasn't so sure I wanted to be there at all. Anxiety flooded my chest at the thought of the brown carpets and stale scent of the bottles on the floor. I wanted to go to the basement, but Alana wasn't there. Uncertain what I planned to do, I landed behind the apartment.

I went up the stairs to the second floor. The first apartment on the left had been the one I shared with Jake. The door was locked, but it took a mere shove of my shoulder to convince the doorknob to give. It swung inward, and I was left staring at an empty room.

The furniture was gone, the beer bottles removed, and even the musty picture of the deer was missing; it had been on the wall so long the wallpaper behind still showed bright blue flowers. There was nothing left, no lead, no scrap revealing where he might have gone. Helpless rage filled me. He shouldn't have gotten away. I had let him escape as much as if I had watched him walk away. He didn't deserve to go free after what he had done. I didn't care about myself; I cared about Alana. He would pay for tying her up and slapping her face when she tried to defend me.

The memory played over and over in my mind. I couldn't escape the leering smile on his face or the glee in his eyes at my pain. I wanted to beat him like I had in the training room. He needed to pay. If he was truly linked to the crime ring, which all evidence seemed to point, he may be the key in bringing it down. All I had to do was find him.

I shut the door behind me as I left the apartment. It swung open a few inches in the broken frame. I walked slowly down the steps and paused on the dark sidewalk outside. The streetlight near the entrance had broken long ago, and no one bothered to repair them in that part of town. It felt fitting that I would leave the apartment for the last time in darkness.

A voice broke the silence. "I was hoping you'd return."

My heart skipped a beat. I spun with my knees bent and hands up, ready for an attack.

"Slow down," the voice said. Officer Donaldson stepped from the shadows. He gave an apologetic smile. "I didn't mean to startle you."

"I got that from the way you were hiding in the dark," I replied dryly, keeping my gaze locked on the gun at his side. He hadn't pulled it, but I knew a second could mean the difference between death and a chance to escape.

"Guess I could have been a bit less stealthy," he said.

I decided not to beat around the bush. "I can't let you take me in. Alana needs me and I've got to find the other female Galdoni."

Officer Donaldson lifted a hand. "I don't want to take you in."

"Then why are you here?" I asked, puzzled.

He hesitated, then shoved his hands in his pockets uncomfortably. "I just wanted to make sure you were alright after my partner shot you."

I hadn't expected that response in the least. "I'm fine," I said quietly.

"I'm glad," he said, but his expression remained unconvinced as his gaze kept drifting to my bandaged hands.

"It, uh, just grazed my head. I was a bit loopy though," I concluded with a wry smile.

"I can imagine."

We stood in awkward silence for a few minutes. Officer Donaldson finally cleared his throat. "You want to go get a bite?"

"A bite?" I couldn't picture that being a good thing.

"Food," he said with a smile. "Do you want to eat?"

I had no good reason to say no, though that wouldn't have stopped me from saying no anyway before I met Kale. Something about the black-winged Galdoni made me want to treat people better. I couldn't explain it. He had a way of talking as if I was the only important person to him at that moment, even though I knew he had countless other cares on his mind with all he handled.

I had never felt important until the moment he sat in the hallway with me across from Alana's room. His words stayed with me, tangling in the back of my mind. "Love can focus your drive and help you understand that there is more to life than fighting." My brief contact with his human friend Jayce and the Galdoni Goliath had impacted me as well. I felt it; I was different because of them. I just couldn't decide if that was bad or good.

"Alright," I agreed hesitantly.

He led the way around the front of the apartment complex. I paused at the sight of the police car.

Donaldson caught my look. "If you think this is a fancy lie to arrest you, keep in mind that I don't take criminals to dinner."

The confined space was the last thing I wanted. I didn't have enough experience with cars to know if I could get out if Donaldson had a way of locking the doors. With my burned hands, I wasn't sure I could work the handle, and my wings wouldn't give me enough room to break the window and climb through.

Officer Donaldson chuckled. "Tell you what. There's a diner about three blocks north of here. Why don't we just walk?"

"I should have brought my jacket." A pang went through me at the thought that I no longer even had the jacket I used to hide my wings. Jake had taken everything from me; bitterness welled up in my chest at the thought that he had also given me everything I thought I had.

"Saro, you don't need to hide who you are. Galdoni can do what they want."

I glanced at him, but refused to let him know how uncomfortable I felt walking down the street with my wings showing. It was late, but cars drove past and a few people hung around the steps of the nearby apartments. I felt eyes on me, but kept my gaze straight ahead. If they wanted to start something, I would finish it regardless of my hands.

Chapter Fifteen

The scent of hamburger, eggs, and coffee drifted out when Officer Donaldson opened the door to a place called The Mmm Mmm Good Café. My stomach rumbled at the pleasant smell. The eyes of the few late night diners turned to us as I followed Donaldson to a booth near the back wall. He was about to take the seat closest to the wall when he paused. "Usually I like to keep an eye on the room, but I think you'd be more comfortable facing the crowd." He sat down with his back to the diner and gestured for me to take the other seat.

I slid onto the red vinyl booth seat, grateful and surprised by his insight. Galdoni were trained to be alert for attack. Though none of the other tables' occupants appeared anything more than curious at the entrance of a Galdoni with a police officer, I wasn't about to take chances. The table closest to us held an elderly couple. The woman had her back to me, but the man poked at an over-easy egg and shot glances in my direction. They both sat in a silence that felt familiar and comfortable instead of awkward as though they did the same thing often.

Two tables from them sat three middle-aged men. They had been talking animatedly when we entered; now their voices were low. None looked in our direction, but it was easy to guess that we were the topic of conversation. On the other side of the door, a mother with two boys was busy cutting up food for her energetic children. I doubted any of them had noticed our entrance.

"Have you figured out how to kill everyone in here?"

My gaze shifted back to Officer Donaldson. I gave him a wry look. "Work with Galdoni often?"

He shook his head. "You're the first, actually, but with that look in your eyes, I wouldn't mess with you."

I dropped my gaze to the table. He may have been joking, but I really did have a plan that involved the napkin holder on our table, a glass mug near the cash register, and a few moves considered beneath the training at the Academy. I wasn't proud of the fact, but it was life. When every day from birth was spent learning how to defend oneself from any attack, it came as second nature.

A woman came over with a pad of paper in one hand. "What can I get for you?" she asked in a forced bored tone even though her eyes lingered on my wings for the briefest moment before flitting back to her paper. Her hair was in a messy bun held in place by a pencil, and her hands were red and cracked as if they were often in water. Her crooked nametag said 'Mel'.

"Coffee and a Joe Burger," Donaldson ordered. He glanced at me. "It's like a normal hamburger with an egg on it. You should try it." At my nod, he said, "Make that two."

"You got it, honey," Mel replied. Her black flat shoes gave a squeak when she turned and walked away without looking at me.

"It's okay to relax."

I shook my head at his tone. "It's okay for *you* to relax," I replied. "Your badge and uniform tell everyone not to mess with you. My wings, on the other hand, scream target and tell people to either run away or attack."

"Did Jake teach you that?" he asked, his tone gentle.

I gritted my teeth. I wasn't used to being contradicted. I let out a slow breath. "Call it the product of a violent upbringing. If you assume everyone is out to get you, you're not surprised when it happens."

"So being out a year and a half hasn't taught you differently?" The curiosity in Donaldson's voice took away any sting the question might have held.

I told him the truth. "It confirmed my feelings. This world is run by greed, just as ours was. Violence is an end result of fear, which is in turn the product of ignorance. If people realized just how easily their money can be taken away, maybe they wouldn't value it so much."

Officer Donaldson nodded. "Good observation. So you've learned something during your time as a burglar."

"How to avoid fire," I replied dryly, lifting my hands.

He smiled. "The chemical traces from the Molotovs you used helped us link the thefts together. Twenty-four, if I'm not mistaken."

That triggered my curiosity. "Twenty-seven. The first were a little sloppy because we used gasoline before Jake began experimenting with Molotovs. So why not press charges?"

He shrugged a bit uncomfortably. "I think you're a bit young for solitary."

I picked up my fork and toyed with it. "I've been in solitary more times than I can count."

I saw his eyebrows lift out of the corner of my eye, but kept my gaze on the metal tines.

"That doesn't make it right," Donaldson replied. "The Galdoni who are thrown in prison don't survive long. Apparently quite a few inmates were into gamboling. They started putting Galdoni in solitary for their own safety."

"They should do the same for our entire species," I muttered.

"You don't really think that, do you?" he asked.

There was an innocence to his tone that angered me. He shouldn't trust us, any of us. We were worse than the

140

humans, and that was saying a lot. I met his gaze and he sat back at the sight of my rage. "Do you really want Galdoni around your kids?" I gestured toward the mother and her two little children at the other end of the small diner. "Every time a Galdoni walks by, he's already figured out how to kill you. Do you truly believe that's healthy in society?" I spread my gauzed hands. "I stole because I was so *afraid*," I spat the word, "to go back to the Academy that I would do anything to stay out. I knew burning houses was wrong, but I didn't care. I hated the families who lived within the walls so safe and secure in their world that they couldn't care less about people being raised to kill for no reason other than the greed of a money-hungry society."

I dropped my voice so that he had to lean closer to hear me. I watched my reflection in the spoon near my hand. It showed my head and body small and upside down with massive golden wings emphasized by the metal's contour. I grimaced. "Killing a child when I was only a child myself took something from me. Call it my heart, my soul, anything you want. I'm broken, and I shouldn't be here. I should be in solitary where I'm not a threat to anyone, because if I can't kill myself, I'll surely hurt someone else."

There it was; the bare truth. It had been swirling through my head since our release from the Academy. I had never spoken it aloud before. Fear that I couldn't control it surged through my veins. I was a born killer along with every other Galdoni in the world.

My heart skipped a beat. Every Galdoni but Alana.

I took a shuddering breath. Officer Donaldson's hand touched mine. He opened my gauze-covered fingers and removed the spoon I hadn't remembered picking up. My hand ached and fingers trembled from the pain. I slipped it under the table where he wouldn't see it. He pretended not to notice.

Footsteps crossed to our table. I didn't have to look up to recognize the sound of the flat rubber soles. "Burgers up," Mel said. She slipped two plates of burgers and fries in front of us, then filled up our white mugs with strong-scented coffee. "Enjoy," she said flatly before she turned with another squeak and walked away.

The scent of the burger rose tantalizingly to my nose. I wondered how I had an appetite after spilling what was left of my soul to Officer Donaldson, a stranger who probably was wishing he had never invited me to take a bite.

"Take a bite," he said.

I stared at him, surprised to hear my thoughts repeated when he should have been calling for backup or shooting me.

He lifted his hamburger. "You won't regret it."

"You might," I replied before I could stop myself.

He gave me a searching look before he took a bite out of his hamburger. The sound of the pickles crunching was loud in the air between us and he smiled with full cheeks. "Try it," he said, his words sloppy.

I sighed and gave in, picking up the hamburger gingerly to keep my gauzed fingers clean. The bread was soft and sprinkled with sesame seeds. The hamburger was at the bottom of several tomatoes, pickles, lettuce leaves, orange cheese, and the white outline of the egg. It looked almost too good to be edible.

I took a bite, then closed my eyes. A tidal wave of flavors rushed over my tongue. The seasoned meat was tempered by the mellow flood of the salted and peppered egg. The tomatoes were crisp along with the pickles, touching my taste buds with the perfect mixture of sweet and sour. A hint of ketchup lingered in my mouth when I swallowed. I heard Officer Donaldson chuckle and opened my eyes.

"As good as I said?" he asked.

"Better," I replied. A grin spread across his face. I took another bite.

"You'd miss it, right?" His tone was serious again.

At first, I thought he meant the burger, then I realized he meant the world. I wanted to lie, to tell him I wouldn't miss a thing if they threw me into solitary and tossed the key like I deserved. One glance told me he would know if I lied. I chewed slowly, enjoying the flavors as much as I knew I would hate the bitter taste of the truth.

"I'd miss everything about it," I said quietly.

"Which parts?" he pressed.

I lifted my wings slightly. "Flying, especially." He smiled and nodded for me to continue. "Warm sun. It was always a bit cold at the Academy; made us keep moving to stay warm. Couches."

"Couches?" he repeated, surprised.

An unbidden smile touched my lips. "I've been sleeping on one at the Galdoni Center. They're very comfortable. I've never slept so deep."

Officer Donaldson's smile deepened, but his eyes were touched by sadness. "You should try a bed sometime." He took a sip of his coffee. "What about the food?"

I pretended nonchalance. "It's not the best."

Somehow Mel had managed to reappear just as I spoke. She gave me a look of distain. "I'm just, uh. . . ." I couldn't find the right word.

"He's kidding," Donaldson supplied. "Saro's very sarcastic."

She rolled her eyes. "I'm sure." She marched away with her pot of coffee after ascertaining that our mugs did not yet require refilling.

Officer Donaldson burst out laughing. It caught me in a wave and I couldn't fight the chuckle that rose from my stomach and turned into a full-throated laugh. I held my sides; they hurt, but I couldn't stop until tears filled my eyes and my face ached so much from smiling that I thought I would be sore the rest of my life.

Donaldson leaned over the table and slapped me on the shoulder. "You're alright, Saro."

"I don't know about that," I replied. "But you're the one who needs a psychological evaluation." His eyes held his questioning amusement, so I expounded. "First you try to shoot me and your companion succeeds in nearly knocking the sense clean out of me, then you stalk me outside Jake's place, hiding in the shadows and acting all suspicious, and now you're eating dinner with someone deemed fit for a five by five cell and no windows. You sure you're alright?"

He looked quite pleased with himself. "More than alright."

"Why is that?" I asked suspiciously.

He grinned. "Because anyone who can laugh like that has something left of worth in him. If you can laugh, you can cry, and if you can cry, you can get rid of all the pain from the past and move on. You're better than the lot you've been given, Saro. You just need a chance to believe it."

We finished our burgers in silence. I let his words fill me. I didn't believe them; I couldn't. Yet they soothed the tattered pieces of what was left of the little boy on the screen with the tears running down his face and his friend dying from his sword at his feet.

Officer Donaldson left money on the table and I followed him to the door. The mother and children were gone, but my muscles tensed when we passed the table with the three men. They didn't speak, but the hostility in their eyes said enough. We walked up the road. It wasn't toward Jake's apartment or Donaldson's car, but it was casual, as though we were wandering. I liked the feeling.

"I've always wondered what it would feel like to fly," Donaldson mused.

I glanced at him; his eyes were on the dark sky. I knew there were stars out, but they were hidden above the light pollution of the city. "Like there's nothing in your way but the wind and any whim you want to take."

He shook his head. "It's not for me. I'm afraid of heights."

That brought a smile to my lips. "Then why do you wonder what it'd be like?"

He grinned. "I wonder if I would die of fright or from the fall because I'd be too terrified to remember to flap my wings."

I chuckled. "You'd forget your fear the minute you were in the air. Trust me."

We walked in silence for about a half hour before we turned back toward the car. Officer Donaldson glanced at me. "Is there anything else you can tell me about the houses you hit? Anything that links them together?"

I thought about it for a second. "They were nice houses, rich, definitely well to do. Some had kids, some didn't."

"How do you know that?"

"The pictures on the walls."

Donaldson nodded. "There must be something that ties them all together, or else why those houses?"

"It could be random, couldn't it?" I asked. Curiosity was getting the better of me. Did Jake have a hidden motive besides money when he picked a house?

Donaldson's brow furrowed thoughtfully. "In cases like these, it's usually not random. There's a reason behind it; we just don't know what that may be." He glanced at me. "What was in those safes you opened?"

"Money, usually cash, sometimes gold bars."

His eyebrows rose at that, but he continued walking in silence.

"There were also envelopes. If I forgot the envelopes, I got whipped." The admission stung. I shouldn't have let him do that to me. I should have fought back; but at the time, he was all I had. His little apartment and my bed of blankets on the floor represented my only security in the world.

"Envelopes," Donaldson mused, his tone interested. "I wonder what was so important about them." I was grateful he didn't ask about the whipping. The scars on my chest gave a dull throb. I ignored them.

"He cared about them more than the gold, I suppose." I thought back. Why hadn't I been more curious? It could have saved us a lot of trouble.

"Did the envelopes have anything on them? A crest or name of some sort?"

I nodded. "They did. Each had the letters 'AC' in red on the front right corner." I glanced at him. "Does that mean anything to you?"

He shook his head. "I'll run it through the system and let you know. It's something to go on."

We were walking past the diner when a man ran out followed by Mel the waitress. "They stole our money," she cried when she saw us.

Indignation flared in my chest. The man turned down the next alley, his footsteps loud in the night. I pushed down hard with my wings, flying faster than a man could run.

"Saro, wait!" Officer Donaldson called.

I landed at the entrance of the alley because my wingspan was too large for the buildings. All three men were waiting. It was a trap.

I ducked a punch and threw an elbow into one face, dropped to my knee and knocked the legs from another, and rose with another elbow to the last man's jaw that carried the force of my momentum and dropped him like a dismembered dummy. I drove my head into the stomach of the first man and slammed him against the wall; he fell gasping to the ground. Something hit the side of my head. I spun and kicked, connecting with the second man's face. When I landed, I drove an elbow into his groin. He doubled over and I slammed another one into his back.

"Saro!" Officer Donaldson shouted as he and Mel rounded the corner. Both of them stopped at the sight of the fallen men. Mel's hand flew to her mouth.

I stepped around them. "Don't worry. I didn't kill any of them," I told the officer. A plastic bag near the wall caught my eye. I picked it up and glanced inside. "I think this is yours." I handed the bag to Mel. Her hands shook as she took it from me and looked inside at the money.

"They set you up," Donaldson said, his eyes on the groaning men.

I nodded. "I'm just glad they didn't have a gun."

He let out a half-laugh that didn't carry any humor. "They meant to kill you, Saro."

I shrugged. "I'm used to it."

He shook his head, but the humor returned to his eyes. "I need to call for backup. We'll have to report this and take these guys in."

"I'd better get back to the Galdoni Center. I told Kale I wasn't going to be very long. Need any help?"

The shadow of a smile touched his mouth. "I think you've handled it. Take care of yourself."

"You, too," I told him, surprised that I really meant it. I was glad I got to the alley before the officer. If they had jumped him, I would have one less friend in the world, and friends were hard to come by.

I stepped back to the street and noticed the elderly man and woman from the diner standing with the other two diner employees near the door to the café. I was about to spread my wings when a hand touched my shoulder. It was too soft to mean harm, but I still had to fight to keep from defending myself with the adrenaline that raced through my veins.

I turned to find Mel, her eyes wide and hands clutching the bag of money. "I just wanted to say thank you," she said. "That was very brave. I didn't know a Galdoni would do that."

I smiled, feeling more like myself than I had in a long time. "I'm not sure all of them would, but I was happy to help."

Officer Donaldson's smile and nod over the head of the waitress filled me with warmth as I spread my wings and soared over the city. I couldn't explain why I had gone after the men; I hadn't thought, just acted. A smile wouldn't leave my face even after I landed at the Galdoni Center and made my way to Alana's room.

Chapter Sixteen

My smile faded when I saw her lying there in the same position, the tubes still connected and machines beeping disharmoniously. I let out a slow breath and stepped into the room. A chair had been pulled next to her hospital bed. I wondered who had sat with her while I was gone. A pang of guilt rose at the thought that she might have awoken when I was away. I shoved it down and sat on the chair, letting my wings relax on either side to ease the healing ache from the burns that still irritated the joints.

"I don't know what's going on with me, Alana." The words broke out even though she couldn't hear what I said. It felt right to talk to her, as though she was awake and smiling her beautiful smile, her brown eyes filled with light. "I chased down robbers today." I snorted at the thought. "Me, catching robbers. I think for the first time in my life, I understand true irony."

I chuckled. "I didn't even think about it. It just happened, and Mel was so grateful. I've never had anyone look at me that way before, as though I had just given her life back and made everything right in the world. Things are definitely not right if three grown men are robbing nice little diners."

The side of my head itched. When I reached up, I found a good-sized knot where one man's fist had connected. I grinned. "I'm feeling more like myself every day." A thought tickled my mind, chasing the grin from my face. "Except I'm not. I'm different, Alana. I can't explain it." I shook my head, trying to make sense of how I felt. "It's like the more others expect of me, the more I change; yet it's not like I'm leaving me behind. The me that's filled with the need for violence and revenge is still there waiting for its chance."

I clenched my hands, and remembered Officer Donaldson taking the spoon from my grip. My palms ached. I hoped that meant the burns were healing and I hadn't stressed them too badly. "But there's something else. It's like I want to be the person Kale and Donaldson think I am. I know I'm not," I quickly put in before my thoughts could contradict me. "But I'm trying to be." My head ached. I rested it in one bandaged hand, ignoring the pain the weight brought. "I just don't want to disappoint them," I concluded softly.

The silence that met my words filled me with longing. I wanted her to answer. I wanted her to be alright. She needed to know that she was safe, and that there were people other than me who wanted to take care of her. She didn't need me. My heart gave a sharp throb. I let out a slow breath. She at least needed me there to reassure her that she was safe. After that, I could leave the Galdoni Center behind.

"Her numbers are better."

I stood so fast my chair hit against the small couch by the wall and fell over. My hands were up and I stood in a defensive stance before I realized the voice had been feminine and soft. I blinked, and found myself looking at a young woman in nurse's scrubs holding a tray of food.

"I didn't mean to startle you," she apologized, one foot turned toward the hallway as if she was ready to run in case I attacked.

I willed my muscles to relax and shook my head. "I'm sorry. I overreacted. I, uh, I'm not used to being caught off-guard."

She gave a small, uncertain smile. "They should turn the bed so you can see the door when you sit there. It might make you more comfortable."

I grimaced. "Or I could learn that the staff here isn't out to kill me." I gave her what I hoped was an apologetic smile. "It's been an interesting night."

She took a step into the room. I crossed to the couch and stood the chair back up using my elbow and a foot. When I turned back, the girl had set the tray on a small rolling side table and was watching me with a hint of a smile playing around her mouth. "I could have done that."

I scooted the chair back toward Alana's bed. It made a loud screech on the linoleum floor. The girl and I both winced and glanced at Alana as if afraid the sound might have awoken her. We looked at each other again and she gave a little laugh. "As if waking her up would be a bad thing," she said.

I nodded. "Maybe I should do it again."

She laughed out loud, then covered her mouth with a hand as though surprised such a thing had come out of it. She quickly dropped her hand again. "Here." She pushed the tray toward me.

"You're the one who's been bringing me food?" The thought made me feel even worse about scaring her.

She shrugged. "It's my job."

She was different than the other nurses I had seen at the center. Her hair was black and cut short at the back, but left longer at the front so that it fell in front of her eyes when she tipped her head down. The ends had been colored bright red, which contrasted starkly with her light blue eyes. Black marks traced her skin, peaking above the collar line of her scrubs, and then lacing along her arms like vines that ended in thorns around her wrists.

"What are those?" I asked. I wanted to kick myself for talking without thinking. It was none of my business; I had just never seen anything like it before.

Surprise lit her guarded gaze. She turned her arms, revealing more of the marks swirling up past her elbows. A small red flower had been crafted on each forearm about midway between her elbows and wrists. The distinction was beautiful. "Tattoos," she said quietly. She glanced up at me through her red and black hair. "I'm supposed to wear a long-sleeved shirt, but they don't seem to care if I *forget* during the night shifts. Never seen tattoos before?"

I shook my head. "I haven't exactly been around many sophisticated women before."

The laugh burst from her again as if she couldn't hold it in. Her hand covered her mouth, but mirth still showed in her eyes as if despite her efforts, it bubbled beneath the surface. She shook her head. "Sophisticated. That's a first."

My cheeks burned. "Did I use the wrong word?"

She looked at me again with the same gaze as though she was trying to read my heart through my eyes. My heart responded by performing what felt like a backflip. My breath caught in my throat. "You used it right," she said, her expression curious and head tipped slightly to the side. "I just don't think you have enough experience in the world to realize why it doesn't apply to me."

I nodded, willing to accept the explanation. She looked back at her tattoos. "Tattoos are made with ink and needles. They inject the ink into the skin as they draw; that way, it's permanent."

She appeared pleased that I had asked, but also uneasy as though she warred with hiding how she felt. It made me feel better to know I wasn't the only one who had to struggle to keep my emotions from view. "Did you like getting them done?"

The hint of humor surfaced in her gaze once more. "Most people ask if it hurt."

I shrugged. "I don't mind pain."

She looked at my hands. "I think I guessed that about you."

I didn't know what to say to that.

She fell silent for a moment, then said, "I'm sorry. That was rude. I shouldn't make assumptions." She hesitated before continuing, "I'm Skylar, but everyone calls me Sky."

"That would be a good Galdoni name," I said without thinking.

Instead of taking it as an insult, she gave a true smile. She turned and lifted up the back of her scrubs shirt without saying a word. My heart caught at the sight of wings skillfully crafted along her skin in the same black ink as her arms. They were inked from her back below her pants hem up to what I could see of her shoulders. The vines from her arms twisted along her back, entwining the wings in an artistic tangle of thorns. A single red flower had been worked between the wings close to the base of her neck. The middle of the petals was red, while the tips had been colored black, like the opposite of her hair.

My hands itched to trace the delicate lines along her skin. I wondered how soft it would be, if it would feel like feathers or the smooth fabric of the sheets on the couch Kale had ordered brought up for me. I held my hands behind my back, dismayed at the urge and discomfited at the thought that with the gauze I wouldn't have felt it anyway.

"They're beautiful," I said before my tongue could show the same restraint as my hands.

She lowered her shirt and turned. "Not as beautiful as yours," she replied. The embarrassed smile that followed was heightened by the blush that rose to her cheeks. She shook her head. The neon light overhead caught the small rings and

153

gems that lined her ears. She glanced at the watch on her wrist. "Do you want to see something?"

I wanted to say no, but like with Officer Donaldson, I hesitated.

She took that as my answer. "Come on."

She led the way to the hall. I glanced at Alana, but despite our conversation and the noise I had made with the chair, she showed no sign of stirring. "I'll be back," I promised in a whisper.

I followed Skylar down the hall wondering about how different she seemed from the other humans at the Center. She led the way to the elevator and pushed the up button. Her foot tapped impatiently and she checked her watch again. The doors slid open to reveal the empty box.

I had avoided the elevators during my stay at the Center, though I had watched my share of the staff enter and depart on the various floors. The concept seemed simple enough, but the box itself intimidated me. The thought of being caught inside such a small place without any means of escape sent a shudder down my back.

Skylar turned to push a button; surprise showed on her face that I hadn't followed. "You coming?"

"I might stay here," I replied uncomfortably.

The shadow of a smile appeared again. "You're not afraid of an elevator, are you?" Her tone was partially teasing, but carried a hint of humored curiosity. "I guess if you consider the weight of the elevator combined with the fact that it's hauled up and down by cables smaller around than my arm, it makes sense." She shrugged. "But I've survived this long and if we take the stairs, we might miss it." Her expression grew serious and she gave me her soul-searching gaze. "Trust me, Saro."

I couldn't refuse. There was something about the way she said the last words as though they were both a question and a statement, beckoning and asking me to trust her at the same time. I held my wings close and stepped inside the box.

She gave a satisfied nod. "It's easy to fear something you haven't tried before, especially when you look at it logically." She pushed a button and the elevator doors closed. It gave a slight jerk and ascended with a soft whoosh. "But sometimes logic isn't the best way to look at things."

I glanced at her. She studied the buttons that glowed as we passed each floor. The button for floor twelve that she had pushed stayed lit as we raced upward.

She seemed comfortable with my silence, and even glanced at me with her curious look before turning her attention back to the numbers. The elevator slowed. The button for the twelfth floor lit up and the box gave a lurch as it stopped. Adrenaline spiked in my veins. I put a hand on the door in alarm. It opened with a breathy hiss.

"We survived," Skylar said before stepping out.

I watched her walk nonchalantly through a wide, empty room. Tables lined the edges with a great view of the dark city beyond.

"You coming?" she called over her shoulder.

Chapter Seventeen

I took a deep breath to collect myself, then crossed the room to the door she held open at the end. Short cement stairs led upward. She followed them quickly as though worried we would miss something. I jogged to keep pace with her. She threw open the door at the top. A brisk breeze chased down the steps. I stepped into the cool air and smiled.

The Galdoni Center had been built a short distance from the city. Because of that, it felt as though we stood above the city of Crosby. Light touched the horizon, basking the buildings in hues of purple and gold. I could only stare. It was the first sunrise I had seen. Our cramped apartment faced the wrong direction, and Jake always made sure we were inside well before dawn so we could never be questioned about our escapades. The Academy's windows had been tinted dark with bullet-proof glass. The only sunlight that made it through was dull and faint.

Warmth brushed against us as the sun appeared. "This is my favorite part," Skylar said quietly beside me.

I glanced at her. Her face was turned toward the sun and her eyes were closed. The sun heightened the small smile on her lips. I willed my walls to fall, letting down my guard enough to close my eyes. A sigh escaped my lips as the sun bathed my eyelids in rosy hues. The light felt like warm breath on my cheeks and fell on my shoulder as though I was being wrapped in a warm blanket. I had never felt such a thing before.

Skylar spoke softly beside me. "Whenever I struggle to remember why I'm alive, I come up here." Her voice caught slightly. "It reminds me to keep fighting."

My eyes opened. "Why wouldn't you be alive?"

She opened her eyes as well and glanced at me. She crossed to the edge of the roof without a word. I followed her. The thought that Officer Donaldson would be extremely uncomfortable so high up brought a smile to my face. I gazed at the city stretched in front of us. It wasn't as large as the city that surrounded the Academy, but it was big enough to get lost in.

"I've always wondered what it would feel like to jump off."

"To fall?" I asked, keeping my voice emotionless.

"To fly," she replied. A slight smile touched her voice as though she spoke something she had never said aloud. "I sometimes imagine that the wings on my back are real, and I could fly into the sun and never look back."

"It's too far away," I said.

She turned and I gave myself a mental kick for the stupid response. "I know," she humored me. "It's a dumb daydream. That's all."

The derision in her tone reminded me of the voice in my head that pointed out whenever I did something stupid. I felt like she deserved better than that. "Want to fly?"

She turned an incredulous gaze my way. "I should trust a strange Galdoni and step off the roof?"

Her comment hurt. Defensiveness colored my voice. "I was going to carry you."

She ducked her head. After a moment, she looked up at me through her red and black hair. "Sorry. Sometimes I talk before I think about what I'm going to say."

"That makes two of us," I admitted.

She smiled. "Alright."

"Alright?" I repeated, confused.

She nodded. "I would love to fly."

Now that she had agreed, trepidation filled my chest. I forced it down and scooped her up before I could take back my offer. She gave a little squeak of surprise, but with one arm beneath her knees and the other behind her shoulders, I was able to keep the pressure off my hands.

"I don't know if this is a good idea," Skylar protested.

I smiled and stepped off the roof.

A small scream escaped Skylar. She clutched my neck tightly as we plummeted toward the earth. The windows of the Galdoni Center raced by. I spread my wings. They caught the wind before we reached the ground. Skylar's scream turned into a bubble of laughter as we lifted over the trees and soared toward the city.

"You did that on purpose," she said, slapping my shoulder lightly with one hand before wrapping her arms back around my neck.

I smiled at her. "Don't you know you shouldn't trust strange Galdoni?"

She laughed again and turned her attention toward the city. I tipped my wings slightly to catch the morning breeze and let it lift us high above the buildings. "It's just how I imagined it would be!" she exclaimed.

"I'm glad," I replied, and it was true. I loved flying with all of my heart. It was a part of me as much as breathing or seeing. When we were released from the Academy and I had truly flown for the first time, the feeling of freedom that came with riding the wind was every bit as great as I had hoped. Over the last year and a half with Jake, I had gotten used to it. I loved it and it still thrilled me, but seeing the world below through Skylar's eyes filled me with joy again.

I lost count of how many times I circled the city. It was different seeing the people and cars below in daylight. So many times I had flown through the darkness, but Jake had forbidden me to do so during the day. It made the world feel less sinister, more like the lives I saw on the pictures inside the homes I had burned, and less like darkness and shadows waiting to take me back to the Academy.

Skylar checked her watch. A small sigh escaped her lips. "We've flown for an hour," she said in amazement. "I've got to get home."

"Do you have a car?"

She shook her head. "I usually take the bus."

"Want me to drop you off?" I felt reluctant to go back to the Galdoni Center; I didn't want Alana to wake up alone, but she was well cared for and Dr. Ray didn't seem to think she would be awakening any time soon. Sitting by her bed without knowing was tearing me apart.

Skylar glanced up at me. "Are you sure you have the time?"

"My schedule's pretty full," I replied.

She shook her head with a little smile and said, "Alright."

I followed Skylar's directions to a little neighborhood with apartments on one side and homes that looked like they had been squished together on the other.

"They're called town homes," Skylar explained when I landed and set her gently on the sidewalk in front of the furthest one north. "It's like having a house with really close neighbors, but better than an apartment because we have a little yard."

"You mean grass?" I asked. I didn't know why someone would go to so much trouble to own a patch of grass.

She smiled at my tone. "If you've ever been cooped up in an apartment, you'd understand. It's nice to be in the sunshine without feeling like you share your quiet place with the rest of the world." A hint of red brushed her cheeks as if she had said more than she planned. She turned to go up the sidewalk, then paused. "Want to come inside?"

I shook my head quickly and raised my wings. "I really should get back."

"For your busy schedule?" she countered.

I nodded.

She waved me over. "Come on. My brother would love to meet you, and I think my mom's still in denial that Galdoni exist, so it'd be good for her, too."

"Doesn't she know you work at the Galdoni Center?" I asked. My heart pounded. I couldn't put into words why the thought of meeting her family made me so nervous. I stayed on the sidewalk, unable to get my feet to join her.

"She knows, but it makes her uncomfortable when I talk about it."

I gave her an incredulous look. "How is bringing me here supposed to help with that?"

She crossed to me with an exasperated look on her face. "Come on, Saro. They're not that bad."

I followed her reluctantly to the door. She pulled a key from her pocket and unlocked it. She pushed it open and voices immediately flooded out.

"Sky, Sky!"

"I made you some breakfast, honey."

A boy raced down the stairs. He grinned at Skylar, then his gaze shifted to me. He froze in the act of setting his foot on the bottom step.

"William, Saro, Saro, William," Skylar introduced us.

I expected the boy to be afraid, but instead he stepped around his sister and looked me up and down. I guessed his age to be about ten. He had Skylar's black hair and serious blue eyes. After a moment, his face lit up with a bright smile. "You're a real live Galdoni!" he exclaimed.

"I am," I replied, though it felt silly to say something so obvious.

"Sky, don't leave the front door open," a woman's voice called.

"Sorry, Mom," Skylar said. She ushered me inside.

William followed and I felt his fingers touch my feathers. The feeling was unnerving. I wanted to fight, to run, to get out of the small townhouse filled with pictures and memories like so many of the homes I had burned. I shouldn't be seeing how a real family occupied the walls. I had done so much damage; I didn't belong there.

Skylar caught my arm, unaware of my battling emotions. I followed her blindly, feeling as if I walked in a haze down a set of carpeted stairs, through a small living room, and into the kitchen where a woman with dark blond hair and glasses sat at a round table.

"Saro, this is my mom, Sylvia Jamison. Mom, this is Saro. He's from the Center."

Skylar's mom glanced up from the papers she was holding. She looked at her papers again, then her head bobbed back up so fast her glasses slipped down her nose. "I, uh. . . ." She rose quickly; her chair slid back with a loud screech.

"He's a Galdoni!" William exclaimed behind me.

"Y-yes, I can see that," Mrs. Jamison replied, her voice almost level.

"Want to see my action figures?" William asked.

I gave Skylar a questioning glance. She looked like she was about to laugh at my discomfort, but she held it inside. "Go ahead. He won't bite."

I followed the boy back up the stairs.

"Are you sure it's William we should be worried about?" I heard Mrs. Jamison ask.

"It's alright, Mom. Trust me."

"It's just that I never expected you to bring one of *them* home with you."

I grimaced at the way she said the word 'them' as though I was a species of animal better left alone.

Chapter Eighteen

William entered a room on the right and immediately took a seat on the carpeted floor by his bed. Light blue curtains covered the one window, and a blue and white checkered blanket lay askew on the bed as if he had given up straightening it about the same time that he started.

Strange objects filled every space, small animals made of soft material, plastic bugs in a clear box, a plaid cotton snake that wrapped around one of the bed posts, little green men holding guns were evenly spaced across the top of a dresser, and small figures that looked like replicas of creatures I had never seen sat anywhere they could be placed.

"What are all these?" I asked, confused as to why any boy would want them in his room.

William's dark eyebrows rose. "Toys," he answered in surprise. "Haven't you seen toys before?"

I shook my head. "We weren't allowed to play with toys when I was your age."

William looked aghast at my admission. "What did you do then?"

"Fight," I replied, not willing to expound.

He nodded as if that explained everything. He grabbed a few of the little green soldiers off his dresser and handed them to me. Taking some for himself, he sat on the bed and began to make shooting noises.

After a minute, he glanced up. "Play," he said.

I sat down slowly on the bed and studied the little green men, turning them in my gauzed hand.

"Make sounds for them, like this." William began to speak in a gruff voice that sounded hilarious coming from a young boy. "What are your orders, Captain?" He held up another man. "Surround the building. Take out the snipers." He bounced the first one up and down. "Yes, sir."

William then looked up at me. "If their hands could move, I would've had him salute, because you do that to a captain. Do you understand?"

I nodded, but it was clear to both of us I had no idea what he was talking about.

Footsteps sounded in the hall. We looked up at Skylar's entrance. She leaned against the door frame. "What are you guys doing?" Humor showed in her blue eyes at the sight of the army men in my hands.

"Saro doesn't know how to play," William said with as much dismay as if I didn't know how to slam someone's jaw with a haymaker at just the right angle to lay him out cold.

Skylar's brow creased. "Give him a break, Will. I'm guessing he had to grow up pretty fast."

She looked at me as if she wanted to ask questions, but wouldn't in front of her brother. I settled for a nod.

"Did you have anything to play with when you were my age?" William pressed.

"Will," Skylar said quietly.

He watched me with his eager gaze, ready to soak up anything I could tell him. I hesitated, then said, "Wooden swords."

"Cool," he replied. "I have a plastic sword that Dad gave me, but he was the only one who would play with me. Now nobody will."

His tone caught my attention. "What happened to your dad?"

Skylar took a step into the room. William's head lowered, his gaze on his little green soldiers. "He died last year from an accident at work. There was an explosion."

Death was something I was used to, something cold and tangible. I had looked at death so many times in my life it felt like an old friend, almost. Yet looking at William brought it all back, full force. I saw VA579 again, his body crumpled at my feet. He used to laugh, one of the few who dared to still do so at our age. The guards would beat him for it, but he didn't care. He said that laughter was something nobody could take from him, yet I had managed to do it. After my best friend's death, there was no more laughter at the Academy.

I glanced at Skylar; there were tears in her eyes that she refused to let fall. I think I understood why she covered her mouth when she laughed. Perhaps the laughter had also vanished inside of her when her dad died. Maybe there was nothing left to laugh at.

On a whim, I held up one of the little green men. I attempted to imitate William's gravelly voice. "I blew my arm off, Captain. What should I do?"

He looked up at me in surprise. A grin filled his face. "Get to the medic tent, stat!" he commanded with his plastic man.

"Uh, okay."

He laughed. "Soldiers don't say 'okay'. They say 'roger' or 'yes, Captain, sir', or 'ten hut!'"

"What does 'ten hut' mean?" I asked. I glanced up at Skylar. She gave me a warm smile before she disappeared back down the hall.

"I don't know," William said. "I just know that's what soldiers say."

We played for a few more minutes. It felt strange to sit on the bed with William surrounded by all the toys and figures that occupied a normal youth. I wanted to go back there, to forget everything at the Academy and have the chance to be young again without the training and violence. I wanted to know what the guy on the shelf with the red stick in his hand was for, and why there were shoes with wheels sitting on the floor of William's open closet. There was a stick leaning next to them that turned at an angle near the end that would have been perfect for tearing the weapon from an opponent's hand, but I guessed that wasn't what it was really for.

A worn cotton dog sat near his pillow on the disheveled bed. Its nose was scratched and one of the eyes looked as though it had been sewn on crooked, but the matted fur and bedraggled look let me know that the creature was well loved. I wondered why a child would hold something so dear.

"You bored?" William asked, bringing my attention back to the soldiers in my hand.

I shook my head. "I'm just new to this."

He nodded. He thought for a minute, then his eyes lit up. He dropped to his knees on the floor and reached underneath the bed. "Look at this." He pulled out a box and set it on the blanket, then opened it to reveal the contents.

My stomach twisted at the sight of more small figures, only this time, I recognized them. William held up a small replica of a tiny Galdoni with black wings and hair. It was accurate down to the tiny details on the armor. "Kale is my favorite," William explained. "He's the hero. He broke the Arena down."

"It's still standing," I replied numbly.

He nodded. "But it's broken just the same."

He sorted through more of the Galdoni. I recognized a few, the giant Goliath, a small red-head I had seen a few times in the Academy cafeteria, and one with orange wings I had fought occasionally in practice.

I glimpsed something familiar in the box. Without a word, I reached in and pulled out a Galdoni with gray wings and black hair. He held a sword in one hand with a detailed serrated blade, the very blade he had been named for.

"Did you know him?" William asked.

I glanced up at his accurate assumption. "I did."

He shook his head. "Blade's the bad guy. He tries to kill everyone." He took the Galdoni out of my hand and moved the Blade and Kale figures as though they were fighting together. I watched, entranced, as he made combat noises and flipped one over the other. It felt almost like I was in the Arena again, watching Galdoni fight to the death for values that were as empty as the freedom they gave us when the gates were opened.

"William!"

I jumped at the sound of Skylar's voice, torn from my thoughts.

She took the Galdoni from her brother's hand. "Where did you get these?" she demanded.

"Nate, at school," he rushed to explain. "I won them with my slammer. You should have seen his face!"

"You know I'm against this, and Mom is, too," Skylar said. She threw the Galdoni replicas into the box and shoved the lid on, then gave me an apologetic look. "I'm so sorry, Saro."

"It's alright," I said. I couldn't hide how the Galdoni figures shook me. The plastic Galdoni, the Arena, everything I had stood for and bled for made my life into a sham. I wasn't real; I was a toy just like those in the box. Men created and destroyed us with the heartless abandon of the green soldiers scattered around the bed. We weren't real; we were the toys of men who had decided to play god.

"Are you okay?" Skylar asked.

I rose. "I just need to get some fresh air." I walked unseeing past Skylar and back down the hall.

She caught my arm when I turned toward the stairs. "This way," she said. She guided me through the kitchen to the back door. I could feel her mother's eyes on my wings as I pulled the door shut behind me. I followed Skylar up four short cement steps to a square of grass surrounded by a high white fence.

"Come on," Skylar said. She laid on the grass, then motioned for me to do the same. She closed her eyes and turned her face toward the rays of sun that spilled into the yard. "You should try it," she encouraged.

I glanced around again. The only way someone could reach us was from above or through Skylar's house. We were relatively safe unless a Galdoni came looking for me, and nobody had a reason to worry about my absence from Kale's Center. I gave in and sat by Skylar on the grass. She didn't open her eyes, but patted the green growth near her, emphasizing that I should lay down as well.

I gave in and settled onto my back. The grass still held the chill of night. It felt good against my wings where they were still recovering from the burns. I spread out my arms, imitating Skylar. After a moment, I stretched out my legs as well.

Skylar's hushed voice broke the silence between us. "Do you feel it?"

"What?" I asked.

I could hear the smile in her voice when she said, "The peace." She fell silent for a few minutes, then said, "Let everything down, Saro. Drop your guard, let your muscles relax. Pretend you are nothing more than the grass. You'll feel it if you stop trying to."

Her words didn't make sense. My mind argued against it. My muscles fought to relax. I felt tense on my back, vulnerable, ready to spring up at any sign of an attack.

Something light touched my hand. I opened my eyes instead of shying away like I normally would. The sight of Skylar's hand resting on top of mine made my heart give a few strange little beats. I closed my eyes and turned my face toward the sun, willing my heart to slow.

"Breathe," Skylar whispered beside me.

I took a deep breath, held it in my lungs for a few seconds, then let it out in a quiet rush. I did it again, and willed my limbs to relax as I did so. To my surprise, they obeyed. Each breath calmed my nerves and helped me will myself to let go. Muscles I hadn't even known were tense eased. After a few more breaths, I felt more relaxed than I ever remembered being.

When I was no longer so in tune with my instincts, the outside world became crisp, clear, as if it was the only thing that mattered. I heard dogs barking in the distance, and a bird chirped in the tree at the front of the town home. The steady hum of cars made their way up and down the busy city streets even given the early hour of the morning. Honking sounded, and a siren wailed.

Yet I felt distant from it, apart. I felt as though none of it mattered, like I was an ant watching everything from my little patch of grass. The world didn't affect me and I didn't impact it. I was separate, alone, yet not lonely. Skylar's hand on top of mine had everything to do to that.

"Now you know why a little yard can be so important," Skylar said quietly.

I nodded. "I need to get me one of these."

She laughed again, a little sound that was more of a breath than a chuckle, but I heard the soft brush of fabric when she lifted her hand to her mouth.

"Don't do that," I said, opening my eyes.

She tipped her head to look at me. "Do what?"

169

"Don't cover your mouth when you laugh." I met her gaze solemnly. "It's the most beautiful thing I've ever heard."

She stared at me, her blue eyes wide and reflecting the golden rays that streamed down past the fence. She sat up and looked down at me, her black and red hair brushing along each side of her chin. "I don't understand you, Saro."

The statement hurt. I tried not to let it show as I watched her from my place on the ground.

Skylar's eyebrows pulled together. "They told me to be careful around you."

My heart twisted as though her words wrapped around it, strangling it. I sat up and pulled my wings close behind me. "Did they say why?" I asked, refusing to look at her.

"They said. . . ." She let out a breath, then continued. "They said you were dangerous."

"All Galdoni are dangerous," I replied bitterly. I pulled a handful of grass and let it sift through my fingers, hiding how much her words bothered me, how they tore at my heart.

"That's what I told them," she said with a touch of humor. She let out another breath in a huff. "The reason I told you is because I think they're wrong, Saro."

She waited in silence for me to look at her. I refused. My knees were up and my arms were locked around them. My hands ached as I clenched my fists. I wanted to hit something so badly it was all I could do to hold still. I could feel myself wanting to snap, needing to snap. I couldn't keep it inside.

"Look at me." It was more of a question than a statement. There was something in her tone, something I couldn't deny.

I lifted my gaze to hers. There was a look of understanding on her face so soft and caring that it brought tears to my eyes. I blinked quickly, looking away. "They're not wrong. I shouldn't be here."

"Saro."

I stood. "No, Skylar. All I want to do right now is hit someone, to tear them apart. I want to leave somebody bleeding on the ground." My burned hands ached. I forced them to unclench. The gauze pulled at liquid from the blisters that had broken. I let out a breath between my clenched teeth. "You shouldn't trust me." I opened my wings.

Skylar grabbed my arm. "You didn't ask me to trust you," she said.

I looked down at her. One part of me wanted to fly away, to abandon the Galdoni Center, Kale, Alana, everyone, and just leave forever; the other part of me was caught in Skylar's gaze, held by the pleading on her face.

"I asked you to trust me," she said. "From the moment you stepped into that elevator, I knew you were different than anyone believed. You've proven that a hundred times over."

"You don't know me," I said. I meant for my voice to be strong, but the words came out soft, barely above a whisper.

"I'd like to," she replied.

Her words took the breath from my chest; they deflated the rage that pounded through my veins. They ate at my heart, tearing me open and leaving my soul exposed, raw and full of pain.

"I know you were born to fight," she said. "I can see the war in your mind. You don't feel like you belong anywhere but a battlefield, but I know that's not true. You can fight with your heart instead of your mind. Show them that you have a soul. I can help you. I want to know you."

The tears that burned in my eyes this time were of anger at myself, at all that I was and everything I had done. I turned my face toward Skylar, and forced the words past the knot in my throat. "You might not like what you find." A tear escaped, sliding down my cheek.

She reached up and brushed away the tear with fingertips so gentle there was only a lingering trail of heat where her skin had connected with mine. "Let me be the judge of that," she whispered.

I stared down at her. For the second time in my life, I wanted to kiss a girl. I couldn't explain it. First Alana, now Skylar. She watched me with her searching, bottomless eyes as if she knew all the secrets I held. I wanted to turn away, but I couldn't. I was frozen, held to the ground as if I was truly another blade of grass, so fragile that a gust of wind could bend me in two.

Skylar reached her hand up again. Her fingers caught my tangled brown hair and pushed it out of my eyes. "Why do I feel so comfortable with you?" she asked quietly. "It's like I've been waiting for you all my life without realizing it until now."

Her touch was familiar and gentle; the heat that raced through me beckoned for me to cover her mouth with mine. Her chin tipped up slightly and the barest hint of a smile brushed her lips.

"Skylar?" her mother called through the closed kitchen door.

She dropped her hand and stepped back. My heart raced in my chest as though I had fought a battle. "I've got to go," I said.

She nodded, the red I had come to be fond of stealing across her cheeks. "I'll see you at the Galdoni Center," she replied.

Her words sent a tingle down my spine. I nodded and lifted my wings.

"Saro?"

I glanced back.

"Thank you for the ride home."

My smile answered hers before I pushed my wings down and lifted above the small town house. I circled once. Skylar watched me, her eyes shielded from the bright sun. She waved before I filled my wings with the breeze that would take me back to the Center.

Chapter Nineteen

"She's awake!"

Kale met me at the balcony to the third floor. The wide grin on his face made him look like the happiest person in the world. "Alana's awake!"

My heart skipped a beat. I rushed down the hall with Kale close behind. We skidded to a stop at Alana's door. She turned her head at the commotion. A sigh of relief escaped me when I looked into her familiar brown eyes.

"I'm so glad you're okay," I said.

She gave a weak smile. "Same to you."

"You can go in," Kale said softly so nobody else could hear.

I glanced back at him. He nodded encouragingly. I stepped inside the room and he followed.

My attention shifted to Dr. Ray as he checked numbers on the monitors and jotted down a few notes in Alana's file. Kale moved the chair back to Alana's side and motioned for me to sit. Now that Alana was awake, I was afraid of doing anything that might hurt her. She must have read it in my face when I sat down.

"I'm okay, Saro. I'll be fine thanks to you."

I looked up at Dr. Ray for confirmation. He nodded. "Her numbers are improving, the wound is healing well, and her collapsed lung from the bullet has responded to treatment." He gave her a kind smile. "You're going to be just fine."

"Thank you, Dr. Ray."

"You've very welcome." He patted her hand. "I'll be back to check on you soon. In the meantime, it looks like you have some attentive visitors who will let me know if you need anything."

He nodded at Kale and I before leaving the room.

Alana smiled at me again before she glanced at Kale. Her eyes widened. "You're Kale!"

He nodded. "Pleased to meet you."

She looked from him to me. "You brought me to Kale's place."

"Just like you asked."

Tears filled her eyes. I stood quickly. "What's wrong? Do you hurt? Should I get Dr. Ray?"

She shook her head. "Nothing's wrong." She gave me a look of such gratitude my heart stood still. "You did it, Saro. You brought me somewhere I'm safe. You promised to protect me, and you did it. I can't believe I'm here."

I didn't know what to say. She made it sound so grand, not like the charred Galdoni who set her on the grass in front of the Galdoni Center because my legs wouldn't hold me any longer.

"You were shot because of me," I said in a low voice.

Her kind smile chased away my self-loathing. "I'm free because of you."

***

"She's resting well," Kale said. He leaned against the railing beside me and watched the busy city beyond the Center.

"I don't know how to thank you for saving her."

"You don't have to," Kale replied. "That's what we're here for." He glanced down at my hands. "How are your burns healing?"

"Dr. Ray rewrapped them." I opened and closed my hands. They felt better with the new bandages. "He said if I stop popping the blisters, they would heal a lot sooner."

He smiled at that. "Sounds like when he told me to stay off my knee after I got shot."

"Did you listen?"

He shook his head. "It healed anyway."

That brought a smile to my face.

Kale chuckled. "I'm surprised we haven't driven Dr. Ray to become a veterinarian."

"He kind of is."

Kale stared at me a second before a true laugh burst from him. He slapped my shoulder. "You're alright, Saro."

The door behind us pushed open. A young man I didn't recognize hurried through. He looked a bit older than me with brown hair and a slender build. "We found it. We found the link!" he exclaimed, rushing over to Kale.

Kale took the paper he held out and studied it. His eyebrows rose. "Nikko, this is a list."

The boy nodded quickly. He glanced at me, then turned his full attention to Kale again. "Officer Donaldson found the pattern with Saro's fires. Apparently there were a few houses we didn't know about, along with papers that linked them together from the information Saro gave the officer."

I stood in silence; being spoken of in third person had the great effect of making one feel nonexistent.

Kale turned to me. "When did you see Officer Donaldson?"

"The other night." I felt like I had been caught doing something bad, and fought back the urge to hang my head. The feeling amused me. I wasn't a scolded child, I was a Galdoni trained to kill; yet I had promised Kale I wouldn't go back to Jake's apartment without him. The thought of disappointing the black-winged Galdoni filled me with shame.

Instead, a grin lit Kale's face. "Well done, Saro! You might have given us the means to find the female Galdoni if we can question anyone involved in the crime ring."

"We have to catch them first," Nikko warned.

Kale shot me a smile that was weighted with his next words. "You ready for some payback?"

***

"Officer Donaldson said they had good reason to believe this house would probably be next. His team has found a pattern to the hits, something about the papers," Kale said in a hushed voice.

We sat on the roof of a house across the block from the one we were watching. Our vantage point gave us a good view of the front yard, while the back was watched by a few of Kale's other comrades. He had officers on radios at the other likely houses on the list in case they struck there first.

Kale glanced at me. "Any idea what that might be?" he asked.

I shook my head. "I only know that each envelope I took from the safes had the letters AC on them."

"Advantage Corp," Kale replied in a surprised whisper.

"You know them?"

"I know of them," he answered thoughtfully. "Advantage Corp was behind the Academy's funding. They had the most to profit from the Arena battles."

"And the most to lose when it shut down," I finished, following his thoughts. "So why take the papers?"

Kale shook his head. "I wish I knew."

I sat in silence for a few moments, then glanced at him. "We can always find out."

"How?" he asked guardedly.

I gestured toward the house we watched. "Hit it first. The papers are in the safe. We get the envelope and catch the Galdoni who are sent to steal it. We can then trace the Galdoni back to whoever they work for."

Kale let out a slow breath. "It's risky. My plan wasn't to add breaking and entering to my list of credentials."

I gave him a wry smile. "It's already on mine."

He was silent for a few minutes. When he spoke again, it was musing as though he planned as he talked. "Can you open the safe?"

"Maybe, depending on the safe. I wish I had my tools." I remembered last minute that Jake had them. "At the very least, a stethoscope. I might need a drill depending on the safe."

"We can get one if you need it," he replied. He fell silent again, then said, "The house is empty."

I nodded. We had watched the occupants leave an hour before. Kale's sources told us they were the Jorgensens. It bothered me to know the family's name.

"Better now than wait for the Galdoni thieves to show up," I replied.

He let out a small breath. "Alright."

He touched his earpiece. "Nikko, you heard all that?" I couldn't hear the reply on the other end. Kale's eyes narrowed thoughtfully. He nodded. "Will do. Thanks."

"What was that about?"

He tipped his head toward the house. "The alarm code is 5839. Officer Donaldson mentioned you might need it."

I chuckled at the thought of my first encounter with the officer. Apparently he was willing to help me avoid the same blunder; though part of me questioned whether it had really been an accident at all.

Kale jumped off the house. I followed him on silent wings. His feathers were jet black, making him a mere shadow in the night. I tilted my wings slightly, flying just over the top of the back fence behind him. We landed on a lawn that was only a little bigger than Skylar's. A garden had been tilled near the fence line. The scent of tomatoes on vines touched the air.

Kale gave one short wave to the officers who were watching the backyard. They would split so that several could cover the front where we had been. I marveled at their efficiency. If this had been my house to hit, my story would have turned out differently.

I walked around to the garage.

"Where are you going?" Kale whispered, following.

I glanced back at him. "Habit. Bear with me." The garage door wasn't locked.

I pushed it open and Kale gave a huff of approval. "Nice."

I crossed to the next door. "I guess people think their cars are safe inside a garage. Not many think to lock the door."

"Semblance of safety," Kale said.

I nodded, glancing at him. Jake had mentioned the same thing. If something appeared safe, people didn't worry about it. That was the very reason a safe was so aptly named. I was living proof safes could be cracked, yet the peace of mind they gave their owners made them worth the very miniscule chance someone might steal what was hidden inside.

I turned the door knob. The door swung inward to reveal a dark kitchen. The alarm started to beep.

"Where's it coming from?" Kale asked, a slight edge of worry to his voice.

"Probably the front hall or the closet," I replied. "Don't worry; we have sixty seconds to disarm it with the code." I led the way down the hall. By habit, I counted the beeps to ensure I had enough time as we crossed the kitchen and made our way to the front door. Sure enough, a blue panel glowed in the darkness. A yellow timer counted the increasing seconds.

"What was the code again?" I asked.

He paused and I chuckled. "Just kidding." I entered the numbers. The beeping stopped. "I used to write the codes on my hand because by the time I lit the Molotovs, I was close to forgetting." I threw him a wry smile. "Funny how not racing against explosives makes this job easier."

Kale grinned. "Strange how that happens." He gestured down the stairs. "Our source said the safe is in the basement."

I followed him down. "I wonder who Jake's source was working with."

"What do you mean?"

"Well," I mused aloud. "He always knew the alarm codes and safe locations, the same as your people. Who would have that information?"

Kale put a hand to his ear, then chuckled. "Apparently Nikko's working on that as we speak."

Appreciation for the efficiency of Kale's team filled me. If they could find Jake's source, perhaps they could find Jake. I would definitely make sure I was there when that happened.

"Here it is." Kale swung open the bottom cupboard on a fancy claw-footed desk. Looks were deceiving. With the floorboards recessed, it looked like the cupboard was too small for the safe we needed; yet with the door open, we saw that the bottom of the safe actually rested on the ground and was covered by the front of the desk.

"Clever," I said, dropping to my knees. I began to unwind the gauze from my right hand.

"Is that necessary?" Kale asked, concerned.

"It's the only way I can feel the clicks. Lucky for us, this is an older safe; otherwise it would be easier to wait for the Galdoni to arrive, then take the papers from them after they've done their job."

"That's leaving a lot to chance," Kale said. "There's always the gamble that the Galdoni aren't coming here." He tipped his head slightly, then said, "I'm mistaken; they just arrived." His eyes widened slightly.

"What?" I asked.

"There's a few more than we expected."

"How many's a few?" Trepidation built in my chest.

"Seven." He put his hand to his earpiece. "Make that eight."

"Seems like overkill," I replied.

He nodded. "How about that safe?"

I touched the dial. Even the soft contact sent pain up my fingers. I took a stealing breath and held it as I turned the dial. My fingers were so tender I wasn't sure I would feel the click above the pain; even so, the faint click thrummed. I let out the breath and turned the dial to the right.

"You've got this?" Kale asked.

I nodded, my full concentration on the dial. His footsteps disappeared upstairs. A crash sounded. My fingers slipped and I felt the dial pass the turning point.

Chapter Twenty

I sucked in a breath through my teeth and turned the dial to start over. Another crash sounded overhead. We should have brought more back up. None of us had expected more than one or two Galdoni. Eight seemed like a whole lot more than was necessary to crack a safe and steal the contents.

I forced myself to concentrate and turned the dial again. The first click sounded; I spun the dial to the right. The second click felt strong through my aching fingers. I turned the dial left again. Turning slowly, I held my breath and felt each miniscule click with my fingertips. Someone yelled. I closed my eyes. I was almost to the starting point again. Footsteps rushed down the stairs. I focused on the dial. Click. I pulled and the door opened.

Something slammed into my back, knocking me against the desk. I staggered to my feet and turned in time to block the chair the Galdoni threw at me again. It splintered into pieces against my arm. I grabbed a broken piece from the floor, ducked under a punch, and drove the wood deep into the Galdoni's thigh. He fell back with a yell. I slammed a knee into his head. It snapped back and he dropped unconscious to the ground.

I opened the safe. Stacks of cash filled the front half of the box. I pulled the cash out and let it fall forgotten to the floor. In the back of the safe lay the envelope. Footsteps sounded down the stairs. I grabbed the envelope and spun in a defensive crouch.

A Galdoni with black and white wings jumped from the bottom step and tackled me. I fell against the desk and used his momentum to propel us both backwards over it. He slammed into the wall. I punched his stomach, then elbowed him in the jaw. He staggered, but caught my hand in a vice-like grip. Pain raced up my arm from the burns. I fell to one knee and head-butted him in the stomach. He doubled over. I brought my head up with a jerk, slamming the back of it into his jaw. His eyes rolled back and he slumped to the ground.

My chest heaving, I tucked the envelope in my back pocket and ran up the stairs. I followed the commotion to the kitchen. Two officers in black uniforms lay on the floor moaning with pain. A tan-winged Galdoni had collapsed next to them with a dart in his neck. Kale battled three Galdoni against the cupboards. Another lay unconscious near his feet. I was about to step in, but Kale's expression stopped me.

Steel burned in his dark eyes. He ducked a punch and slammed a heel-palm into one Galdoni's jaw, blocked a kick with his forearms and drove his elbow into the next Galdoni's stomach. He turned with his wings spread, using his momentum to drive a haymaker into the jaw of the third. The Galdoni fell to the tile floor.

Kale jumped and pulled his black wings around to propel a kick into the first Galdoni's chest, then spun again and landed a second across the other Galdoni's face. The first Galdoni staggered against the table while the second collapsed in a heap. The first attacked again. Kale ducked so that the Galdoni's punch barely grazed the top of his head. He slammed a fist into the Galdoni's ribs so hard I heard them snap. He followed it with a punch to the Galdoni's stomach, then to his face. The Galdoni fell back against the table, then slid to the floor.

Fury showed in the line of Kale's jaw and the coldness of his eyes as he checked each Galdoni, making sure they were down. An Academy rule whispered in the back of my mind. Don't assume, ensure. An enemy can be just as deadly from the ground. I grimaced at the remembered chant of hundreds of voices repeating the words.

Kale's eyes met mine across the room; the battle rage in them reminded me again how dangerous he was. As much as he acted like he fit into normal society, the inbred Galdoni bloodlust still filled his veins. He shook his head and the look faded. A trickle of blood dripped down one side of his face and he fought for breath. "The two that made it downstairs are incapacitated?" It was more of a statement than a question, but I nodded without a word.

"They got past me."

"I noticed," I replied as men in black uniforms hurried inside the house. Officer Donaldson followed them in. He nodded when he saw me. One of his men pulled a small gun from a holster and shot the fallen Galdoni with their darts.

"Stops them faster when they're already down," Kale said dryly.

Donaldson chuckled. "Took a while for the Galdoni outside to fall; a few of my officers will be feeling the effects of this fight in the morning. These should drop an elephant; I don't think the tranquilizers come any stronger.

"Time to check," Kale said.

Officer Donaldson nodded with a smile. "Will do."

I pulled the envelope from my pocket. "Hopefully this will give us what we need; I don't think the Galdoni will be up to questioning for a while."

Donaldson accepted the envelope with a chuckle. "I'm just glad you guys are on our side."

***

The worry on Alana's face erased when we walked into her room.

"Dr. Ray said you were on a mission," she said. "I was so worried!"

I sat by her bed and took her hand in my wrapped one. "We were safe enough, and I think we found something that might give us the link for the robberies."

"I'm glad," she replied. The frailty of her body was countered by the life in her beautiful gaze. The relief in her smile filled me with joy. It was so good to see her recovering. Her fingers traced the back of my hand and warmth rushed up my arm.

A girl with long brown hair and dark brown eyes appeared at the door. The smile that spread across Kale's face softened his features and filled his eyes with warmth. He wrapped her in a hug. She held onto him for a moment, then stepped back and gave him a searching look. "I thought it was supposed to be a quiet bust," she said. She reached up and gently touched his forehead. He had wiped away the blood before we entered Alana's room, but the goose egg forming at his hairline was obvious.

He smiled. "Nothing we couldn't handle." He turned to us. "Alana, I understand that you and Brie are already acquainted."

The girls exchanged warm smiles in answer to his question. "We are," Brie replied.

Kale looked pleased at that. He nodded at me. "Saro, this is my girlfriend Brie."

I held out my hand, but Kale caught it before she could shake it. "Saro, you need to get this looked at." I followed his gaze to my palm. When I removed the gauze to open the safe, the burns had been exposed to the fighting. All the blisters had burst, and blood showed in places where the chair leg I had driven into the Galdoni's thigh had left splinters in the skin. With the adrenaline fading from my body, the sting of the exposed wounds was growing.

"I'll rewrap it."

Kale shook his head. "You can't risk an infection." He pushed a button near Alana's bed. A beep sounded, followed by a woman's voice. "Can I help you?"

"Please send Dr. Ray to room 32," Kale said.

"Right away," the woman replied.

Brie smiled at the look on my face. "Don't be fooled; Kale was just as stubborn when he was a patient."

Kale snorted, but couldn't hide the smile that appeared at her teasing. He put an arm around her shoulder. "You're just lucky I couldn't fly away."

She grinned and leaned against him. "Yes, I was."

He dipped his head and gave her a kiss. His dark wings rose, shielding them from our view. I glanced at Alana. She grinned up at me. "They're cute," she whispered.

Kale's wings lowered. "Sorry; I couldn't help myself. Should we leave so we don't subject these two to our mushiness?"

"Yes," I replied with a smile even though he had directed the statement to Brie.

Kale laughed. "You get that hand taken care of."

"I will," I replied.

They left out the door arm in arm, one of Kale's wings wrapped around Brie's shoulder.

A smile lingered on Alana's face. "I sure like them."

I nodded. "I do, too."

Her eyebrows rose. "What? Saro, my fierce protector, actually likes someone?"

I sat down in the chair near her bed. "Believe it or not, I think I have friends here, if only a few."

She nodded at that. "I've been making friends, too. Brie visits me during the day and the rest of the staff have been making sure I'm comfortable." A slight blush spread across her cheeks as though the thought of others caring about her made her embarrassed.

Seeing her so happy brought a smile to my face. "I'm so glad you're making friends. How have you been feeling?"

"Just what I was going to ask," Dr. Ray said, walking through the door.

Alana smiled at him. "Better, thank you. It's easier to breathe, and I've kept a few bites of food down."

"I'm glad to hear that," Dr. Ray replied. He glanced at me. "Does that mean you're the reason I'm needed?" I held up my hand without a word. He took one look at it and shook his head. "I shouldn't be surprised. I've worked with enough Galdoni to know you guys seem to have no sense of self-preservation despite what everyone keeps telling me about your survival instincts." He grabbed supplies from a cupboard and pulled the little rolling table over. "Let's see your hand."

I gritted my teeth as he removed the damaged skin from the blisters before working on the splinters. Alana's fingers traced patterns on my other arm, distracting me from the pain. I shot her a smile. The answering one that spread across her face lit her eyes.

"Done."

I glanced down in surprise to see my hand wrapped in gauze again. "You're getting faster," I noted.

He chuckled. "Perk of the job. You take care of those hands. You might need them someday," he concluded with a wink. He rose and paused at the door. "Both of you get some sleep. Alana needs to rest so she'll heal, and Saro you look exhausted."

We listened to his footsteps fade down the hall. Alana's hand gave a little twitch. I looked down to see her open her eyes again. She gave an apologetic smile. "Sorry; I guess I am a little tired."

Empathy filled my heart. "You should rest. You've been through so much."

"You, too," she replied. She reached up and set a hand softly on my cheek. "I wouldn't be here if it wasn't for you, Saro."

I covered her hand with mine. She gave a small smile before her eyes closed and her breathing slowed. "I wouldn't be here if it wasn't for you, Alana," I whispered. I set her hand gently by her side and rose.

Despite Dr. Ray's analysis, I couldn't sleep. Thoughts of the fight with the Galdoni played over and over in my mind. I sat on the couch and willed my heartbeat to slow, but memories of punches refused to go away. I replayed everything over again, including watching Kale take down the three Galdoni without help. I realized with a start how much I had enjoyed fighting, how much I had missed it. I rose and walked to the door. The window across the hall showed the first glimmers of sunrise. I wandered to the stairs.

It bothered me how much I relished taking down the other Galdoni. Despite the year and a half away from the Academy, my body remembered its training. Fighting was easy, familiar. I was good at it.

Chapter Twenty-one

I opened the door to the balcony and spread my wings. Despite Skylar's reassurances about elevators, I felt much better with nothing but the air between me and the ground. I stepped to the edge and jumped.

Wind washed past me, beckoning me to join its carefree flight around the Galdoni Center. I tipped my wings, obeying its call. I circled higher, pushing my wings down and gathering wind beneath my feathers. It was amazing to soar so free, no chains, no walls, nothing between me and the limitless horizon. I still relished the feeling of my freedom. A laugh surprised me, breaking from my chest as I topped the Center and landed on the roof.

"It's nice to see you so happy."

I spun.

Skylar put up her hands. "Just me," she said, her light blue eyes sparkling. "I'm not much of a threat."

"You sure about that?" I asked.

She looked up at me, her red and black hair falling away from her face as she studied me to see if I was serious. "Am I a threat?" she asked.

I smiled. I couldn't help it. She tried to look fierce, but the glimmer in her eyes and her clenched jaw combined with her tiny frame was laughable. I was about to say so, to tell her how even a fly wouldn't be afraid; yet there was something in the depths of her gaze. It held me, beckoned me. I took a step closer. My hand moved of its own volition, cupping her cheek. I wished I could feel her soft skin without the bandages.

"You're beautiful," I whispered. "And so therefore, a threat."

CHEREE ALSOP

A slight smile lifted one corner of her mouth as though she was afraid to let it go any further. She looked like she didn't believe my words, though she very much wanted to. Her eyes traced my face; I felt the brush of her gaze along my skin as if it was her fingers. Warmth flooded my chest.

"Did you hit your face on something?" she asked, her focus lingering on my forehead.

I touched it with my hand. The area was sensitive. I couldn't remember taking a hit; it must have been when I slammed into the desk. "Just another day at the office," I said.

She shook her head. "I guess my office is a bit less violent than yours." The reflection in her eyes changed as she looked past me to the sunrise. Her brown irises filled with golden light.

The rising sun blanketed my wings with warmth. I turned, and was rewarded with the rosy shades of dawn. Clouds blanketed the sky, and the sunrise basked the edges in gold so bright anything that called itself the color paled in comparison.

"Looks like rain," Skylar noted; her tone indicated she looked forward to it.

"Need a lift home?" I asked.

She looked up at me. "I can take the bus." She hesitated and I could see the thoughts in her eyes. She looked as though she wasn't going to speak, then she blurted, "Do you want to go somewhere with me?" She dropped her eyes as if I had already said no.

The thought of leaving Alana after she had just woken up filled me with guilt, yet something told me Skylar didn't leave herself vulnerable often. She looked as though she wished she had never said anything.

191

"It's alright," she said. "I should probably go home anyway. I don't want Mom to worry and—"

"I'd like to," I replied.

She smiled and fell quiet.

"Let me just make sure Alana's alright. I'll be back." I jumped off the roof. I could feel Skylar's eyes on me as I circled around the building once with my wings pulled close to make my descent quicker. I opened them at the third floor and landed on the balcony. I glanced up just in time to see Skylar's face disappear above. The glimpse made me smile.

I shut the door behind me and walked up the hall toward Alana's room. Guilt filled me. Alana was healing from a bullet wound she received saving me. I should be at her side, not off with Skylar. The thought gripped my heart tight. I wanted to be there for Alana, yet another part of me wished to fly with Skylar again, to see the world from her point of view, to feel like I was a part of something simpler and lighter than the path my life had taken.

I was about to walk into Alana's room, expecting to find her asleep, when voices stopped me. I paused outside her door.

"That's when I realized kissing Janice wasn't such a good idea."

Alana laughed, the lighthearted, happy sound I remembered from the basement of Jake's apartment complex.

"Sounds like you were lucky," she replied.

"Lucky Kale was on my side," the male voice agreed. "He definitely saved me from a beating."

"Wouldn't your friends have protected you?"

He chuckled. "Brie felt like I deserved it and Nikko's not much of a fighter. He's more the brainiac type. Takes after his dad."

"Dr. Ray is wonderful," Alana said.

I stepped close enough to the door to peer inside. The sight of Jayce sitting on the chair beside Alana sent a surge of mixed emotions through my chest. I walked back to the balcony and jumped off. I flew for a few minutes, trying to school my face to be expressionless. When I landed on the roof, however, I must not have done a good job.

"What's up?" Skylar asked.

My trust issues made perfect sense to me. Give someone insight into your soul, and it leaves you open for attack. Yet I had seen the same thing on Skylar's face when she asked if I wanted to go somewhere with her. Trusting my thoughts to a human didn't seem like the best idea, but the emotions that warred inside of me were enough to drive anyone mad, let alone a Galdoni who was probably already there.

"What do you know about Jayce?"

Surprise showed on Skylar's face. "Jayce Johnson? What about him?"

I shrugged, already regretting my question. "Never mind."

I turned away, but she set a hand on my arm. "What is it, Saro?"

The sound of my name from her lips sent a little thrill through my heart. I let out a slow breath, willing my thoughts to calm. "I, uh. . . ." I decided to stop stalling and just let the words rush out. "Jayce is talking to Alana in her room and I'm not sure how I feel about it." I felt stupid as soon as the sentence left my lips. I leaned against the railing and focused my attention on the buildings in the distance to distract myself from whatever Skylar would say.

She surprised me. There was no laughter or derision. Instead, she said, "Jayce is a good guy. He was kind-of a lady's man at school, at least from what I saw before I left, but he's always been polite and respectful. It's the guys that don't like him."

"Because he took their girls," I guessed. Her words made the conversation I had overheard make sense.

"Did he take your girl?" Skylar asked quietly, her gaze also on the buildings lit by the rising sun. There was a tone to her words I didn't recognize. It was subtle, but contained a hint of sadness or remorse. It didn't make sense to me.

I hesitated, then shook my head. "She's not my girl." My heart twisted as though admitting as much took something from me. I gave a humorless smile. "I'm not exactly relationship material."

A small laugh left Skylar's lips, though it wasn't funny. The sound caught my attention. "What?"

She shrugged, a small lift of her shoulders. "That's something I'm used to being told from the guys I've dated."

The admission surprised me. I glanced at her. "You're not relationship material?"

She nodded. Red showed on her cheeks, letting me know how much the words had cost her to confess. Her eyes flitted to mine, then back to the glowing horizon.

Resolve solidified in my chest. "What did you want to show me?"

She turned. "You sure you want to see?"

A true smile spread across my face. "If it's important to you, it's important to me."

The answering smile that met my words stole my thoughts. I could only watch her, entranced by her lips and the way they pursed together slightly when she smiled. "We can fly or take a bus."

I snorted. "Why ride when you can fly?"

The joy that lit her face told me she had been hoping I would say exactly that. It filled me with amazement that something I said could bring such an emotion to someone else. I wanted to laugh and run away at the same time. I was getting too involved. My instincts said to back off, while my heart urged me closer.

"You look concerned. Is it something I said?" Skylar asked.

I shook my head. "You confuse me." I regretted the words the instant they left my mouth.

Hurt touched Skylar's light blue eyes as if I had cut her deeply with a knife. I had never seen the pain of words on someone else's face. She turned away.

"Skylar." I grabbed her arm with my gauzed hand. My grip was gentle, but the pressure to my recently debrided skin sent pain shooting up my arm. I let go with a quick intake of breath. Skylar turned at the sound. "I didn't mean it like that," I rushed to explain. "I just, I. . . ." I let out a sigh. "I'm not good with people. Half of me feels like I should leave before I get close to someone just to watch them die, and the other half says to stay because every moment is precious and I might not get another."

Skylar's eyes searched mine. I didn't know what it was about her that brought me to my knees. I was unable to hide my thoughts; hiding them had always kept me safe. Something about her made me completely honest and vulnerable.

"You watched someone you were close to die?"

The empathy in her words gripped my heart, forcing the answer from me even though I didn't want to say it. I lowered my head. "At the Academy, we have no friends. At least, we weren't supposed to. But I had a friend. Only one. The only person I ever allowed myself to care about."

"What happened?" Skylar asked quietly.

I met her gaze. "I killed him. We fought with katanas and I had an opening. We were taught to never hesitate." I blinked. "I've wished from that day on that I did hesitate, and

I never let myself care about anyone after that because it hurt too bad to see them die."

I couldn't look away. The sorrow in Skylar's eyes matched the pain in my heart so completely it softened the edges of my agony.

"How old were you?"

"Six."

Skylar's voice was barely a whisper when she said, "You haven't had a friend since you were six?"

I shook my head, then hesitated. "There was Alana."

She nodded. "You blame yourself for her getting shot. That's why you're here," she said as though that explained something she had wondered.

"It was my fault," I replied. The bitterness in my voice was nothing compared to the guilt and shame that filled me. "If I hadn't burned that house, she wouldn't have been in danger from Jake." The voice in the back of my mind reminded me that she would also still be trapped in the female Galdoni ring without hope of escape. I wondered if she would choose getting shot.

Skylar tipped her head and looked at me through her black and red hair. "Since Dad died, I lost all my friends. It was my own fault. I shut them out because they couldn't understand the pain I was going through. I felt like he didn't deserve to die. I shouldn't be happy if he's dead." She let out a slow breath. "I felt like it should have been me instead of him."

She covered her mouth when she laughed because she felt guilty. The thought struck me hard. It put my pain and guilt in a different light, a light I wasn't quite ready to see it in.

"Let's fly," I said.

Surprised by my change of topic, Skylar's mouth twisted into a wry smile. "Running away?"

I nodded. "As fast as I possibly can, and you're coming with me."

She laughed. Her hand moved toward her mouth, then paused in the air. She dropped it back to her side and nodded. "I'd like that."

I scooped her up in my arms.

"Jump like you did last time," she said, her eyes alive with excitement and a hint of joyful terror.

I couldn't hide the grin that spread across my face before I stepped off the roof.

Chapter Twenty-two

We plummeted toward the ground. A shriek escaped Skylar as though she couldn't help herself, and then it changed to laughter when my wings caught the wind and lifted us high into the sky. Dark clouds edged in the colors of dawn cloaked the sky. I tipped my wings and sent us in a slow spiral, following the directions Skylar gave me. We flew through the heart of the small city to a long building with a domed roof. I landed and set Skylar gently on the ground.

"The best way to travel ever," she proclaimed. She searched her pockets and pulled out a set of keys that jingled in the still morning air.

"What is this?" I asked.

"Trust me," she called over her shoulder.

I grinned and hurried after her. The key turned; she held the door open. "After you," she said with a flourish of her hand.

I stepped inside the dark building and waited while she locked the door behind her. She flipped on a light. We stood in a small lobby with a desk and a few chairs. Behind the desk were small alcoves that contained what looked like shoes with blades on the bottoms.

"What size of feet do you have?" At my confused look, Skylar waved a hand. "Never mind; I'll just guess."

She came back around the desk with two pairs of the bladed shoes in her hands. "Come on," she said, leading the way.

I followed her through another door. My senses picked up a wide expanse beyond us. The room was chilly and completely dark. Skylar fumbled by the door for a moment.

"I know it's here somewhere," she muttered. "Ah-ha!"

Light flooded the room.

Beyond the four foot wide space that ringed the huge arena was a floor of what looked like sheer glass. "Ice?" I asked in surprise.

Skylar nodded. She sat on a long bench and took off her shoes. "I take it you've never seen an ice rink before?"

I shook my head. It didn't make sense to me to have a huge building with nothing but a floor of ice inside. "Why do you have keys to this place?"

She threw me a smile that was becoming more permanent on her face when we were together. "I work here on day shifts as a manager."

"I thought you worked at the Galdoni Center."

She pulled on one of the white shoes and tied it as though she had done so a million times. "When Dad died, Mom couldn't make ends meet. I quit school to help out with bills. Mom wasn't happy about it, but it was either do that or lose our place." She gestured toward the front of the building where we had entered. "I work here during the day, and pick up night shifts at the Center. Mom works ten hours at the grocery store, and can be home for William. Between the two of us, we've managed to make things comfortable again."

She sounded happy about the arrangement as though it meant a lot to her that they had been able to make it work. She stood up with both bladed shoes on. "Plus, it comes with perks."

She stepped onto the ice. She gave a strong push with one shoe and skated on the little blades that looked more dangerous than serviceable. Instead of cutting through the ice like I had imagined they would, she glided across it like a bird through the soft white clouds that sometimes dotted the evening sky. At the end of her glide, she kicked a leg around. The motion sent her into a spin. I counted five complete turns before she stopped short, facing me with a full grin.

"That was amazing!" I said, unable to conceal my shock. "It's like you were flying."

She laughed and I was happy to note that her hands remained at her sides. "I used to skate when I was little. I came here so much that when I asked for a job, Joe said I was already qualified to take up the manager spot they had been trying to fill." She tipped her head to indicate the bladed shoes on the bench. "Put on your skates and try it."

"I don't think wearing knives on my feet is a great idea."

She glided back to the short wall that surrounded the ice rink and leaned against it. "They're not sharp. Here, let me help."

She walked across the black rubber pad that protected the floor from her skates. I sat down and used my feet to remove my shoes. Skylar loosened the laces on one skate, then worked it onto my foot.

"Perfect size," she said. She winked at me. "You'd guess I'd worked with skates before."

I couldn't help but smile at her enthusiasm. "If you like it so much, why did you stop skating?"

She shrugged as she tied the laces. "Life took over. School, friends, dates." She glanced up at me. "I think sometimes our dreams get a little faded when we're faced with reality."

"They shouldn't, though." At her look, I shrugged. "Dreams are supposed to make reality better, like symbols for hope, right?"

Her head tipped slightly to the side, my ice skate forgotten in her lap. "I thought Galdoni don't believe in hope."

I frowned, trying to phrase my thoughts in a way that made sense. "The Academy was no place for hope. I think. . .

." I studied my gauzed hands. "If I didn't dream of something better, I wouldn't be here."

"What do you dream of?" Her voice was soft as if she was afraid of interrupting.

I felt the beginnings of a smile reach my face. "For you, I think." Surprise showed on her face. I waved a hand to indicate the place. "For this, for a normal life."

She ducked her head to put on my other skate. Her hair swooped forward to hide her expression. "To not be a Galdoni?" she guessed tentatively.

I thought about it for a moment. Even though it made sense to say yes, I eventually shook my head. "That's all I am."

She stood up and held out a hand. "That's not all you are, Saro. You're a Galdoni and so much more."

My chest tightened at her words. I wanted to believe them. How could she think so much of me? I rose to my feet and wobbled on the blades. Skylar's arm slipped under my elbow, helping me balance.

"Little steps," she said.

We walked slowly to the ice. She stepped down first. I followed with one unsteady foot, then the other. I leaned forward as my feet immediately decided they were done with the venture and tried to slide out from under me. Skylar caught my elbow in her sure grip.

"Easy now," she encouraged. "Just wait until you find your balance."

I wavered between almost falling backward and leaning precariously forward so far I had to use my gauzed hands to keep my betraying feet from sliding out into the splits.

"Careful!" Skylar warned, leaning into me with her shoulder to help me stand again. When I was upright and had a firm grip on the wall, she laughed. "I thought it would be easier with wings," she said. "Aren't you used to balancing with them?"

Her words made perfect sense, yet testing them meant letting go of the wall that had become the single thing between me and a painful thwack on the icy hard floor.

Skylar skated backwards. She made it look so easy, her feet alternating between gliding across the ice and floating an inch above it. She spun in a slow circle, then kicked out again and jumped, bringing herself around in a fast pirouette. She landed with a sharp slice of one foot that sent the ice up in a small white cloud.

I clapped. "You are so graceful!" I said.

"Thank you," she replied with a touch of red to her cheeks. Her eyebrows rose.

I realized I had drifted away from my precarious hold on the wall. I had two options, scramble haphazardly back to the perpendicular post that was my lifeline and crutch at the same time, or give her advice a try.

I let out a slow breath and raised my wings. Instead of throwing off my balance, I was able to stand straighter.

"Bend your knees," Skylar suggested in a quiet voice as though worried speaking would send me to the floor.

I did as she said. My balance improved. I gave a slight push with one foot. I slid forward, my wings tipping in counterbalance. It was easier. I gave another push. The slight scritch of the blade across the ice made me smile. I had never been a tentative person. It was fly or fall. The thought made me laugh.

I shoved my wings back hard enough to propel me in a rush. It was easier to stay balanced with speed. I moved my feet like Skylar did and pushed my wings again.

"Saro!" Skylar called in surprise.

I bent my knees and moved my feet as she had, lifting each one just enough to clear the ice before putting it back down. My wings worked as if I flew. I leaned forward so that the majority of the force would go directly behind me. My feet moved in time with my wings. The scratching sound of my blades turned into a rhythmic whoosh. I sped around the ring. It felt like flying. No wonder Skylar liked it so much. The air rushed past my face and filled my wings. A laugh escaped me. Skylar danced in the middle on her skates, her own laughter mingling with mine.

I turned my wings enough to bring me close to her. With a quick turn, I swooped behind her and caught her around the waist. Her feet moved in time with mine. She bent low and I followed, pushing us both with my wings. We flew around the ice rink, our feet and the rush of the air past our faces the only sound in the huge room. Skylar's feet moved faster; I followed with my wings, propelling us past the wall that was a mere blur to our right. We completed so many laps I lost track.

Eventually my wings began to grow heavy from the unaccustomed angle. I slowed, steering us toward the opening where we had put on our skates. Skylar stepped onto the rubber. She turned, her face aglow with the smile that lit her eyes in sparkles like the bits of ice carved from our blades.

"That was amazing," she breathed, her cheeks and nose red from the cold. The affect made her light blue eyes stand out like gems. I had never seen anything so beautiful. I was motionless, captivated by the sight of her. I could barely breathe.

I realized she was staring at me. I dropped my gaze. "I'm glad you liked it," I replied. My chest heaved as I caught my breath, both from the exertion and from being with her. I didn't want the moment to end. She watched me for a minute with a little half-smile as though she guessed my thoughts. When she turned away, breaking the spell, I felt a piece of my heart linger as though it stayed in that happy place; it belonged to her and was mine no longer.

I followed her to the bench and she removed my skates. "I've never gone so fast," she said. The smile danced on her mouth, refusing to leave.

I smiled in return, glad to have caused it. "No wonder you like ice skating."

She laughed. "I've never skated like that."

I watched the joy bounce in her eyes as if it could barely be contained. Her hair was mussed as though still caught in the wind of our wake. I reached down and brushed a strand from her cheek. She smiled at me. "Thank you."

Suddenly aware of what I was doing, I dropped my hand. "Thank you for sharing ice skating with me."

"Thank you for coming," she replied.

I waited while she put our skates back behind the desk, then watched her open the door. Driving rain pounded down to meet us. I realized then how secluded we had been, away from the weather, the Galdoni Center, the busy city, and anything to remind us that life went on while we were lost in our shared moment.

Skylar checked her watch. "The buses don't run this way for another hour."

"I'll fly you home," I offered.

She gave me an incredulous look. "In this? We'll probably get struck by lightning."

As if in answer, a flash of lightning darted across the sky. The hair on the back of my neck rose. Thunder rumbled less than a second later.

"That was close," Skylar breathed, her eyes wide. She looked up at me. "Mom's going to be worried if I'm not home before she leaves for work."

"Let's make a run for it," I offered.

"That's crazy," she said.

I shrugged. "Why not?"

She looked out at the rain. Lightning flashed again, but it was further away. The smile she threw back at me made her look like a little girl filled with excitement. "Okay!"

I followed her into the rain. She fumbled for her keys; a shiver shook her as a torrent of water from the roof landed on her shoulders. I lifted my wings, sheltering her from the water. She glanced up in surprise. Gratitude filled her eyes. Before I could move, she drew up onto her tiptoes and kissed me on the cheek. I stared down at her, watching her find the key and insert it in the lock. She locked the door, then shoved the key back into her pocket.

"Ready for this?" she asked? She darted into the rain without giving me a chance to reply.

I could feel the touch of her kiss on my cheek as we ran together through the downpour. She slipped her arm through mine and I sheltered her the best I could with my wings. I didn't care about the rain; I couldn't feel it. I was only aware of her arm in mine and the ghost of her kiss on my cheek.

She led me to her house; I suspected that she may have taken us on a longer route than was necessary, and our jog slowed by the time we reached the townhouse. We lingered on the tiny porch watching the rain fall beyond the eves. It was already slowing. The downpour had eased to a sprinkle that hit the roof with a soft patter. No words were spoken; none were necessary. Another piece of my heart was Skylar's. I would never own it again, and I was grateful.

Chapter Twenty-three

Skylar drew in a breath and opened the front door. "I'm home, Mom," she called.

Mrs. Jamison appeared at the top of the stairs. "You're soaked," she exclaimed. "Didn't you catch the bus?" Her gaze met mine and widened slightly. She collected herself visibly and walked down the stairs. "You two need to get dry. I'll be leaving for work in a few minutes, and I probably shouldn't leave alone." She passed us and called back over her shoulder. "I'll make you a quick breakfast."

"Thanks, Mom," Skylar replied. She motioned for me to follow her upstairs.

"What does she mean, 'I probably shouldn't leave alone'?" I asked.

A little laugh escaped Skylar's lips. "She means that she doesn't want you and I home here alone together."

Curious, I pressed, "How would she keep that from happening?"

Skylar gave a mock serious expression. "You don't want to know. Moms can be scary when they have to be."

I laughed at her expression. "Alright; I won't push it."

She led the way to a bathroom and pulled towels from beneath the sink. Handing me one, she used the other to cover her hair. "Man, I am soaked! Excuse me a minute." She walked down the hall to a room a few feet away and shut the door.

I toweled off my hair the best I could. I glanced in the mirror, then looked away. It showed everything I knew it would, dark brown hair that was curly and messy from the rain; brown eyes that couldn't quite hide the torment of the soul beneath. My face held only a few scars, an s-shaped white trail down one cheek from a whip at the Academy when I was younger, a little gap at the end of my left eyebrow where the hair never grew back after a punch to the face split it wide open.

I avoided my reflection because it showed a seventeen-year-old boy. Inside I felt older, but not wiser. I felt like I had lived too many lifetimes. I had definitely seen too many pass away unlived. Watching death aged a person, just as participating in the passing stole a piece of their soul. I closed my eyes, wondering if I had anything left.

"Much better."

I opened my eyes to see Skylar in a dry red tee-shirt and loose sweat pants. She had dried her hair enough that it stuck up in red-tipped spikes. Something of the thoughts she had broken me from must have shown on my face, because she asked, "Are you alright, Saro?"

"Fine," I replied with what I hoped was a sincere smile.

She shook her head. A hint of worry colored her eyes. "I don't believe you."

A shiver ran down my spine.

"You must be freezing. I'll get you some of Dad's clothes." She left before I could protest.

I couldn't deny that a dry shirt would help. My wet wings and soaked clothes made for an uncomfortable mess. I gingerly worked my elbows into the hem of my shirt and pulled it over my head. The Velcro that held the shirt closed beneath my wings opened and I was able to work it free. I cleared my head in time to see Skylar standing at the door again.

She had a hand to her mouth and her face was pale. I glanced down at my chest, and then looked away. The sight wasn't pleasant; definitely not something a girl should have to see. I turned my back.

"Saro." She said it as though the name hurt.

I wanted to punch the wall, to break the mirror that showed only what was on the surface, not the pain and torment carried by the tattered soul beneath. My hands clenched, bringing pain to the healing burns. "You shouldn't have to see it."

Another shiver ran down my spine when her fingers touched the feathers of my right wing. She set a hand on my arm, the pressure of her fingers willing me to turn back around. I couldn't deny her anything, not even this.

I turned slowly, careful to keep my gaze on the floor. Her hand lifted away. I immediately missed her touch.

My heart stopped entirely when she set her hand in the middle of my chest. I couldn't breathe, I couldn't speak. I could only feel the heat that emanated from her soft palm on my scars.

"Saro," she said again. This time there was pleading in her voice, as if me not looking at her hurt worse than what she had seen.

I closed my eyes for a second, then obeyed, opening them and turning my face toward hers. I was lost, completely and utterly swept into the depths of her bottomless blue eyes. They held me safe and secure, and I knew she would never betray me. She was a rock in my upside-down world. She was the bridge over the torrent, the wind that carried me above the madness.

I leaned down and covered her mouth with my own. Heat rushed through me as she returned the kiss. Her fingers tangled in my hair, pulling me close. I cupped her chin, resting my other hand above the one she kept on my chest. I could feel my heartbeat through her fingers. Heat flared from her touch, filling my chest with fire.

She stepped back, keeping my hand in hers when she pulled it away from my chest. She frowned slightly at the gauze. "We need to get you dry bandages or you could get an infection," she said.

I nodded because it was the only thing I could think of to do. I was filled with her scent and the taste of her kiss. Everything about her clouded my senses.

She began to unwrap the gauze. When the wet dressings fell away, she looked up at me. "You're shaking. Are you alright?"

I nodded again. When she looked like she expected more than a mute answer, I tried to speak. "Y-yes," I said through the knot in my throat; I was always so elegant with words.

She nodded this time, but I could tell by her gaze that she didn't believe me. She picked up the blue shirt she had brought of her father's and opened a drawer next to the sink. She found a pair of scissors and cut two slits up the back of the cloth.

"I don't have Velcro, but it'll have to do," she said apologetically.

I tried to take the shirt from her, but she stepped back and shook her head. "I just unwrapped those hands. You can't touch anything until they've been bandaged. Let me help you."

She gently slipped my hands through the arm holes, then worked it over my head. She stepped around behind me and slid the material down my back. Her fingers lingered, running through the feathers of my wings. "They're so beautiful," she said. "I've never seen anything quite so lovely."

I met her gaze in the mirror. "I have," I replied.

A blush stole across her cheeks. She ducked her head and stepped around to my front. She pulled the shirt down gently over my scars. Her hand brushed the one at my side I had pieced together when Blade tried to kill me.

"How are you still alive, Saro?"

209

"Stubborn, I guess," I replied.

She smiled. "I believe that about you." She gestured to the sweat pants she had brought. "Those were Dad's, too. I would help you put them on, but—"

I lifted a hand at the red that colored her face. "It's alright. I can handle it."

She gave a quick laugh. "That's good. Come downstairs and I'll have the bandages out for your hands."

I rested my forehead against the door frame and listened to her footsteps as she made her way down. After a moment, I let out a sigh and gingerly worked my soaked pants off. I pulled the sweat pants on with my fingertips. They were a bit too short, but they would do. I left my shoes in the bathroom with the hopes that they would dry a bit before I put them back on.

I walked into the kitchen to find both Skylar and her mother there. At the sight of the shirt, something softened in Mrs. Jamison's face. She smiled. "It's good to see that shirt worn again." She gave her daughter a warm look. "Do you remember the last time your father wore that?"

Skylar nodded. "Father's Day. You guys took William and me to see the car exhibit. He loved cars."

Her mother pulled her close for a quick hug. "It was a good day." When she stepped back, she threw me a warm smile as well. "Let's see those hands." I held them out with my palms up and her eyebrows pinched together. "What happened to you, Saro?" she asked gently.

Nobody had ever used such a motherly tone with me. I hadn't realized what I was missing. It felt warm and kind, like being wrapped in a blanket or standing in the sun after a cold night. I pushed down the emotions and gave her a wry smile. "I had a little incident with a Molotov and someone who didn't like me very much."

"What's a Molotov?" she asked, glancing at her daughter.

"A mixture that starts fires," Skylar explained. She shrugged behind her mom's back as if she didn't know what else to say.

I shrugged back and she smiled.

"Well, be more careful next time," Mrs. Jamison recommended.

She spread ointment over some bandages and proceeded to gently dab the wounds. Skylar did the same on the other hand. It hurt, but at the same time, it felt so strange to have them care for my hands. It was far different from stitching my side or bandaging my wounds at the Academy. They cared. It was in the expressions on their faces and the gentle ways their hands wrapped the burns.

"Your hands are shaking," Skylar said quietly. She looked up at me. "Are they hurting?"

I shook my head. "I'm not used to someone taking care of me," I admitted.

She exchanged a warm smile with her mother. Mrs. Jamison nodded as though she made up her mind about something. She finished wrapping my hand, then smiled at me. "Saro, I'd like you to stay for breakfast. I'm making eggs and toast. It's not much, but you're welcome to it. And you don't have to hurry off. I hear the Galdoni Center is nice, but it's not home."

I glanced at Skylar; she was smiling at her mom as though proud of her. I got the impression that such warmth between them was rare and fleeting, that life got in the way and they seldom had the chance just to be mother and daughter. Mrs. Jamison passed behind us, squeezing Skylar's shoulder on the way by. Skylar's smile deepened. She turned her attention to my hand and finished wrapping it with gauze.

"Thank you," I said quietly.

"Thank you," she replied in the same undertones. "I haven't smiled this much in a year." She rubbed her cheeks. "I think my face is going to be sore."

"You should always smile," I told her. "It brings out the blue in your eyes and makes you look even more beautiful."

She stared at me, her elbows on the counter as she sat across from me. The vines running up her arms looked delicate in contrast to her pale skin. "Why do you say that?" she asked.

"Because it's true," I replied.

She shook her head, glanced back at her mom who was busy cracking eggs into a pan on the stove, and drew closer to me over the counter. "You surprise me every minute we're together, Saro. I'm different when I'm with you; it's like I'm a whole other person. I can laugh again, smile again, and it feels right."

She lowered her head and my gaze shifted to Mrs. Jamison's. She was watching us, an egg in one hand and a fork in the other. Her eyes shone with what I realized were tears. She gave me a watery smile before turning back to her pan.

Skylar continued, unaware that her mother was listening, "I've felt so lost since Dad died. I know we've only known each other for a short time, but I swear I've known you forever. I feel so comfortable with you."

Warning bells went off in the back of my mind. My instincts crowded forwarded, heralding danger to those close to me. I was a Galdoni. I was dangerous, raised on blood and violence; yet here I sat in Skylar's home where her mother and brother lived. I didn't deserve such kindness.

"You shouldn't be so comfortable with me," I told her softly.

Skylar looked up at me. Her blue gaze melted deep into me, seeing my soul and the truth of what I was without me telling her. Instead of backing away in horror, the gentlest of smiles curved her mouth and graced her eyes. Her hand rested on my forearm; a tingle ran along my skin at her touch. "You're different, too. We all have many sides, some that we hide, and some we embrace. We get to choose what side we present to the world. When Dad died, I pretended I was alright so people would stop asking me how I was doing. With you, I don't have to pretend. I'm remembering what it feels like to be happy again." Her eyes creased as her smile deepened. "I think that's the same thing that's happening to you."

The warmth in her voice surrounded me with the truth. Around Skylar, I could breathe and relax. I could just be, without worrying about attacks or instinct or any of those things that brought out the animal in me and chased down the emotions and sensitivities of my human side, the side I used to believe didn't exist.

"I'm not very good at this," I said. "I might mess it up." There it was, my deepest fear put to words. I was so different around Skylar that I was afraid I couldn't keep it up. If she saw the other side of me, I feared it would destroy the relationship we had built.

Skylar just gave her tiny shrug and tipped her head to one side. "It takes practice, right? I'm definitely not perfect." I snorted in disagreement. She smiled and continued, "You might get bored being around me."

My eyes widened. "Not likely."

She laughed, light and musical like the few drops of rain that pattered against the kitchen window. She squeezed my arm. "You're a good guy, Saro."

I chuckled. "You really don't know me."

213

She laughed again. Mrs. Jamison surprised us by sliding two plates of eggs and buttered bread in front of us. "Eat up, kiddos. I've got to run to work."

"Thank you, Mom," Skylar said. She rose and threw her arms around her mother's neck, giving her a hug.

Mrs. Jamison's eyes met mine. "Thank you," she mouthed with a smile that said more than a thousand words.

Skylar sat back down and we ate while we listened to her mom leave. My heart turned in my chest. Things were changing. I was changing. I liked who I became when I was with Skylar.

My thoughts turned to Alana. My chest gave a pang of guilt. I let out a slow breath. "I need to get back."

Skylar nodded. "Alana might miss you." Her words were carefully expressionless, giving me no clue as to how she felt.

I grabbed my wet clothes and shoes and Skylar walked me to the door. When she opened it, sunlight streamed through. The scent of rain-washed grass and cement filled the air. I took a deep breath and turned back to her. "Skylar, I—"

She rose on her tiptoes and kissed me. Surprised, I smiled against her lips and returned her kiss. I closed my eyes, enveloped by her scent, her taste, and her hand that rested on my chest above my scars. When she stepped back, a sigh escaped my lips.

She laughed. "Have a wonderful day, Saro."

"You, too, sophisticated Skylar."

That brought another laugh from her, filling my ears with the sweetest music. I stepped off the porch and pushed down my wings. Rising into the rain-washed air, I circled her townhouse once before turning my wings toward the Galdoni Center.

Chapter Twenty-four

Alana was asleep. I collapsed on the couch in her room. I had just shut my eyes when a familiar voice broke through my daze.

"We really need to get you a phone."

I opened my eyes to see Kale leaning against the doorframe. He smiled at me. "You look exhausted."

I gave him a tired smile which seemed to surprise him. "I've been busy."

He pulled the chair over and sat down near the couch. "I would ask busy doing what, but what you do on your free time is up to you. 'It's what we do in our unscheduled time that makes us who we are'." A warm look swept through his dark eyes and he rested his elbows on his knees. "Dr. Ray told me that. I was fresh from the Academy and not used to having time to myself." His eyes narrowed thoughtfully. "With Brie in my life, every free moment I get I spend with her."

I nodded. "I understand that."

He sat up and gave me a surprised look. "You do? A few days ago, you were disputing love, saying that fighting was all Galdoni were good for."

Thoughts of Skylar filled my mind and I smiled. "Someone's changed that for me."

Kale glanced at Alana sleeping in the bed. He looked back at me. "I'm glad to hear it."

I tipped my head against the couch. "I don't think my philosophies on love are what you came here to discuss."

He shook his head. "Nikko's team has managed to trace the paperwork we found in the safe. The details in the documents reveal share holdings in Advantage Corp. We're not sure why anyone wants to steal the papers, except maybe to destroy evidence of the shareholders; though I doubt those papers are their only documentation."

I studied the ceiling. "That doesn't make sense. Maybe it's someone working against Advantage Corp. Anyone with power has enemies, right?"

His tone darkened. "Same lessons outside the walls, huh?"

I shrugged. "Who would have thought the Academy provided real world training?" I felt his stare. After a moment, I chuckled. "Lighten up, Kale. You're the one who brought down the walls, remember?"

He snorted. "I remember. I just didn't think you had a sense of humor."

"I needed one to survive that place."

The remark brought an answering chuckle. "Tell me about it." He rose and slapped my shoe. "Get some shut-eye. Nikko's tracking down the origin of the documents. I'll let you know when we have something to investigate."

"Kale?" My voice stopped him at the door. When he turned, I smiled, trying to keep my eyes open. "You sound like a cop."

That brought a true laugh from him. "Wouldn't that be the day?" he replied. He turned down the hall. I could hear him chuckling to himself all the way to the balcony.

***

"Rise and shine, sleepy head."

I opened my eyes to see Alana sitting up in her bed. The apologetic look on her face filled me with warmth. "I wanted to let you sleep, but Kale stopped by and said they had a lead, whatever that means."

I sat up and rubbed my face in an attempt to chase the grogginess from my thoughts. A glance at the clock showed I had slept four hours.

"Good morning," I told her.

I stood and stretched. Alana watched me with a smile. I sat on the chair beside her and pushed the hair out of my eyes.

"You need a haircut," she noted.

"Who does your hair?" I asked, picking up one of her dark blonde braids.

She smiled. "Brie. She's really nice."

"Do you get a lot of visitors?" I wasn't sure what I wanted her to say. My heart twisted at the way her face lit up.

"I've made some good friends," she replied vaguely. She looked at my hands. "How are your burns?"

I was grateful for the change of subject. "They'd be better if I took it easy."

She laughed. "Saro taking it easy. That'd be the day."

I rose. I wanted to talk to her like we used to, but something was in the way. I felt like there was a wall I couldn't get around. I couldn't decide which of us had built it. "Guess I should get going."

I felt her eyes on me as I walked to the door. "Saro?"

I turned, relieved. "Yes, Alana?"

She gave me a true smile. "Thank you so much for bringing me here. You saved my life."

I shook my head. "It's my fault you got shot."

"You saved me from that house. You bandaged my feet, and you were so nice to me. You almost died for me." Her voice caught.

The same memories swarmed me, the house on fire, Jake's uncaring voice, my arms tied to the chair. I crossed back to Alana's side. "I would die for you a hundred times if it meant your safety." Every word was true. I set a gauzed hand on Alana's cheek. "You are worth everything. My regret is that I should have been the one shot, not you."

She smiled up at me. "I don't think I could have carried you here."

"You're pretty spunky. I think you could have managed it."

She laughed, and the sound took me back to the girl in the basement with the warm eyes and bandaged feet. She winced at the pain in her chest.

"Should I get someone?" I asked, worried.

She shook her head. "It's normal. Dr. Ray said it'll just take time. Don't worry about me."

"I'll always worry about you," I replied.

She smiled again. "You better get going."

"Take care of yourself."

She nodded.

I turned to leave when Jayce entered the room. We stared at each other for a moment. He looked at Alana, then back at me. "I, uh, I just wanted to see how Alana was doing," he explained.

"That's nice of you," I replied evenly. I realized he held a flower in his hand; it had yellow petals and a brown center. It was then that I noticed the vase near Alana's bed. At least a dozen other flowers sat it in, each a different color. I forced myself to nod. "I'll be by later," I told Alana.

"Take care," she said.

I walked through the door filled with confusion. When I was with Alana, all I could think about was Skylar, yet seeing Jayce with his flowers twisted my heart in a way that physically hurt. I cared about Alana, but it felt as though Skylar held my heart in her hands. Every moment I was away, I wanted to be back at her side. Jayce obviously cared about Alana, if the number of flowers was any indication. I couldn't decide how I felt about that. I didn't own her, yet I felt responsibility toward her because of all we had been through together. I didn't know what to do, or if there was anything I should do.

I was almost to the balcony when Kale landed.

"Glad to see you up," he said. "When I stopped by, you didn't even budge."

"I guess four hours of sleep in the last two days doesn't quite cut it," I replied, trying to get my thoughts together.

Kale threw me a searching look, but he didn't press me with questions. Instead, he held out a paper. "Nikko's team traced the documents back to this address."

"What is it?" I studied the numbers. The city was within a half-hour's flight.

"That's the problem." Kale's tone caught my attention. "When he pulled up the address, there was nothing there."

"We should investigate."

Kale laughed. "Now who sounds like a cop?"

I smiled. "Speaking of which, should we involve Officer Donaldson?"

Kale thought about it for a minute, then shook his head. "Let's make sure there's something there first. We don't want to send the police force on a wild goose chase."

We took off in the direction of the address. "My boys will be ready if we need backup," Kale said, his dark wings spread to catch the wind. "Goliath and Varo will leave the second we call. They've had my back for a long time."

I nodded. "Good to know who we can trust." I tipped my wings in time with Kale. We rose high above the city, riding on the currents that pushed the clouds along. I appreciated Kale's silence. It was comfortable just flying. Sometimes that was all I needed to clear my head. Thoughts of Skylar, Alana, and Jayce drifted with me. I wanted to kiss Skylar again, to feel her fingers on my skin. Being away from her reminded me of how much I enjoyed having her near.

"Who's the girl?" Kale asked.

"Taking back giving me my space?" I retorted, throwing him a searching look.

He held up his hands. "I'm not trying to be nosey. I just know that look. You miss someone and I can tell it's not Alana. She's a sweet girl, but you've been absent a lot since she's awoken."

I debated whether to tell him. Keeping Skylar a secret felt like a way to protect her. Yet I owed Kale; every time I looked at Alana, I was reminded that she wouldn't be there if it wasn't for Kale and the Galdoni Center. I glanced at him. "You know Skylar Jamison?"

He nodded. "She works the night shift. Nice girl. Human." He glanced at me.

"Is there a problem with liking a human? You seem to do well enough," I replied defensively.

Kale smiled, banishing the anger that filled me. "I love Brie; she is my girl and she's human. I just didn't take you for the type to trust humans after everything you've gone through. Your attitude about them hasn't exactly been welcoming."

I rode the wind in silence for a few minutes. Finally, I said, "She makes me feel like a real person when I'm around her, like I matter, and not just to anyone, to her. I matter to her and it makes me want to be better."

I glanced at him in time to catch his searching look. He nodded. "The right kind of love asks us to expect more of ourselves and to accept more of ourselves. When you find that person who sees all of you, your flaws, your idiosyncrasies, the little things you hate about yourself, and they love you more because of them, you know you need that person in your life." A knowing smile touched his lips. "And when it's hard to breathe because she isn't at your side, and you feel like your heart will never beat the same unless you are near her, then you truly are lost because the only way you will be found again is when you are with her."

"That's how I feel." The words escaped me before I knew I had said them. I avoided his gaze, focusing instead on the ground that rushed below. Sunset was coming. Skylar would be heading to the Center. "I can't stop thinking about her. We haven't known each other long, but she's different." I glanced at Kale.

He smiled. "I can tell you're different, too."

I nodded without speaking. There was nothing to say.

Kale let out a breath, tipping his wings on the graceful evening breeze. "All I can say is I'm happy for you, Saro." He really looked it. It showed in his eyes, his smile, and the nostalgic look on his face. "Change is hard but inevitable. We were taught to expect the unexpected, but love sweeps you off somewhere so unexpected you don't know where you're going to land." He nodded at the streets below. "Speaking of landing, I think that's our destination."

A building sat where nothing should have been. Kale and I landed behind it in a small, empty parking lot. The walls of the building were white. It stood several stories high and it felt like we were walking toward a hospital. Windows that caught the sunset stared down at us, silent sentinels hiding whatever lay within the building.

"On second thought, we should probably try the roof," I suggested. "We'll be a bit less conspicuous than barging in through the back door."

"Good thinking."

Chapter Twenty-five

We landed on the roof and tried the door. It was locked. Kale was about to kick it in, but I lifted a hand. I found a discarded piece of wire near the roof's edge and straightened it out. Five seconds later, the door creaked open.

"I forgot about your previous employment," Kale said.

I shrugged. "Employment implies that I got paid. Jake's due for a little payback."

He smiled. "Maybe this place will be our link back to him."

"I sure hope so."

We walked quietly down the stairs. Sounds met us, voices, beeping like the Galdoni Center, and the near silent scuff of our shoes on the clean white cement stairs. I didn't spot the camera until it was too late. I let out a slow breath and tapped Kale on the shoulder. At his look, I pointed to the small camera mounted in the top corner above the door we had entered.

"Guess the element of surprise is out of the question," he said. He lifted his phone to call for backup. The door below us slammed open.

"I thought I smelled a coward," Blade said. He glared up at us, his green eyes flashing. Men crowded behind him, but his form blocked the doorway and they didn't look eager to push past. Blade wore armor much like he had in the Arena. Scales had been worked in gold along his chest and shoulders; it fit with the dragon helmet he used to wear, but he had discarded it. Instead, spikes ran up his shoulders and followed a golden harness that attached to his wing joints. The spikes that tipped his joints looked deadly.

"SR029. Of all the Galdoni Kale could side with, he chose the only one I killed who refused to die."

I glowered at him. "I could say the same about you. How's your side?"

I wondered if he felt the throb of the scar I had given him. Mine burned with a searing heat, reminding me of the pain of my improvised stitches and the fever that had almost taken my life.

"You're on my territory, SR029," Blade growled. "I'll tear your limbs from your body and—"

"Leave him alone," Kale barked.

Blade's face twisted in a dark sneer. "Come down here and fight like a Galdoni, Kale. Or are you waiting for your *human* friends to save you again?" He spat the word human as if it was poisonous.

Kale took a step down. I grabbed his shoulder. "Not like this. I know you want revenge, but this isn't the way," I growled in his ear. "We need to find out what this place is. I'll distract him while you check it out."

He shook his head. "Go back up to the roof and enter through one of the windows. Report to me as soon as you know. We'll get out of here when you have an answer."

I wanted to argue. Leaving him with Blade seemed like the stupidest thing I could do. Neither of us should leave the other. That left only one option. "We're going together." I took a step back.

Kale glanced at me, then back down at Blade. If it was either of us against the Galdoni, we might have had a chance, but the armed men who crowded forward at each step Blade took left no doubt as to the outcome of such a foolish risk. He nodded. We backed up slowly.

Blade's eyes widened. "Leaving? You cowards. Fight me!" When we continued to retreat, a vein on the side of his forehead bulged with anger. "Fight me!" His voice echoed up and down the stairs.

I reached the door and threw it open. Kale and I took to the sky.

"There!" Kale pointed to a window on the second floor that appeared to be a walkway. I tucked my wings and dove after him. I lifted an arm to shield my face as we burst through the glass. I rolled once and came up on my feet. Footsteps sounded down the hall. A shadow passed the window.

"This way," Kale shouted.

We ran down the hall lined with doors. "We don't have time for your lock picking," he said. I was about to bash the door in with my shoulder, but he turned the knob and it opened. We rushed inside, then stopped at the sight of an empty bed. Padded handcuffs were still attached to the bars. A file sat on the table. I opened it. Pictures of a black-haired girl with cream-colored wings had been stapled to the left hand flap. Notes on the girl filled the right. I shoved it beneath my shirt.

Kale ran down to the next room; I opened the door across from it. Each was empty, but we found two more files before Blade caught up to us.

"Now I know what you came for," Blade said. A glimmer of cold glee lit his eyes. "You want the girls."

"You know about them?" Kale asked.

"Of course," Blade responded, angling himself between us and the exit. "I also know about the paper trail." He pointed at me. "SR029 was working for Jake, one of the slimiest human's I've ever known. What does that say about you?" he asked me.

Kale held up a hand before I could respond. "We know Saro was stealing the papers, but not why. What makes those documents so important?"

Blade's dark eyebrows rose. "Each investor with AC was entitled to a girl Galdoni of their own. I thought you'd figured that out." Footsteps pounded up the hall. Guards appeared around the corner. Blade stopped them with a look.

Kale and I exchanged a glance. We needed more information. We had to keep him talking. "So why steal the papers, then?" Kale asked.

Blade chuckled. "The founders of Advantage Corp got greedy. Why give up the girls when they can keep their little experiments to themselves?"

"No papers, no female Galdoni," I said.

Blade clapped. "Well done, *Saro*, is it?" he asked, twisting the name. "You should try one. You might find a female Galdoni to your liking." He winked. "Oh, I forget, you already have one, don't you?" His smile deepened. "You probably shouldn't leave her alone. Bad things can happen."

My heart did a backflip. Alana was in trouble. Blade wasn't trying to fight us, he was distracting us! I dove at him. Blade ducked to the right. Kale had anticipated the move and connected with a haymaker that sent Blade reeling. The men down the hall raised their guns. Bullets tore into the walls around us. Kale and I ran for the window. We jumped, clearing the glass. I opened my wings and pushed hard. The sound of bullets tearing through the air drove me higher. Kale's shadowed form ghosted at my left. Neither of us spoke. We directed our focus toward the Galdoni Center.

***

Flames danced on the horizon. We passed several dark forms, Galdoni heading back to Blade. I wanted to attack them, to finish what they had started, but my thoughts were occupied by the burning building. Skylar and Alana were there. I had to help them.

I could see Skylar on the roof where she had no doubt been waiting for the sunrise. She leaned against one of the railings. Flames reached from the gaping doorway that led up from the twelfth floor. She had no way down.

I tipped my wings. Windows shattered. Each floor looked consumed by fire. Galdoni flew to and from the building, trying to save anyone they could find. Thoughts of Alana trapped in her bed crowded my mind. My heart raced as fear of the fire engulfed me in its deadly orange grip. I couldn't go inside. The flames were too much. I couldn't face the fire again.

"Third floor," Kale shouted. "You get Alana. I'll find Brie. She said she was visiting the children. I need to make sure the sixth floor is clear."

"Got it," I shouted back over the roar of the flames.

Kale pulled his wings in. He turned slightly so that the glass wouldn't catch his wings. He shielded his head with his arm. The slight crash made by the broken window was lost in the hungry roar that devoured the building.

I had to save her. I had to fight my fears and fly into the building.

I repeated the words over again in my head. I was running out of time. My heart thundered in my ears. I couldn't breathe. The smoke would be too much. My hands ached as if I had burned them again. I couldn't think.

One image surfaced, a vision of Alana in her bed unable to run from the flames that lapped around her. She had been shot because of me. She wouldn't die because of me.

I tucked my wings and dove.

Air rushed past my face. I turned as Kale had, but not far enough. The glass shattered around me. I felt it pull at my right wing. I rolled on the floor and came up on my feet, slightly dazed from the landing. The fire had ruined the electricity to the building. Dark shadows warred against two emergency lights that flickered on either end of the hallway. I ran down it, shouting Alana's name. Smoke snaked down my throat, threatening to choke me.

"Saro!" a male voice responded.

I stumbled into Alana's room in time to see Jayce pick her up in his arms. Alana's eyes were wide with fright. She was struggling to breathe through the smoke. Jayce's face was white with terror.

"I don't know where to go," he said.

I grabbed his shirt. "To the balcony."

He carried her back the way I had run. I checked the rooms we passed. Most were empty. The charred remains of a Galdoni in a bed near the end drove a dagger through my heart. I led Jayce through the room to the balcony. Fire exploded around us as the flames found oxygen containers. I shielded Jayce and Alana with my wings. The ceiling began to collapse. The heat beat against us.

"Take her," Jayce shouted. "There's no time!"

He held her out, willing me to save her and leave him to the flames. I couldn't do that.

I grabbed them both just as there was a loud explosion behind us. We fell from the balcony, plummeting toward the ground. Time slowed. Figures ran around below; the lights from three fire engines cut through the darkness beyond the flames. Sirens met my ears; their wailing sounded like creatures in pain. I opened my wings.

I kept my wings at a sharp angle so they wouldn't break with the sudden force. Even so, the weight nearly snapped them. I bit back a cry as they caught the air, slowing our descent before we slammed into the ground. The friction tore at my hands. I struggled to hold onto Jayce and Alana. I could feel the gauze tearing my skin instead of protecting it. I clenched my teeth and tipped my wings, bringing us to a stop on the grass.

I let them go and forced my wings down.

"Where are you going?" Jayce shouted.

"To get Skylar," I replied.

I sped upward as the heat from the building beat against me. I passed Kale on his way down with two children in his arms. They were crying and clutched his shirt in terror.

"Where's Brie?" I shouted.

"Safe on the ground." The relief in Kale's voice was stark.

"Are there more children?" I asked.

"Goliath just left on the other side with three. I couldn't find Koden," Kale answered.

I nodded. "I'll get him."

I sped to the top of the building. Skylar stood on the railing. Tears streaked her cheeks. When I landed, she ran to me.

"I knew you would come," she said. I could feel her shaking. I wrapped her tight in my arms. "I knew you wouldn't forget me."

"Never," I whispered into her hair. I tightened my hold. I jumped off the roof just as it caved in. Two seconds later and Skylar would have been engulfed in the flames and ash that rose high into the air. I tightened my grip. She leaned against me.

"There's someone we have to get out of there," I shouted above the roar.

"Let's do it," she replied. Soot colored her cheek and her hair stood up on one side. I had never loved her more.

Chapter Twenty-six

I turned in a tight circle that dropped us to the sixth floor. Skylar followed me into the room. "Koden!" I called.

Skylar took up the name. "Koden, where are you?" she yelled.

The fire was so hot. I dropped into a crouch and Skylar did the same. Every breath I took burned in my lungs, filling them with smoke. We didn't have any time left.

I threw couches over, ignoring my damaged hands through the rage that filled me. Blade knew about this. He had stalled us long enough to ensure people would be killed in the Galdoni Center. He had to pay.

"Koden!" Skylar ran to the corner.

I hurried after her. A beam fell from the ceiling. I stopped short before it crushed me. Sparks rose, blanketing the air in flaming red dots. I ran to the wall and worked around the beam in time to see Skylar kneel at the side of a motionless form. I fell to my knees beside her and gathered the boy up in my arms. Skylar shrieked when another beam fell, pinning us against the wall.

There was no way out. Skylar held my arm, her eyes wide with fear and reflecting the fire around us. I might have been destined to burn because of all I had done, but Skylar and Koden didn't deserve that. I handed the unconscious boy to Skylar.

"What are you doing?" she asked, panic in her voice.

I grabbed the fallen beam that blocked our way. Fire raced along the gauze, eating through it to my skin. I gritted my teeth, but the pain was too much. A yell broke from me as I lifted the beam. I threw it to the side, clearing the path. Adrenaline coursed through my veins, chasing away the pain from my hands. I took Koden from Skylar and led the way through the debris. Someone must have set off explosives on each level of the Galdoni Center for such mass destruction. Blade would pay; he had purposefully distracted us. All who died were on his head.

We reached the balcony. I was about to hand Koden to Skylar so I could pick her up like I usually did. Before I could move, the entire north side of the Center fell. Skylar screamed. I grabbed her hand and dove off the building. We plummeted through the smoke and debris. I couldn't see. I needed to fly, to get us away before the building crushed us.

I opened my wings. A sharp yell tore from my lips as my grip tightened on Skylar's. She hung in the air, suspended with only my burned hand keeping her from plunging to the ground. I tried to shift Koden, but my grip on his body was precarious. I could feel my skin giving way beneath the tattered remains of the gauze. I couldn't get to the ground fast enough. I was going to lose Skylar.

"Kale!" I shouted.

Suddenly he was there, catching Skylar around the waist. "I've got her," he reassured me. "You can let go."

I had to will the damaged muscles in my hand to respond. Tears blurred my vision at the pain.

Kale grabbed my shoulder. "Easy," he said. "Let's get to the ground."

He kept one hand on my shoulder as we rode the wind down. When we landed, I dropped to my knees and lowered Koden to the grass. "Come on," I spoke quietly, watching him for a response. His curly blonde hair was singed, and his red wings were dark with soot. "Breathe!" I shouted.

"Saro?"

I heard Skylar's voice, but couldn't turn away from the boy. I felt a hand on my shoulder. I shook it off. Tears clouded my vision, clearing the smoke from my burning eyes.

"You've got to breathe, boy," I said. Frustration at the way events had unfolded filled me. We had fallen into their trap. We had left the Galdoni Center unprotected. Koden should not have to pay for that mistake.

I slammed a fist down on his chest. His back arched and he began to cough, drawing in ragged breath after breath. His blue eyes opened. He tipped his head to look at me.

"Thank goodness," I breathed. I rocked back on my heels. Skylar beamed down at me, her eyes filled with tears. My hands hurt. I tried to ignore them. My Galdoni training to put aside pain seemed to have neglected to point out that burns were a different kind of pain, the kind that was hard to think through.

Kale patted my shoulder on his way past. I glanced up at him. There was determination in his dark eyes and the line of his clenched jaw.

"Where are you going?"

"To make them pay," he replied in a growl.

I stood. "I thought you were above revenge."

His eyes narrowed. "They targeted my family. Brie, Jayce, and Nikko were all in the Center when it was hit. They barely made it out. You don't mess with my family."

My heart raced. "I'm going with you."

He shook his head, his eyes on my hands. "Get those taken care of."

"Wait for me."

He let out a breath. "There's no way, Saro."

I stepped closer to him so that we were eye to eye. "Try to stop me, Kale. They almost killed Alana and Skylar. Koden barely made it. I saw a Galdoni who died in his bed because of this." I motioned toward the fallen building. "I am going." My tone left no room for argument.

Kale finally nodded. "Alright, but get those hands looked at first. I'm going to see who can go with us. We leave in ten minutes."

Skylar helped Koden toward the ambulances. I followed them, cradling my hands against my chest. I couldn't look at them; it hurt in some places, but in others, the lack of pain concerned me. Dr. Ray's familiar face appeared out of the chaos.

"Skylar, Saro, thank goodness!" he exclaimed. He picked up Koden and led us to the back of one of the ambulances. "Jayce said you saved him and Alana. I don't know how to thank you."

I held out my hands. "Could you re-bandage these so I can go with Kale?"

He settled Koden on the small ambulance bed, then turned back. His eyes widened. "Saro."

I shook my head. "I don't want to know. Just bandage them so I can get going. Kale needs someone to watch his back."

"Someone who can use their hands," he pointed out. He stepped out of the ambulance. The team hurried inside to help with Koden. Dr. Ray gently picked up one of my hands. I hid a wince at the pain. His voice lowered. "Saro, you need to go to the emergency room."

"He's right," Skylar said. "You've got to get these burns taken care of."

I met both of their eyes, willing them to understand. "I can't. Kale will leave without me and he can't take Blade by himself."

"Blade?" Dr. Ray's face washed pale. "He's behind this?"

I nodded. "He distracted us to keep us from coming back. He knew the Center was going to be attacked. We need to find out who gave the orders or everyone will be in danger." I gave him a searching look. "Is there a safe place the Galdoni can go?"

Dr. Ray nodded. "We'll secure the hospital; I've already contacted the police department. They'll have it protected when we arrive."

I held out my hands. He sighed. "As long as you get these looked at when you come back."

"I will," I promised.

I sat on the back bumper of an ambulance while Dr. Ray did what he could to protect my hands. Skylar's hand rested on my shoulder, squeezing once in a while when my muscles tensed at the pain. I looked up at her. The worry in her eyes let me know her fear. When Dr. Ray was done, I wrapped her carefully in my arms.

"I'll be back," I said quietly in her hair.

"You promise?" she asked.

I nodded. She tipped her face up and I kissed her. We stood apart from the chaos that swarmed around us. People cried in pain; the wailing of ambulance and fire engines filled the air. We stood in a little bubble for that moment, away from everything that threatened to tear us apart. All I wanted to do was stay there forever, holding her in my arms with my lips pressed against hers. She filled every place I was empty. My heart thudded and I wondered if she could feel it where her hand rested against my chest. I hoped so, because it beat for her.

"You need to go home; your mom and brother will be worried."

"I will," she said, blinking up at me. "Please be careful."

"I will."

She nodded and stepped back just as Kale and three other Galdoni landed.

"I've sent everyone else to the hospital to keep the Galdoni and staff who were injured safe while we're gone," Kale told us. His gaze shifted to Dr. Ray. "I told them you're in charge. If you feel there's a threat, don't hesitate to evacuate."

"Will do," Dr. Ray replied. He held out a hand. Kale shook it. "Take care of yourself."

"I will," Kale promised. He tipped his head to indicate the Galdoni behind him. "Saro, you already know Goliath. Varo and I fought together in the Arena, and this is Lem."

My eyes met the Galdoni's and memories crashed forward.

"Scream for me, SR029," Blade had said with glee in his voice.

I couldn't help the scream as he sliced my side open with his blade. When he walked away to leave me bleeding on the ground, Lem was the one who had stepped forward.

"Want me to cut his head off?" he asked.

I saw Blade's smile through the darkness that crowded my mind. "Leave him. His death from that wound will be slow and agonizing, just the way he deserves it."

I blinked, willing my eyes to focus. "LH308."

Lem stared at me for a moment; soot was smeared across one cheek and his red hair was streaked with it. His eyebrows pulled together, and he nodded in recognition. "You're the one Blade killed in the Arena when you were pinned by five other Galdoni. I guess should say *almost* killed. You had your revenge."

"And you wanted to cut my head off," I growled.

Kale stepped between us before I could attack him.

"Lem's different, Saro. All of us are." His gaze bored into mine. "He's been with me for the last year."

"He was one of Blade's cronies," I argued.

Kale nodded. "Back when we were all trained killers and fought to survive. It was a different world."

Lem held up his hands, his green eyes wide. "I just want to help. I'm sorry about the past. Blade had to take you when he had the advantage to keep from fighting you when he didn't; he was a coward like that."

I shoved past Kale and stood toe to toe with the orange-winged Galdoni. "You would have killed me when I was already dying."

Lem met my gaze without flinching. "Call it mercy."

My chest heaved as I stared at him. I wanted to take him down. He deserved to pay for all he had done at the Academy under Blade's tutelage. Who was worse, the monster or the one who followed him and did everything in his name?

A hand touched my arm. Goliath spoke, his deep voice rumbling through the night. "We don't have time for this, Saro. Every moment we waste takes us further away from catching Blade and finding out who is at the bottom of the attack."

The giant Galdoni's reasoning found its way through the red haze that filled my mind. I let out a breath and nodded. "Fine." I pointed at Lem. "But we're not through."

He shrugged, his eyes already on the sky. "I'd get the ground crew clear in case the Center collapses," he told Kale. "That was quite the fire."

My hands balled into fists. I winced at the angry pain, but it worked to clear my mind. "I'll find you at your house when we're done," I told Skylar.

She nodded, her eyebrows pinched together and her gaze shifting from me to Lem. "Are you going to be okay?"

I gave her a forced smile. "Don't worry. We've got bigger things to worry about than settling private battles."

The other Galdoni rose into the air. Skylar stood on her tiptoes and kissed me. "Come back to me," she whispered.

I smiled at her and lifted my wings. We flew through the smoke and left those on the ground far behind.

Chapter Twenty-seven

"Watch each other's backs," Kale commanded when we reached the building. "Get what information you can. We need to find the female Galdoni and any links from AC to the attack on the Galdoni Center."

He pulled his dark wings tight against his back and dove. Goliath followed close behind, his huge form dwarfing the rest of the Galdoni. Varo spun to the left, using his gray wings to guide him in a tight circle. Lem motioned for me to go next. I shook my head, unwilling to let an enemy at my back. Despite the time away from the Academy, our training and my instincts held true. Lem shrugged and dove, holding his light orange wings along his body to streamline him through the drop. I let out a breath and followed.

Uncertainty filled me. It didn't feel right to return to the building. Blade no doubt knew we were coming back. Blade was never unprepared; we were flying into a trap.

At the last minute, Kale pulled back and dove through the glass above the floor we had previously entered. He motioned for the other Galdoni to hit the windows on either side. I smiled at that. He also knew it was a trap. The others broke windows along the same floor but in different rooms so they wouldn't be cornered if there was an ambush. On impulse, I chose the same window Kale had used.

I tucked my wings and rolled when I hit the floor. I came up in the middle of a firefight. Bullets hit the floor around me. Men with ballistic shields swarmed from the doors on either side of the large room. I could see Goliath and Varo taking down guards in the next room.

I grabbed a shield, throwing the guard who held it into two more. Kale held two shields on the other side of the room. He spun, taking down three guards before throwing one of his shields into a forth. I searched for Lem. The Galdoni was nowhere to be found. Uneasiness filled me at his absence. If he was on Blade's side, our backs wouldn't be protected.

Bullets peppered my shield. I ran forward, barreling the guards who shot at me into the room from where they had attacked. I shoved them back and pulled the door shut, then used the shield to snap off the door knob. Pounding followed gunshots; the door wouldn't hold long.

A roar of rage tore through the air. I looked back in time to see Blade dive through one of the windows closest to Kale and grab him in a tackle that took them both through a wall to the next room. I was about to follow when three more Galdoni flew through the window, barring my way.

I recognized the first as PF220, one of the Galdoni who had held me down when Blade sliced through my side. I recognized the other two from the Academy, one who shaved his head and always had a bit of drool down the lopsided right side of his face from where Blade had broken his jaw, and a Galdoni close to my age with white and yellow wings. I had fought both of them before; Picasso was definitely the biggest threat.

"Wrong place, wrong time, boys," I said.

PF220 popped his knuckles. I rolled my eyes at the cliché. "Ready to die, SR029?"

I couldn't take all three of them together. Kale might have, but he was bigger and stronger. My scrappy style would only protect me for so long. I had to separate them. "You tried to kill me once before; I don't think it's happening now."

"Wanna bet?" PF220 asked.

If I had owned a coin and the use of my hands in order to flip it, it would have been a great distraction; however, given my limitations, I had to work with what I had. I dove out the window.

I glanced back to see the three Galdoni exchange surprised glances before jumping out after me. I pushed my wings hard, ducking around the building just as they cleared the window. I expected them to split up. Training at the Academy taught us to head off an escaping enemy. We had often practice in the Arena, swooping the wide dome and tackling the Galdoni who branched away from the protection of their team.

Common sense said two would pursue me while one went the other way to catch me off-guard. If I could eliminate one, I would have a much better chance with the others. I glanced back in time to see the yellow-winged Galdoni and PF220 fly around the corner. I pushed my wings harder, holding as close to the building as I dared. Picasso was huge. Timing would have to be on my side or the attack would turn into the worst decision of my life.

I surged forward, giving one last hard push with my wings. Picasso appeared a second before I reached the edge; his eyes widened. I hit him, slamming the Galdoni into the building. A snap sounded as one of his wings broke under the force. He screamed as we dove through a window. Glass shattered around us, glittering off the marble floor. I shoved him away from me and glanced back to ensure that he was no longer a threat. He huddled in the corner, his broken wing a tattered mess beneath him.

I was about to jump back out when a form barreled into me, slamming me to the floor. I struggled against PF220's grip. Yellow landed close behind him. PF220 punched my face, then my ribs. I felt them give.

"That all you got?" I forced a laugh.

241

Anger colored his face. He grabbed one of my wings. "You hurt Bulldog, this is what you get!" He bent my wing in his hands; I screamed at the pain of my protesting joint.

I rolled toward him and punched, using the momentum of my roll to drive my fist into his face. He staggered back, one hand on his jaw and the other thrown back to keep his balance in the crouch. I dove at him; his head hit against the marble floor. He kicked, shoving me backward toward the gaping hole that was once a window. I staggered back in the hopes of escape, but Yellow grabbed me in a bear hug from behind, pinning my wings and arms.

PF220 lowered his head and slammed into my stomach like a battering ram. I gasped for air. Stars danced in my vision. I felt him hit my face and my stomach, but I couldn't draw in enough breath to fight back. Each blow made it worse; I was suffocating. He was going to kill me. I couldn't protect Kale; I wouldn't keep my promise to Skylar.

A blur tackled PF220. I elbowed Yellow in the stomach, followed by an elbow to the jaw. He spun and dropped. My vision cleared enough for me to see Lem trading punches with PF220.

"Protect Kale," Lem yelled over his shoulder.

I jumped out the window trying to grasp what had just happened. The Galdoni I had thought was my enemy had attacked PF220, the scum he used to hang out with at Blade's side. He had saved my life. I flew around the building with my thoughts spinning. I had to focus. I had to find Kale.

I flew back into the main room where we had started. It didn't take long to follow the sounds of fighting to Kale and Blade. Room after room showed the effects of their battle. Doors had been broken off hinges, bodies of guards lay motionless on the floor, and drywall was everywhere. I entered the last room in time to see Kale motion for Blade to attack. The room was the size of the lunchroom at the Galdoni Center and had the same linoleum floor and tables pushed to either side. A few guards lay hapharzardly among the white tables without moving.

Both Galdoni looked as though they had received the beating of their lives. Kale limped and blood ran down the side of his face. One of Blade's wings was missing enough feathers to make flying difficult, and his left eye was swollen almost completely shut.

"Enough with the guards," Kale said. "Finish this with honor." He threw down his shield.

"I can do honor," Blade replied. He threw down his shield as well and gave a smile I recognized.

Blade didn't have honor. The scar along my side was a testament to that. "Don't trust him!" I yelled. The ceiling was too low to fly. I ran toward the pair, dodging tables and bodies.

Kale walked to meet Blade, his fists up and a look of expectancy on his face. Blade's smile mirrored the toothy grin he had given me as he pulled the sword through my skin.

"No!" I shouted.

Two shots rang out. Kale stumbled backwards. He looked from Blade's gun to me.

I tackled Blade against a table. The table collapsed beneath us, sending both of us to the ground as the gun flew from Blade's grasp. He hit me in the head twice. I slugged him in the jaw, then drove my forehead against his with a sharp crack. Lights exploded behind my eyes. I stumbled backwards and saw Blade's eyes roll back. He shook his head and tried to rise.

A hand grabbed my shoulder. "Get Kale out of here!"

I met Varo's eyes. The Galdoni's right wing hung crookedly against his shoulder. His face was pale with pain, but his gaze was stern. "Get Kale to safety."

I nodded and ran to the black-winged Galdoni. He moaned when I touched him. There wasn't time to see where the bullets had hit. A glance showed Blade getting back to his feet. Varo stood in the way but Blade looked ready to tear through the Galdoni to get to us.

I slid my bandaged hands beneath Kale's knees and behind his shoulders.

"Don't you dare leave, SR029," Blade growled. He dove at us, but Varo tackled him. Blade grabbed the gray-winged Galdoni by the throat. Varo kicked him in the groin.

"Fly, Saro!" he yelled.

I jumped out the window.

Chapter Twenty-eight

Kale was heavier than Skylar. It took all of my energy to push my wings hard enough that we could soar. I flew high above the dark buildings. I didn't know where to go. I only knew that Blade would be after us soon and it would be best if I found a place to hide Kale. My shirt grew sticky with his blood. I didn't know where he had been shot, but I could tell by his ragged breath that it was taking a heavy toll on him.

I stopped on the roof of a building long enough to assess Kale's wounds. I didn't want to risk him bleeding to death before I could find help. A quick check showed that one of the bullets had pierced low through his right shoulder; the other was embedded in his thigh. Both bled freely. I ripped off my shirt and pressed half to each wound. Kale's eyes flew open at the pain. "Hold these," I told him.

"Where. . . ?" he managed to get out. Blood touched his lips.

I gritted my teeth at the sight. "To find help," I replied.

"Blade," he said, his voice weak.

I shook my head. "Varo stepped in. When I get you somewhere safe, I'll make sure he's taken care of."

His head tipped from side to side and he looked at me as if it took every ounce of his willpower to keep focused. "He's. . . too. . . strong."

I nodded. "I noticed. Glad to see you have such faith in me."

A half-smile pulled at his mouth as his eyes began to close. I shook him. "Stay awake, Kale. Whatever you do, keep your eyes open. You've lost too much blood, and you've got too much to live for to give up now."

He let out a breath that gurgled slightly. His eyes opened again, focusing on my face. I ignored his cry of pain as I slipped my arms beneath him and lifted. I suspected he had a shattered femur and perhaps a pierced lung like Alana, but I wouldn't know for sure unless I got him help. There wasn't much time.

I flew as fast as I could. Despite my efforts to keep him awake, Kale's head eventually lolled back. I pushed faster, driving myself on.

By habit, I headed toward the Galdoni Center. It was only when I reached Crosby that I remembered it no longer existed. I couldn't take Kale to the hospital Dr. Ray had commanded all the Galdoni and staff be taken to; it would be the first place Blade would look. Frustration filled me at the smoke that tainted the growing sunlight. Sunrise reminded me of Skylar. I tipped my wings.

She could reach Dr. Ray. Kale would be safe with Skylar as long as it would take me to find Blade and ensure that he was no longer a threat. As long as the Galdoni threatened those I loved, I wouldn't rest. Kale's warning that Blade was too strong echoed in my mind. I clenched my jaw and pushed the worry aside. Nothing mattered as long as the threat he represented was real. I had to stop Blade and find the female Galdoni. Unless that was accomplished, my own safety mattered little.

I landed in Skylar's backyard. She must have been waiting for me because the door opened as soon as my feet touched the ground. Mrs. Jamison appeared behind her. Skylar's hand flew to her face.

"Saro, is that your blood?"

I shook my head quickly. "It's Kale's. He's shot. I need you to get Dr. Ray here as soon as possible."

I led the way into the house. Mrs. Jamison pulled the door wide to let us pass. She motioned toward the couch.

"You can lay him there. I'll get some towels." She hurried up the stairs.

Skylar helped me ease Kale down. He moaned, but didn't open his eyes. "You've got to hurry," I told her. She nodded and ran to get her phone.

A noise in the doorway made me look up. William watched me, his blue eyes wide. I kept pressure on Kale's wounds. "It's alright, Will. You can come in." I tipped my head to indicate Kale. "He's my friend. We're trying to save him."

Kale coughed. His eyes opened partway. A hint of a smile showed. "Thought you didn't have friends," he said. He winced in pain.

I blinked back tears. "I wouldn't have if it wasn't for a stubborn Galdoni who refused to leave me alone."

He closed his eyes and his smile deepened. "You were the stubborn one."

I nodded. "You got that right. Now you've got to be stubborn. Remember Brie. You can't leave her like this."

"I'm. . ." he took a breath and winced, "not going anywhere."

"Good."

A motion caught my eye. I looked up and saw that William had stepped into the room. His gaze was on my chest. My heart clenched at the look on his face as he studied the scars colored by Kale's blood.

I opened my mouth to speak; I didn't know what I was going to say, but there was something he needed to hear.

Skylar ran back into the room followed closely by her mother. "Dr. Ray's on his way over. He said to keep pressure on the wounds."

I nodded at Mrs. Jamison. She pressed the towels on top of my shredded shirt, taking over my post. I dropped to my knees next to William. "You have to take care of them," I said, wiping off the worst of the blood on a towel Skylar brought to me. "Protect your mother and sister. Keep them safe until I get back. Can you do that?"

He nodded. Determination filled his gaze. "I know where Dad kept his gun."

I glanced up at Skylar. She gave a small nod. "I know how to shoot it. We'll be alright."

I stood back up and patted William's shoulder. "Help Dr. Ray."

"I will," he promised.

I crossed through the living room to the backyard. Skylar followed close behind.

"Where are you going?" she asked as soon as the door shut behind us.

"I've got to stop Blade. He's our key to finding the female Galdoni, and he's a threat to Kale and all the others if he gets away."

Tears filled Skylar's eyes. "Look at Kale," she said, her heartbreak in her voice. "What if you don't make it back?"

Deep down, I knew her concern was very real. A heaviness filled me, certainty that what she said would come to pass. If Blade killed me, when Blade killed me, the voice in my mind whispered, I would never hold her again. He had to be stopped. Somehow, I knew I was the only one who could stop him. I had to do it. I owed it to Kale for all he had done for me. I owed it to the Galdoni from the Center because they deserved a chance at a real life. I owed it to the female Galdoni because they needed a life of freedom away from the craziness of the world they had been brought into.

Above it all, though, tangling around the inevitability of the situation, was the little voice reminding me that I could stay. I could fly away and pretend that none of it had happened; I could stay with Skylar and tell myself that the threat of Blade didn't hang above those I loved. I could forget about everyone who suffered because of Blade's existence.

I stood torn, tempted to stay with the girl I loved instead of facing an enemy who had almost killed me once and would do whatever he could to fix that mistake.

I closed my eyes, but there wasn't really a choice; not to me, at least.

I wrapped Skylar in my arms. "No matter what happens, I love you. My heart, my soul, my everything is yours and always will be." I stared down into her light blue eyes that sparkled with tears. My chest filled with so many different emotions that I wanted to laugh and cry and kiss her over and over again. I tried to put what I felt into words. "You taught me what it meant to really live, Sky. You filled my life with so much light it chased away all the darkness. You are my sun, my moon, and my stars. You are my guiding light, and I will follow you home."

"I love you, Saro," she replied, holding me tight.

The words I had never heard before filled me with such joy it was almost painful. The fact that I had to face Blade made it bittersweet. I took a shuddering breath and kissed the top of Skylar's head. "I've got to go."

She nodded and stepped back.

"I need you to do one thing for me."

"Anything," she said.

"Call Officer Donaldson; ask him to bring every officer he has." I gave her the location and lifted my wings.

Chapter Twenty-nine

I met Officer Donaldson just south of the building. The rising sun lit the place in yellow and orange. It looked far too beautiful from the outside for what had happened inside to be true. Officer Donaldson handed me an earpiece. When I slipped it in my ear, he said, "You know what to do."

I nodded and flew to the upper floor.

"Take care of yourself, Saro," he said into the earpiece.

"You, too," I replied.

I landed on the floor I had left. My heart turned over at the sight of Varo laying again a wall, his head at an unnatural angle to match his broken wing. I bit back a growl of frustration. Blade was gone. I had failed.

"Saro, is it?"

I turned at the dark chuckle.

"Sad name for a pitiful Galdoni." Blade chuckled again, pushing off from the wall he leaned against. "Fitting, really."

The sight of him set my heart pounding. "Tell me about the female Galdoni, Blade," I replied.

He cocked his head to one side. "I thought you already had your own female Galdoni, Saro," he taunted. He pursed his lips thoughtfully. "Although I heard from several of the Galdoni we tortured here that you had a new female you were fond of. Someone named Skylar."

My heart clenched. I willed my face to remain expressionless.

"Keep him focused," Officer Donaldson said into my earpiece. "I've sent officers to Skylar's house. She'll be safe."

I took a shuddering breath. "You're sidestepping the subject, Blade. Tell me what I want to know."

He circled to the right, keeping himself in silhouette from the sunlight that filtered through the broken windows at his back. "What's it to you? You're just as dead as he is." He gestured toward Varo.

"You take so much joy in killing," I said.

He gave a little half-bow. "Why thank you."

"That's not a compliment."

He shrugged. "Guess it's how you take it. Galdoni were meant to kill, you know."

I followed his circle, carefully to keep my back protected by the wall. "We can change our ways."

He shook his head. "Old dog, new tricks. Doesn't work out that way."

I dove at him, hoping to catch him off guard. He turned at the last minute and grabbed me by the throat, shoving me against the wall. "Have you heard the saying, 'Birds born in a cage think flying is an illness.'?" When I struggled to get free of his grip, he held my throat tighter. "Alejandro Jodorowsky, smart fellow. Proves there may be hope for the human race yet."

He stepped slightly to the side. His face that had been hidden by shadow was revealed. I stared at the blood that marked his cheeks and his forehead. It traced down the bridge of his nose in dots, and ran along the edge of his jaw. I wondered if it was Varo's blood, or if he had used his own.

My struggling slowed. Craziness lent its own form of strength. In the Academy we had been taught that when an enemy suffered from crazed thoughts, he could be stronger than he would normally be because his body was no longer inhibited by the natural survival instincts inborn to the Galdoni. He would fight like an animal because that was all that remained. He was the enemy not to be trifled with.

"Where are the female Galdoni, Blade?" I asked, keeping my tone light.

"In the basement," he answered flippantly. He blinked as though remembering something. "They're under lock and key, the lock being, well, the lock, and the key being the bombs that are going to go off probably sometime in the near future." He chuckled. "The key frees them, get it? When they die, they're free to fly away. Birds in a cage no longer. It's a beautiful thing, really." He smirked. "We don't need them watering down our race any more than we need those Advantage Corp suits doing the watering, if you know what I mean."

"On our way to the basement," Officer Donaldson said into my earpiece. "We don't know if there's a detonator or a timer. Stall him in case he can blow the place."

"You're not going to get away with this," I said.

Blade's eyes narrowed thoughtfully, a bone-chilling look with the bloody patterns on his face. "Don't you want your revenge on Jake?"

I shook my head, even though my instincts surged at the thought of taken down the man who had betrayed me. "I want to kill you."

He grinned. "I don't believe you, Saro. You don't have it in you to kill; you should have finished me at the Academy when you took your revenge with the sword. You don't have what it takes to be a murderer, but I do, and I also know where Jake is." He brought me closer to his face. His teeth were red with blood. "He's dead."

Something protested deep inside of me. He had to be lying. I needed the chance to avenge the way I had been treated. He couldn't take that from me. "You're lying."

He smirked. "I thought you would say that. Advantage Corp sent me to kill him. He was a loose end, and I'm good at taking care of loose ends." He smiled his crazed smile. "I knew you wouldn't believe me, so I tortured him first." He winked. "They don't teach you that at the Academy. We only got the gritty stuff, not the fun stuff."

I tested his grip; his fingers tightened. He was holding me against the wall with enough pressure to remind me that he could snap my neck, but he wanted to talk. I gave in. "What did you find out?"

"That there was one thing he told you whenever he dropped you off at a house, one thing that would let you know he was the one I killed."

My chest tightened. I didn't want to hear what he said.

His eyes bored into mine. He leaned closer and I could smell the iron scent of blood on his breath. "He said, 'The green light will guide you home.'"

I struggled to pull in a breath. Jake was dead. He had tied me up and left me to burn in that house. I should have been relieved; yet I felt empty, torn, as if there was a hole in my chest.

"Hurts, doesn't it?" Blade said. "How do you like your revenge taken from you? Ripped from your hands so that you're left with nothing?" His voice rose into a yell. "You did that to me, Saro! You took Kale away before I could finish him!" He pulled me closer to his face. "He took everything away from me when he brought down the Arena. I was meant to kill; that's all I was created for. I don't do anything but kill!"

His grip loosened in his rage. I saw an opening. I brought both my hands down hard on his arms, bending his elbows. I drove my hands into his face, both damaged palms slamming into his chin with all the force I could summon.

He dropped me and staggered backwards. I wavered on my feet, gasping for a full breath of air.

Officer Donaldson's voice spoke in my ear. "We found the girls and the AC employees. We're getting them out, but we can't disarm the bomb. It's set to a timer and there's not enough time to get a bomb squad here. Keep stalling."

I gritted my teeth. "What do you want, Blade?" I ducked a punch, blocked a kick with my forearms, and tried to answer with one of my own, but he blocked my leg to the side and slammed a fist into my stomach.

He glowered at me as I stumbled backwards. "Death."

I shook my head, forcing my lungs to suck in air. "You fight too hard to want to die."

I dove, tackling him around the legs. He fell onto his back. I punched him twice in the face. He slugged my ribs where PF220 had already hit. I winced at the pain. He kicked, slamming me into the wall. He was up before I could get set. I tried to block his blows, but he hit my ribs and my stomach before driving a haymaker into my face. I fell back against the wall.

"The Academy was my life," Blade yelled, wrapping his hands around my throat. "It was your life. What are you going to do? You're a killer, a trained murderer. Now you have nothing to murder! What do you do when your hands itch to choke the air off in a throat, and there's no more throat? What do you do when you long for the feeling of a blade through flesh? What do you do when all you want is to feel bones crush beneath your hands and see red run from the nose and mouth?" His hands tightened and he gave a maniacal laugh. "It's a beautiful thing, Saro."

"We're out," Officer Donaldson said in my earpiece.

I let my knees go. Blade wasn't ready for the sudden weight. I dropped from his hands, then rose and drove an elbow into his stomach. He doubled over and I slammed another elbow into his back. He fell to the floor. A rumble shook the building. I grabbed the wall for balance.

Blade gave a pained laugh. "There goes your female Galdoni, Saro. You enjoyed talking to me too much."

"Why kill them?" I pressed, anxious to give the officers enough time to get the Galdoni to safety before Blade realized what was happening.

He rose to his feet and wiped a hand down his face, smearing the blood he had put there. "Nobody deserves to live," Blade replied. He threw a punch. I ducked under it. "The Galdoni need to die because it's a circle; killers must die so they don't kill. The humans need to die because they created us." He gestured below. "All the Advantage Corp employees are now in little pieces, unable to play God anymore because they're busy answering to their own." He grinned, pleased with himself. "Poetic, isn't it?"

He feinted to the left, then swung right. It clipped me on the ear, but I spun and slammed an elbow into his face. His nose broke beneath the blow. He ignored it and grabbed my hand. "Remember what we were taught at the Academy, Saro?"

He gripped the hand tight, sending pain shooting up my arm. I fell to my knees. He leaned close, his face inches from mine. "Weakness can be your biggest strength." He saw the earpiece in my ear and his eyes widened. "You distracted me!"

"I used a page out of your book," I replied, fighting to keep focused through the pain.

He let go and ran to the window. "No!" he screamed at the sight of police cars disappearing through the dawn.

The building shook. The floor began to sink.

"Get out of there, Saro," Officer Donaldson commanded in my earpiece.

The floor dipped, then fell away. Blade grabbed me, trapping my wings. We plummeted toward the wreckage. I elbowed him in the stomach, then the face. His hold loosened. I forced my wings free. The Galdoni held my legs. I tried to land on a jutting floor. Blade grabbed a slab of cement and used our momentum to swing me into broken rebar that twisted from the wall.

A scream tore from my lips as the rebar forced all the way through my shoulder and left side, effectively pinning me to the wall. Blade raised his gray wings. "You'll die and I'll make sure Skylar pays for your intervention. She'll curse the day she met you before she crumples broken to the floor." He flew closer. "She'll die loathing the day she ever heard of Galdoni. She'll cry your name when I carve it into her flesh. She'll—"

I grabbed his wings. Time slowed. I pulled him toward me in one last desperate attempt to stop him. He struggled in my grip. My hands were beyond the point of feeling, but they responded as I shifted my grip from his wings to his armor. The rebar that punctured my shoulder pressed against his chest. My strength rushed in one last surge.

"You will never hurt her!" I yelled.

I felt the rebar pierce through his armor. I gritted my teeth and forced it through his chest right where his heart was. Blade's eyes widened in shock and disbelief. He opened his mouth; blood filled it. Fear colored his crazed eyes. His legs kicked, twitching in defiance. He shook his head, but already his movements were lethargic. The glaze of death brushed his gaze.

He blinked as if he suddenly saw things clearer. "I just wanted to fix this world," he forced out. Blood dribbled down his chin brighter than the dried blood that already stained it.

"I think you just did," I replied.

A strange smile crossed his face. He closed his eyes. A breath gurgled from his throat. He twitched, then became still.

The instincts for a Galdoni to survive were strong, but Blade couldn't face the thought of peace and freedom. His love for violence had outweighed his ability to be a part of it. He had to die, I told myself. As the expression of hatred faded from his face, relief filled me at the thought that the other Galdoni would be safe, and he would never be able to hurt Skylar or anyone else ever again.

I gathered my strength and shoved his body away. The movement sent such fiery pain through my shoulder and side that I couldn't bite back a yell. I willed my wings to work, but I didn't have the strength to free myself. I forced a breath into my lungs. Black spots danced at the edges of my vision. I shook, and wondered if it was the building collapsing with me inside. I couldn't fight the fog that filled my thoughts. My eyes closed against my will.

"Saro!"

I forced my eyes to open. Lem flew carefully down through the destroyed building. "Saro, where are you?"

I tried to shout, but my voice caught in my throat. The building shifted and the rebar moved with it, pulling at both wounds. A cry broke from my lips. Lem's head turned. "Saro!"

His hands touched my shoulder. I gave into the darkness.

Chapter Thirty

I awoke to the sound of voices and a siren. I blinked. There was something clear around my nose and mouth. I tried to push it away. Pain filled me at the movement and somebody caught my hand.

"Saro, it's me, Officer Donaldson." He leaned over me, his grizzled gray hair and kind eyes coming into focus as the haze left. "You're safe," he said. "We're taking you to the hospital."

"Skylar." The name croaked from my lips. I tried to push the oxygen mask away again. I needed to get to her. Blade knew about her. She might be in danger.

"I have officers at her house. She's alright. You need to relax." Officer Donaldson's eyes shifted.

I followed his gaze to a man in green scrubs. "We need to get these wounds taken care of; you've lost so much blood I don't know how you're awake. Please keep still."

Something poked my arm. I looked down to see a needle entering my skin. The instinct to survive rushed through my veins, fighting down weakness and filling me with adrenaline. I sat up and tore the needle away, followed by the oxygen mask.

Officer Donaldson held up his hands. "Easy, Saro. You're safe here. You need to go to the hospital."

"I need to go to Skylar," I replied. I rose shakily from the tiny bed. The ambulance swayed and I almost fell over.

Officer Donaldson grabbed my arm. "Trust me, Saro. She's okay."

The words made my need to see her grow. I trusted her. It was the first thing I had known about Skylar besides her captivating blue eyes and the tattoos that defined her. I trusted her and I needed to see for myself that she was unharmed. She had trusted me to protect her. I couldn't rest until I was sure she was safe.

"I need to go."

Officer Donaldson shook his head. "You need a hospital. You could die out there like this. When the orange-winged Galdoni and that huge one brought you to the ambulance, I thought you were already dead. Do you want to push that?"

I shoved open the ambulance door. "There's something I have to do," I yelled over the sound of the road.

"You need to live," Officer Donaldson shouted.

My words to Skylar filled my mind. *You taught me what it meant to really live, Sky.*

"Exactly," I replied with a laugh. I lifted my wings and jumped out of the ambulance.

Training at the Academy didn't cover jumping from ambulances, or else I would have been warned about the wind currents and speed. Our training had been a little short on practical applications; apparently, they didn't think we would need to know more than five billion ways to kill someone. Go figure. As it was, I barely had the strength to rise above the road. Officer Donaldson stared at me from the back of the ambulance. Weakness filled my limbs and my wings wavered. Perhaps I had been hasty; I tipped my wings.

The bandages they had put on my wounds in the ambulance held as I flew. A light rain began to fall as I forced my weary body toward the city of Crosby. The patters fell against my face, beckoning me on. I used them as a guide, closing my eyes. My body faltered. I fell toward the ground.

I managed to catch myself, soaring low enough to land on the outskirts of the city. I was close to the Galdoni Center. The remains of the once great building were hidden behind the rain that began to pour in earnest. I ducked my head against it and walked the last few blocks to Skylar's place.

She must have been watching. She ran out the door the instant I came into view. I tried to say her name, but I was too exhausted to do more than watch her dash through the rain as if she couldn't hold back any longer. My knees gave way at the sight of her safe and beautiful, my sun, my moon, my stars, my Sky.

Skylar dropped to her knees and wrapped her arms around me. Sobs tore from her as she held me tight. I took a shuddering breath and wrapped my good arm around her.

She cried against my shoulder. "I didn't think you would be back. I was so worried."

"I had to make sure you were okay," I told her. Her head was bowed under my cheek. I closed my eyes and memorized the feeling of her soft hair against my chin.

She sat back. "Are you alright?"

I smiled down at her and gently wiped the tears and rain from her cheeks with my gauzed fingers. "I am now."

"I love you so much, Saro."

I pulled her close. "I love you, Sky."

My world was safe. Blade was gone. The female Galdoni had been found and rescued, and the Advantage Corp employees would undergo the punishment they deserved. I could breathe again, I could fly again, and all I wanted to do was hold Skylar in the rain and remind myself over and over again that she was safe. She was indeed my everything.

*** If you loved this book, please review it online so that so that others can find it as well!

About the Author

Cheree Alsop is the mother of a beautiful, talented daughter and amazing twin sons who fill every day with joy and laughter. She is married to her best friend, Michael, the light of her life and her soulmate who shares her dreams and inspires her by reading the first drafts and adding depth to the stories. Cheree is currently working as an independent author and mother. She enjoys reading, riding her motorcycle on warm nights, and playing with her twins while planning her next book. She is also a bass player for their rock band, Alien Landslide.

Cheree and Michael live in Utah where they rock out, enjoy the outdoors, plan great adventures, and never stop dreaming.

Check out Cheree's other books at www.chereealsop.com

A Quick Thank You

I just want to say thank you to the many people who helped make this book possible. Thank you to my husband for patiently reading each draft, for finding plot holes, and for adding depth to scenes and helping them come alive. I couldn't do this without you!

Thank you to my children, my beautiful daughter Myree and my twin sons Ashton and Aiden. Your adventures, laughter, and love fill every corner of my life. I love every moment I'm with you. You are truly amazing and can accomplish anything you put your mind to. Thank you for your patience while I write, and for only destroying one computer in the process (the result of a sippy cup disaster). I hope someday you will lose yourself within these pages and fall in love with the world of your mother's imagination.

Thank you to those who have read drafts and given me valuable feedback, as well as catching as many typos as possible (and I apologize for those mistakes that still managed to sneak their way through). Thank you to Sue Player for your editing and your feedback. Thank you to Andrew Hair for designing the beautiful cover; it always comes back far more amazing than I ever could have imagined.

Thank you to my family for being patient with my runaway imagination and lapses into the world of fiction. I love you!

Thank you most of all to my readers. I am so grateful for your time, for your reviews, and for the emails I receive. I used to escape into books when I was younger and I always wanted to give the same escape back to others. I hope you found Galdoni 2: Into the Fire and the Galdoni Series enjoyable and heartfelt. This was written for you.

With love, Cheree.

5729525R00147

Printed in Great Britain
by Amazon.co.uk, Ltd.,
Marston Gate.